THE ROARING
BOY

ALSO BY EDWARD MARSTON

In the Nicholas Bracewell series:

The Queen's Head
The Merry Devils
The Trip to Jerusalem
The Nine Giants
The Mad Courtesan
The Silent Woman

In the Domesday Books series:

The Wolves of Savernake
The Ravens of Blackwater

The Roaring Boy

[A N O V E L]

Edward Marston

ST. MARTIN'S PRESS ✠ NEW YORK

ISBN: 0-312-13155-0

First Edition: June 1995

10 9 8 7 6 5 4 3 2 1

To
my good friends
Tom and Enid Schantz
in appreciation of their twenty-five
tireless years
as
Moguls of Mystery

We'll have him murdered as he walks the streets.
In London many alehouse ruffians keep,
Which, as I hear, will murder men for gold.
They shall be soundly fee'd to pay him home.

— ANONYMOUS,

Arden of Faversham

THE ROARING
BOY

[CHAPTER ONE]

Death came calling at a most inconvenient hour and in a singularly inappropriate place. The play being performed that afternoon, before an attentive audience in the yard of the Queen's Head, was still deep in Act Three when its main character was summarily excised from the *dramatis personae*. It was an eerie sensation. Out went Alonso, the exiled Duke of Genoa: in came panic and confusion among Westfield's Men. Each actor who stormed offstage brought fresh protest into the tiring-house.

'Ben Skeat has fallen sick.'

'The man is drunk.'

'Fast asleep.'

'I could get no sound from him.'

'His memory has crumbled with age.'

'Fright has seized him.'

'Madness.'

'Sorcery. Ben is plainly bewitched.'

Nicholas Bracewell, the company's book holder, had only a limited view of the actor from his station behind the scenes but he could see enough to sense a crisis. In the habit of a friar, Ben Skeat sat silent and motionless in his chair. Instead of dominating the scene as the play required, he was completely detached from it. Nicholas felt a stab of pain as he realised what must have happened. It gave him no satisfaction to be able to contradict the other diagnoses of Duke Alonso's condition. Ben Skeat was the oldest and most experienced member of the troupe, known for his prodigious feats of memory and for his total reliability. There was no chance that he was ill, drunk, asleep or lost for words. Still less had he taken leave of his senses or become spellbound.

Only one explanation remained and it gave Nicholas another sharp pang. Skeat was an unsung hero of Westfield's Men. A versatile and talented actor, he was imbued with a deep love of the theatre, steeped in its traditions and wholly committed to his volatile profession. The irony was that he had a rare leading role in *The Corrupt Bargain*. Skeat's more usual place was in the second rank of players where he habitually offered rock-solid support as a loyal earl, a worthy archbishop, a fearless judge, a conscientious seneschal or a white-bearded sage. He exuded a benevolence that invariably got him cast as a symbol of goodness.

Now, for once, he was being accused of downright evil.

'He is thwarting me!' said Barnaby Gill as he flounced into the tiring-house in the costume of a court jester. 'There is wanton malice at work here. Ben Skeat is determined to ruin my performance.'

'Not by design,' said Nicholas.

'I gave him his cue, he merely stared at me.'

'Ben had no choice in the matter.'

'I would expect *you* to take his side,' said Gill with a characteristic snort. 'It was on your foolish advice that he was given the role in the first place. And what does the idiot do? He dried up on me. I wait for his twenty-line speech and he stays hiding under his cowl.' He stamped a peevish foot. 'I'll not abide it,

Nicholas! His conduct is unforgivable. Had I not delivered a speech extempore to cover the gap in nature, the play would have fallen apart.'

Nicholas nodded. 'You must do that office again.'

'Never!'

'Ben Skeat has spoken his last line.'

'Do not look to me to rescue him.'

'I look to all of you.'

'Why so?'

'He has passed away,' said Nicholas, quietly.

'What!' howled Gill. 'While *I* was acting with him! That is an insult that cannot be borne. I am mortified.'

His exclamation sent the rest of the company into a state of wild alarm and it was all Nicholas could do to calm them down so that the commotion would not be heard by the spectators. The book holder confided the awful truth in a whisper. Ben Skeat was dead. Cold terror spread quickly. Superstitious by nature, the actors turned the tiring-house into a Bedlam of speculation.

'We shall be chased off the stage.'

'This is a judgement on us.'

'Someone has poisoned him to bring us down.'

'I spy a devilish plot here.'

'There is a murderer in our midst.'

'Who will be his next victim?'

'Abandon the play!'

'Take to your heels!'

'Run for your lives!'

'Stop!' ordered Nicholas, planting his burly frame before the exit and holding out his arms. 'Ben Skeat has died but it may well be by natural means. Would you desert him at a time when he most needs you? Will you behave like cowards when valour is in request? Will you inflict such a dark stain on the reputation of Westfield's Men?' He pointed a finger at the makeshift stage behind the curtains. 'The play must go on.'

Gill was distraught. 'How can we act with a corpse?'

'You have already taught us the way,' soothed the book holder. 'When no words came from Duke Alonso, you provided your own. Listen carefully and you will hear that both the Provost and Count Emilio follow your example.'

As they strained their ears, the company became aware that a small miracle was taking place out there in the sunshine. With its central character reduced to the role of a stage property, the play was somehow continuing on its way. Edmund Hoode, the company's actor-playwright, was in somnolent vein as a kind Provost who escorts the disguised Duke to the condemned cell so that they may comfort the hapless Emilio. In the latter role, Owen Elias was at his best, suffering in the shadow of the headsman's axe while busily plundering all the speeches for which Ben Skeat no longer had a use.

Edmund Hoode was not to be outdone. He had laboured long and hard over *The Corrupt Bargain*. The sudden departure of its main character was not going to disable his play as long as he had breath in his body to rescue it. Renowed for his comedies, Hoode had tackled a more tragic theme in his latest offering. *The Corrupt Bargain* was set in Genoa. The exiled Duke Alonso returns in disguise to seize power from his tyrannical younger brother, Don Pedro. Injustice runs riot in his unhappy land. Alonso is particularly struck by the plight of a devoted brother and sister, Emilio and Bianca.

Wrongly accused of a crime he did not commit, the brave Count Emilio is sentenced to death. The beautiful Bianca goes to Don Pedro to plead for her brother's release. The tyrant is consumed with such a powerful lust for her that he offers her a corrupt bargain. If she consents to give her body to him, her brother will be set free. Bianca is duly horrified by the choice confronting her. She must lose either her virginity or her brother. Which is the more precious? While his beloved sister agonises over her predicament, Emilio spends anguished hours in prison. When Alonso calls upon him in the guise of a friar, he tries to offer a modicum of comfort to the prisoner.

Owen Elias was not going to waste the most telling speech in the scene. Leaning in close to the lifeless Ben Skeat, he cocked an ear and wrinkled his brow.

'What says my holy father?' he asked.

Edmund Hoode seized gratefully on the cue. Bending over the hooded figure, he pretended to listen to the friar's words of wisdom before relaying them to the condemned man.

> *Hearken to his advice.*
> *Subdue this groundless fear of death's approach*
> *And fast embrace him as your dearest friend.*
> *You run from him who can your pain remove,*
> *Your sins redeem, your sister's honour save,*
> *And all the rigours of this woeful world*
> *Lift from your back. The end of life is but*
> *The start of joy. Speak thus to welcome death.*
> *"Light my way to heaven with burning torch*
> *And take me from this hell of durance vile."*

The Provost was not merely recovering words from beyond the grave, he was giving the rest of the company invaluable time to consider how to proceed. In the version of *The Corrupt Bargain* that they had rehearsed that morning, Duke Alonso went on to overthrow his brother, restore good government, pluck Emilio from the block itself and marry the grateful Bianca. Such a resolution was now impossible. A cruel tyrant could not be ousted by a dead friar.

Frantic rewriting was needed and Nicholas Bracewell rose to the occasion with customary speed. Since he held the only complete copy of the play, he knew the piece almost as well as its author and saw the advantage of having Edmund Hoode in a role where he might help to pilot them all home. Sudden decisions were made with an instinctive skill.

'Take note,' said Nicholas to the remainder of the cast. 'The Provost will banish the usurper, Don Pedro. The new Duke will be Count Emilio. We lose Alonso but his place in the action will be taken by the Jester. Bianca will marry the Provost.'

The firmness of his voice instilled confidence into his fellows and most of them were content to obey. There was one notable exception.

'This is lunacy, Nicholas,' complained Barnaby Gill.

'It is our only hope of salvation.'

'Then we are doomed. I am a court jester not a friar.'

'Could you not be both?' argued Nicholas. 'To aid the company in its hour of need, could you not be two or twenty characters if it preserve our good standing?'

'I have my *own* reputation to consider.'

It is difficult to stand on one's dignity while wearing a cap and bells. When Barnaby Gill folded his arms and lifted a defiant chin, he simply appeared ridiculous. He was Petulance incarnate. His bells jingled in mockery.

'Think of Ben Skeat,' urged Nicholas.

Gill was unmoved. 'Did he think of *me* when he went to his Maker in the middle of my performance?'

'We have a duty to our audience.'

'That duty is to give them *The Corrupt Bargain*, not some mauled and tattered version of it.'

'Our patron is here today.'

'Then we must not abuse him with this profanity.'

'Would you rather send him away with two acts of the piece yet unplayed?' said Nicholas. 'Lord Westfield would be affronted, his companions would be disappointed and the rest of the spectators will demand their money back. Is that your wish?' His final point was his most persuasive. 'Master Firethorn would never forgive you.'

'What care I?' retorted Gill. 'It is because of him that we are in this parlous state!'

But his resistance was now only token. The name of Lawrence Firethorn had brought him to heel. Firethorn was the company's actor-manager and acknowledged star, the man for whom the role of Duke Alonso had been specifically written. Ben Skeat had only been elevated to the part because Lawrence Firethorn was indisposed. Their absent leader would pour molten contempt upon them if they dared to abandon a play in mid-performance, and the chief target of his attack would be the reluctant court jester. Barnaby Gill was Firethorn's greatest rival, a brilliant clown who felt that his own art was vastly superior to that of any other player and that he himself was chiefly responsible for the continued success of Westfield's Men. He could not permit himself to be seen as the architect of their downfall.

There was a more tempting consideration. With Lawrence Firethorn off the stage, Gill's ascendancy would go unchallenged. He could rule the roost like a Chanticleer. Improvising scenes in order to cover the untimely death of Duke Alonso would place an immense burden on him but it was one he would cheerfully bear in view of the potential reward. Instead of merely stealing the occasional scene as the court jester, he could now pillage the whole play.

'Take your positions,' said Nicholas.

Act Three was coming to a close as the Provost offered a final crumb of comfort to Count Emilio. Both men were due to leave the prison cell in the company of the exiled Duke but the latter was clearly in no position to join them. Ben Skeat's removal from the action was the main priority and Nicholas Bracewell took the matter into his own hands.

'Dick Honeydew,' he called.

'Yes?' said the boy apprentice.

'We will have your lament now.'

'But I do not sing it for two more scenes.'
'It is needed presently.'
'As you wish.'
'Sing loud and clear, Dick.'
'I will do my best.'

The boy apprentice cleared his throat and tried to stop his hands from trembling. In a dark wig and a brocade gown heavily ornamented with jewels, Richard Honeydew was a most winsome Bianca. Nicholas sent word up to the balcony overhead where Peter Digby and his consort of musicians waited to introduce the next scene with a fanfare. On the instructions of the book holder, the trumpets were replaced by the strains of a lute. Bianca stepped gracefully on to the stage with Nicholas himself in attendance. He crossed to the inert figure of Duke Alonso and gave an indulgent smile.

> *Our holy friar sleeps softly like a child.*
> *I'll straight convey him to a proper bed.*

Ben Skeat was lifted bodily and taken swiftly away. His exit was covered by a tearful Bianca, who wept bitterly into a handkerchief before singing a lament to the accompaniment of the lute. Caught up in the emotion of the moment, the audience soon forgot the strange behaviour of the friar but it continued to exercise his fellows behind the scenes.

Nicholas lay the corpse down in the tiring-house.

'Whatever has happened to him?' wailed Edmund Hoode.

'He is gone,' said Owen Elias sadly. 'I saw his eyes flicker, then it was all over. Poor Ben!'

Hoode shuddered. 'Dead? What a comment on my play!'

'It may yet be saved, Edmund,' said Nicholas.

He acquainted the newcomers with the changes he had made in the action of the piece, drawing a groan of protest from the author. Owen Elias took a more practical view. If the afternoon were not to end in chaos, then the amended version of *The Corrupt Bargain* had to be played to the hilt. Duke Alonso had evidently gone into permanent exile.

Nicholas ordered the participants in the next scene to stand by, then signalled their entrance as Bianca swept off to sympathetic applause. The villainous Don Pedro was now onstage for five minutes or more with his cohorts. Temporary relief was offered. As in most of his plays, Hoode rested the central character in Act Four so that his protagonist could burst back into the action—restored and refreshed—in the final act. Nicholas Bracewell took advantage of the lull.

He carried Ben Skeat to a quiet corner and laid him gently on the floor. As he pushed back the hood, he saw the unmistakable signs of death. The mouth was slack, the skin white, the eyes stared sightlessly. No breath stirred, no pulse could be felt. An old man had passed peacefully away among his fellows at the very height of his career.

It grieved Nicholas that he was unable to treat the corpse with all due reverence but the play had prior claims. Raising the body up a few inches, he carefully divested it of the friar's habit so that the disguise could be used by the court jester. He then covered Skeat with a cloak and looked up at the sorrowful faces all around him.

'Play on, sirs. It is what Ben would have wanted.'

'We owe it to him,' agreed Owen Elias.

'But my work is being mangled!' hissed Edmund Hoode.

'Would you rather call a halt to the proceedings?'

Nicholas threw down a challenge that he knew would be ignored. Unlike Barnaby Gill, the playwright would never put selfish concerns before the good of the company. Survival was the order of the day and Hoode recognised that. It was time to unite with his fellows to bring *The Corrupt Bargain* safely into port, even if the harbour was not the one that the author had originally intended.

'Tell us what to do, Nick,' he said. 'Guide us through.'

'Stand close and hear me out.'

Snatching up the prompt book once more, Nicholas flicked through the pages and reiterated his decisions. Westfield's Men listened intently though their eyes occasionally strayed to the supine figure of their colleague in the corner. Ben Skeat had spent a lifetime responding to the various crises that were thrown up regularly by a capricious profession. It fell to them to meet this dire emergency with the courage and imagination that the old actor would have shown.

Two plays now ran side by side. What the audience saw was an attenuated version of *The Corrupt Bargain* but the drama taking place behind the scenes was much more intense. Actors rehearsed new roles in a matter of seconds. Music was changed, entrances were altered, costumes were reassigned. George Dart, the smallest and most lowly of the assistant stagekeepers, was in a state of near-hysteria as the scenic devices he was due to move were given fresh locations. He soon had no idea what scene, what act, and what play they were engaged in, and simply hung on the commands of Nicholas Bracewell, praying that he would come through the ordeal without earning himself a sound beating.

Most of the actors adapted swiftly and successfully. Owen Elias, an ebullient Welshman, set a fine example as Count Emilio, turning speeches that he should have addressed to Duke Alonso into moving soliloquies. Edmund Hoode, too, was able to mould his part into the required shape, growing in confidence with each scene and slowly emerging as a worthy contender for the hand of Bianca. In this role, Richard Honeydew, youngest but easily the most gifted of the four apprentices, gave a faultless performance as the tragic maid and had the entire audience ready to defend his virginity.

The nature of the double drama was best illustrated by Barnaby Gill. Onstage, he was a revelation, expanding his role in all manner of ways to give other actors more time to think and to adjust accordingly. As the court jester, he was the licensed fool who was able to speak the harsh truth—albeit

couched in riddles—to the wicked Don Pedro. He now introduced a range of jigs and hilarious songs that were a blaze of
light in an otherwise dark tragedy. Gill borrowed freely from
other plays in which he had shone and gave what was effectively a free-flowing exhibition of his remarkable comic skills.

Offstage, the actor's Janus-face came into view.

'I will not wear that friar's habit!' he snarled.

'You must,' insisted Nicholas.

'It is a shroud lifted from a corpse!'

'Ben Skeat has no more use for it now.'

'Take it away. It smells of decay.'

'We have no other costume fit for you.'

'Find one!' demanded Gill. 'I'll not touch that.'

A bell chimed to announce the scene in the cathedral. There
was no time for niceties. Nicholas Bracewell grabbed the friar's
habit and fitted it unceremoniously over the spluttering Gill
before propelling him on to the stage with a firm shove. The
raving actor changed instantly into a serene friar and padded
across the stage with measured tread to play a scene with the
distraught Bianca. Nicholas allowed himself a sigh of relief. It
was all too premature.

They were now into Act Five and exploring uncharted terri-
tory. With the friar re-entering the action, the scope and deli-
cacy of their manoeuvres increased sharply. They had to pick
their way line by line through the text, making constant revi-
sions and refinements. Mistakes soon crept in. Speeches were
either forgotten or delivered in the wrong sequence. Indeed,
there was one moment when both Edmund Hoode and Barnaby Gill declaimed the same rhyming couplet from Duke
Alonso in unison. It produced a restrained laugh in the assem-
bled throng but that laugh became derisive when George Dart
blundered onstage as a servant and promptly collided with a
bench which now occupied a wholly new position. Instead of
imparting his one line and quitting the stage, Dart stayed
rooted to the spot and perspired dramatically with naked fear.

The Provost hustled him roughly towards the exit.

'*Come, man. Your message. What is't?*'

George Dart was pushed out of sight before he could deliver it and fresh sniggers arose. Barnaby Gill quelled them at once with an impromptu prayer. Since the audience believed him to be Duke Alonso in disguise, he used a voice as deep and mellifluous as that of Ben Skeat. A master of deft comedy, Gill showed that he could cope with more serious material when necessary. His sure-footed performance led the rest of the cast safely across the stepping-stones of the play and inculcated fresh hope in their hearts. The final scene at last came into view.

The stage was set for the execution of Count Emilio and the grim ritual was enacted with all due solemnity. Soldiers rushed on to the stage in the nick of time to pull the condemned man from beneath the axe, then arrest Don Pedro. Thanks to the intercession of the friar, the tyrant was finally deposed but he did not accept his fate meekly. He roared and ranted at all and sundry. Breaking free from his captors, he ran to the friar to throw back the man's hood with a yell of *"Cucullus non facit monachum"*—the hood does not make the monk. There was a gasp from the audience.

Instead of revealing Duke Alonso as they expected, he exposed the head of the court jester. It was a moment of pure theatre, at once so startling and so comic that they did not know quite how to react and simply gaped in astonishment. Barnaby Gill gave them no time to discern the more farcical aspects of the play's resolution. Showing admirable invention and no small degree of authority, he announced that the exiled Duke had died of a fever contracted during a visit to the prison. Alonso's last wish was that Don Pedro should be overthrown and replaced by the more worthy rule of Count Emilio. The liberated prisoner was greeted with general acclamation by his new subjects.

There remained only one more strand of the play hanging loose and Owen Elias tied it off neatly. Beckoning his sister and the Provost to him, he joined their hands together in a symbolic gesture. Their marriage would be the first public event of his rule. The play ended with a formal dance, then the whole court went off to church for the nuptials.

The audience was pleasantly mystified. It was not the conclusion they had anticipated, and some of them felt obscurely cheated, but the mass of spectators glowed with approval. Applause was most generous. When Barnaby Gill led out the cast to savour their ovation, there were very few who noticed the absence of the exiled Duke of Genoa. While he lay dead in the tiring-house, *The Corrupt Bargain* was hailed. London had never seen anything quite like it before and, though the play had some puzzling elements and some baffling twists of plot, it also had an undeniable novelty.

Nicholas Bracewell remained behind the scenes and knelt beside his old friend with a sad smile. Ben Skeat deserved his fair share of that applause. Until the moment when he suddenly stepped out of the play, he was giving the finest performance of his career, clear-voiced, expressive and full of rich detail. Death had perhaps not intruded at such an unseemly hour, after all. It could be argued that Ben Skeat had been offered the most perfect exit for an actor.

'Nobly done, friends!'

'I hated every moment.'

'We plucked triumph from disaster.'

'It was intolerable.'

'Have you ever known such excitement?'

'Nor such misery.'

'We have a victory to celebrate.'

'But no strength left for celebration.'

Torn between exhilaration and exhaustion, Westfield's Men came pouring into the tiring-house. The last echoes of applause were fading as they retired to their lair. Some were buoyed up by what they saw as a signal achievement while others merely wanted to collapse and lick their wounds. Owen Elias belonged to the former party and gave all within reach a hug of congratulation. Richard Honeydew, by contrast, was shivering with fear, all too conscious of the narrow escape they had just had. The other apprentices—Martin Yeo, John Tallis and Stephen Judd—were putting on a brave face but their knees were also knocking beneath their farthingales. George Dart was so grateful to have come through it all that he lapsed into frenzied giggling.

The twin poles of emotion were exemplified by Barnaby Gill and by Edmund Hoode, respectively. Gill was suffused with joy, thrilled to have survived a harrowing experience with such honour and basking in the glory of having led Westfield's Men as its undoubted star. An audience which would normally flock out into Gracechurch Street with the name of Lawrence Firethorn on its lips would now talk of little else but Barnaby Gill. Hoode collected no such bounty from their two hours upon the stage. For him, it was a headlong descent into chaos. His play had been cut to shreds and his own performance, he felt, was a cruel travesty.

The severe strain had attacked his moon-shaped face like the slash of a knife. Pale, drawn and sagging with despair, he dropped down on to a stool beside Nicholas Bracewell.

'That was the most corrupt bargain I ever made!'

'How say you, Edmund?'

'I was paid money for writing a dreadful play.'

'A fine play,' said Nicholas. 'And well-received.'

'No, Nick,' moaned the other. 'It was an assault on the intelligence of the spectators. They came to see a well-tuned tragedy and we gave them that discordant comedy of errors. Instead of displaying our art, we foist base, brown paper stuff on to them. It was shameful. I'll never call myself "poet" again.'

'The company did what was needful, Edmund.'

'It destroyed my work.'

'No,' said Nicholas, 'it refashioned it so that it might live to be played afresh another day.'

'Never! *The Corrupt Bargain* died out on that stage.'

'So did Ben Skeat.' It was a timely reminder and it checked the flow of authorial recrimination. 'We all regret what happened to your play this afternoon but it is Ben who deserves our sympathy. Your art continues: he will never tread the boards again.'

Edmund Hoode was chastened. He nodded in agreement, then lowered himself on to one knee before taking the edge of the cloak and lifting it back from Skeat's face. The old actor gazed up at him with a look of posthumous apology. He was deeply sorry for the injury he had inflicted on his friend's play but the exiled Duke had no choice in the matter. A tear of remorse trickled down Hoode's cheek.

'Goodbye, Ben,' he said softly. 'I do not blame you, old friend. Your death has changed my life. You taught me the folly of my occupation. I thank you for that. Over your corpse, I make this solemn pledge. My writing days are past.'

'Do not be so hasty,' said Nicholas.

'I never wish to endure that torture again.'

'Nor shall you, Edmund.'

'Indeed not.' He let the cloak fall back across the face of Ben Skeat once more. 'I am finished with it, Nick. Westfield's Men can find some other fool to pen their plays. No more corrupt bargains for me. Nor more long nights bent wearily over my work. No more sighs and no more suffering. No more *pain!*' His voice hardened. 'I will never—never take up my quill again.'

It was a vow that he would soon wish he had kept.

[CHAPTER TWO]

Shoreditch had once been a tiny hamlet, growing up at the junction of two important Roman roads, and offering its inhabitants clean air, open fields and a degree of rural isolation. That was no longer the case. The relentless expansion of London turned it into yet another busy suburb, tied to the city by a long ribbon of houses, tenements and churches, and further entwined by the commercial and cultural needs of the capital. Shoreditch could still boast fine gardens, orchards and small-holdings—even common land for archery practice—but its former independence had perished forever.

Chief among its attractions were its two splendid custom-built playhouses, The Theatre and The Curtain, and the populace of London streamed out of Bishopsgate on those afternoons when the flags were hoisted above these famed arenas to indicate that performances would take place. Shoreditch competed with Bankside as a favourite source of entertainment but not all of its denizens were happy with this state of affairs. As well as the largely respectable and law-abiding spectators, theatres also attracted their share of whores, cheats and pickpockets in search of easy custom. Rowdiness, too, was a constant threat but the major complaint was against the barrage of noise that was set up during a performance.

Occupants of houses in Holywell Lane were especially vulnerable as they dwelt between the two theatres and thus at the mercy of rival cacophonies. They cringed before explosions of laughter and bursts of applause. They recoiled from strident fanfares and deafening music. Alarums and excursions afflicted them in equal measure. Even on the most sunlit and cloudless afternoons, thunder, lightning and tempest had been known to issue simultaneously from both playhouses as cunning hands usurped the role of Mother Nature. Gunpowder was frequently used with deafening effect. To live in Holywell Lane was to live cheek by jowl with pandemonium.

'Arghhhhhhhh!'

A new and terrible sound shattered the early evening.

'Noooooooooo!'

It was a roar of pain fit to waken the long-dead.

'Heeeeeeeelp!'

Was it some wild animal in distress? A wolf caught in a trap? A bear torn apart by the teeth of a dozen mastiffs? A lion in the menagerie at the Tower, speared to make sport?

'Yaaaaaaaaaa!'

The voice was now recognisably human but so full of grief, so charged with agony, and so laden with despair that its owner had to be enduring either the amputation of both legs or the violent removal of all internal organs. The cry came from a house in Old Street but everyone in Shoreditch heard it and shared in its fathomless misery. Was the poor creature being devoured alive by a pack of hungry demons?

'Ohhhhhhhhhhhh!'

Lawrence Firethorn was not one to suffer in silence. When he was in travail, the whole world was his audience. He lay in his bedchamber and bellowed his torment, quivering all over as a new and more searing pain shot through him.

Firethorn had toothache. To be more precise, he had one badly infected tooth in a set that was otherwise remarkably sound. The actor could not believe that so much tribulation was caused by such a minute part of his anatomy. His whole mouth was on fire, his whole head was pounding, his whole body was one huge, smarting wound.

His wife came bustling into the room with concern.

'Is there anything I may get for you, Lawrence?'

'A gravedigger.'

'Let me at least send for a surgeon.'

'A lawyer would be more use. To draw up my will.'

'Do not talk so,' she said, crossing to the bed. 'This is no time for jests. You have a bad tooth, that is all.'

'A hundred bad teeth, Margery. A *thousand!*'

An invisible hammer struck the side of his face and he let out such a blood-curdling yell that his neighbours thought he had just given birth to a litter of giant hedgehogs. Margery Firethorn wanted to put a comforting arm around him but she knew that it was inadvisable. Her husband's cheek was twice its normal size and throbbing visibly. The handsome, bearded countenance of the most brilliant actor in London was distorted into an ugly mask of woe. On the posted bed with its embroidered canopy, they had spent endless nights of pleasure but it was now a rack on which his muscular torso was being stretched to breaking-point.

'Let me fetch you another remedy,' she suggested.

'Dear God—no!'

'This one comes with the apothecary's blessing.'

'More like his curse!'

'It may reduce the swelling in your gum, Lawrence.'

'I will take nothing!' he snarled.

Firethorn had already submitted to three of his wife's well-intentioned remedies and each had signally failed. The last—a compound of vinegar, oil and sulphur—had not only sharpened the pain to unbearable limits, it caused him to vomit uncontrollably. He vowed that nothing else would go into his diseased mouth. A fresh spasm made his eyes cloud over for a second. When he rallied slightly, he was hit by a tidal wave of guilt.

'I have betrayed my fellows!' he wailed.

'Put them from your thoughts.'

'How can I, Margery? Westfield's Men rely on me and I was found wanting. For the first time in my life, I was prevented from doing my duty and exhibiting my genius as a player.'

'You are not to blame,' she said.

'The name of Lawrence Firethorn is a symbol of true quality in our profession. Where was that true quality this afternoon? Flat on its back!' He slapped his thigh with an angry palm. 'I failed them. I, Margery! Who once played Hector with a broken toe. Who once conquered the known world as Antony with my arm in a sling. Who once led the company to triumph in *Black Antonio* when the sweating sickness was upon me. Disease and discomfort have never kept me off the stage until this fateful day. They needed me at the Queen's Head as the exiled Duke of Genoa but I have been imprisoned here by this damnable toothache!'

In an unguarded moment, he jabbed a finger at his cheek and prodded the inflamed area. Another roar of agony made the low beams tremble. In his anguish, he believed that he could actually hear the stabbing pain as it beat out its grim message, but Margery placed another interpretation on the repetitive sound. Someone was at their front door.

'We have a visitor,' she said. 'Will you receive them?'

'Not unless it be Nick Bracewell. He is the only man I would trust to see me in this dreadful condition and not mock my plight. Nick has real compassion and I am in sore need of that.'

A servant admitted the caller. Margery stood at the door of the bedchamber and listened to the voices below. Feet began to clatter up the oaken staircase.

'Barnaby Gill,' she announced. 'I'll head him off.'

'He is the last person I want at this hour.'

'Leave him to me. He shall not pass.'

Margery closed the door behind her and confronted the newcomer on the narrow landing. She was a big, bosomy woman with an iron determination. When fully roused, she was more than a match for her husband, so Firethorn was confident that she would soon send the visitor on his way. A dozen armed soldiers would not be able to force their way past his wife. He lay back on his pillow and gently closed his eyelids. A tap on the door made him open them with a suddenness he instantly regretted. His swollen jaw ached vengefully.

Easing the door ajar, Margery put her head around it.

'Barnaby brings sad tidings,' she said.

'I'll none of that leering clown today!'

'They concern Westfield's Men.'

'Send the rogue on his way without further ado.'

'His news will brook no delay. Please hear him.'

Before he could protest, she stood aside to let Barnaby Gill strut into the bedchamber. Wedded to ostentation, he wore a high-necked bombasted doublet in the Spanish fashion with its collar edged at the top with pickadils. The doublet was slashed, pinked and embroidered with a centre fastening of buttons from top to bottom. Its startling lime green hue was thrown into relief by hat, gloves and hose of a darker green. Short, squat but undeniably elegant, Gill doffed his hat in greeting, then gazed down at his stricken colleague with a mixture of sympathy and cold satisfaction.

'What ails you, Lawrence?' he asked with token dismay.

'*You* do, sir!'

'But I have saved all our lives this afternoon.'

'Mine is far beyond recall.'

'Listen to Barnaby,' prompted Margery. 'It is needful.'

Firethorn turned a bloodshot eye on his visitor.

'Well?'

Gill sighed. 'Ben Skeat is no longer with us.'

'He has no choice in the matter. His contract binds him to Westfield's Men in perpetuity.'

'You do not understand, Lawrence. The poor man is dead.'

'If he feels the way I do, I am not surprised. I expect to pass out of this world myself at any moment.' Firethorn gulped as he heard what he had just been told. 'Dead? That dear old work-horse, Ben Skeat? Deceased? Can this be so?'

'Sadly, it can.'

'When did this tragedy befall us?'

'In the middle of Act Three.'

Firethorn sat up. 'Ben Skeat died *onstage?*'

'In full view of the audience.'

'What happened?' asked Margery. 'Did you bring the play to an end? Did you send all the spectators home?'

'Did you return their money?' said Firethorn in alarm.

'No,' said Gill with studied nonchalance. 'I stepped into the breach and rescued us from a gruesome fate. Had I not led Westfield's Men with such spirit and authority, there would not be any of them left to lead.'

'Nick Bracewell took control, surely?' said Firethorn.

'Yes,' added Margery with brisk affection. 'Nicholas steered you through, I'll wager.'

'Not this time, alas!' lied Gill. '*I* was the saviour.'

They listened with rapt attention as the visitor told a story that he had rehearsed very carefully on the journey from the Queen's Head to Shoreditch. According to Barnaby Gill, the book holder and the rest of the company had been ready to abandon the play as soon as Ben Skeat's death became apparent. It was left to the court jester to berate them for their faint-heartedness and to insist that they press on with the performance, albeit in an amended form. The new version of *The Corrupt Bargain*—Gill emphasized this—was his brainchild. As actor and as author, he had led from the front and dragged an unwilling company behind him.

Lawrence Firethorn knew him well enough to be able to

separate fact from fantasy. He was so closely acquainted with Nicholas Bracewell's handiwork that it could not be passed off as someone else's. Margery, too, sensed that the unassuming book holder had been the real hero in this crisis as in so many previous ones. One consolation remained. The performance had continued in such a way as to disguise the true nature of the emergency from the audience. No money had been returned but a high price had still been paid.

'Ben Skeat dead?' Firethorn was shocked. 'May the Lord have mercy on his soul! He will be greatly missed.'

'As were you, Lawrence,' said Gill pointedly.

'Not from choice, I assure you,' said Firethorn.

'Indeed not,' agreed Margery. 'He was laid low.'

Gill raised a derisive eyebrow. 'By a mere toothache? It would take more than that to keep me from the practice of my art. The plague itself would not detain me from my place upon the boards. Thank heaven I was there this afternoon! Ben Skeat dying on us. Nicholas Bracewell failing us. Lawrence Firethorn deserting us.'

'I did not desert you!' howled the other man as the pain flared up once more. 'I was unfit for service. Felled by some malign devil.' He waved a dismissive hand. 'Leave we my condition until another time. Ben Skeat must now be our prime concern. What was the cause of his death? Who has examined the body? Where is it now? Have his relatives yet been informed? How stands it, Barnaby?'

'I left all that to Nicholas Bracewell,' said Gill with evident boredom. 'Cleaning up a mess is the one thing at which he has some moderate skill. My task was to ride post-haste to Shoreditch to put you in possession of the full facts. We have lost one of our sharers, Lawrence.'

'The best and sweetest of men.'

'I'll say "Amen" to that,' said Margery soulfully.

'When I was a raw beginner,' continued Firethorn in nostalgic vein, 'it was Ben Skeat who helped me, advised me and taught me all I know about the craft of acting. He let me feed on his long experience. There was not an ounce of selfishness in that dear creature. Ben was a rock on which we all built our performances.'

'Yes,' said Gill with heavy sarcasm. 'Ben was a rock. But this afternoon—like a rock—he could neither move nor speak. If it had not been for my sterling courage in the face of mortal danger . . .'

But his hosts were not listening. Margery Firethorn was too busy recalling a thousand and one pleasant memories of an actor who had served Westfield's Men with honour since the inception of the company, and who had always been a most welcome visitor to the house in Old Street. Her husband was concentrating on practicalities. Ben Skeat was a sharer, one of the ranked players who were named in the patent for West-field's Men and who were thus entitled to a portion of such profits as it might make. Sharers also took all the major roles in any play. They had real status and a qualified security. To become a sharer with one of the London companies was to join an exclusive brotherhood. Ben Skeat had just resigned from that charmed circle.

Lawrence Firethorn weighed all the implications.

'Ben must be mourned,' he decreed, 'then replaced.'

'You are too hasty,' said Gill. 'One less sharer and the rest of us have a slightly larger slice of the pie.'

'Fresh blood is needed in the company.'

'I beg to differ, Lawrence.'

'When do you do otherwise?'

Gill tensed. 'I am entitled to my opinion.'

'No question but that you are, Barnaby,' said the actor-manager with light irony. 'I value that opinion. I shall, of course, ignore it as usual but I can still respect it. The matter is decided. As one Ben Skeat leaves us, another must be found to take his place.'

'The issue has not even been discussed.'

'We just discussed it—did we not, Margery?'

'What more debate is needed?' she said.

'Much more,' argued Gill, irritated that she should be brought into their deliberations. 'Edmund has a voice here. When he hears reason, he will side with me.'

'Reason will incline him to my persuasion.'

Lawrence Firethorn had no doubt on that score. He could invariably win the resident playwright around to his point of view. All the sharers had a nominal voice in company policy but it was effectively decided by its three leading personalities. Of these, Barnaby Gill and Edmund Hoode were allowed only the illusion of control. It was Firethorn whose guiding hand was really on the tiller.

'Think back, Barnaby,' he counselled. 'When Old Cuthbert retired from the company, what did we do? We promoted from within. Owen Elias rose from the hired men to become our new sharer and he has been a credit to us ever since.'

'You bitterly opposed his selection,' reminded Gill.

'That is all in the past.'

'You hated Owen because he joined our sworn enemies.'

'We have put the incident behind us.'

'It was the one time when you were overruled.'

Firethorn breathed in deeply through his nose and tried to remain calm. Owen Elias's elevation from hired man to sharer had taken place in exceptional circumstances and was largely the work of Nicholas Bracewell. The book holder's astute stage management of the situation had overcome Firethorn's serious qualms about the Welshman. Although Owen Elias was now an established player of the first rank in Westfield's Men, the recollection of his promotion was not untinged with bitterness for Firethorn.

'We will look outside the company,' he said firmly.

'Why look at all?' countered Gill.

'A new sharer would invest money in Westfield's Men.'

'Owen Elias did not.'

'Forget Owen. He has no place in this argument.'
'I believe that he does.'
'So do I,' said Margery.

The men stared at her. Ordinarily, she would have no right
to be present—let alone involved—in the dispute. Acting was
a male prerogative. No woman was permitted to take part in a
play, still less to assist in the running of one of the companies,
but Margery Firethorn had a habit of breaking rules that hin-
dered her. Gill was patently annoyed by an intrusion he had no
power to stop, while a weakened Firethorn was unable to assert
himself over his wife. Margery stated her case with blunt clarity.

'Choose the best possible man,' she said.
'Why, so we will,' consented her husband.
'Then turn to Owen Elias.'
'We cannot make him a sharer for the second time.'
'Take him as your example, Lawrence,' she said. 'You
looked within Westfield's Men and the right choice came.'
'More or less.'
'Do the self-same thing again.'
'How so?'
'Nominate the only person fit for the honour.'
'And who might that be, my dove?' he wondered.
'Who else but Nicholas Bracewell?'
'*Anyone* else!' exclaimed Gill. 'I forbid it!'
Firethorn pondered. 'Margery guides us along the path of
logic,' he said. 'Nick Bracewell is the obvious choice.'
'Where would you be without him?' she said.
'Consigned to oblivion.'
'No!' said Gill with outrage. 'This is madness. He is just one
more hired man. You cannot turn a mere book holder into a
sharer. Who is to be next in line? Hugh Wegges, the tireman?
Nathan Curtis, the carpenter? George Dart, that shivering
idiot of an assistant stagekeeper? You make a mockery of our
standing.'

Margery's eye kindled dangerously. 'Nick Bracewell is as

good a man as any in the company.' She shot a meaningful glance at Gill. 'Far better than some I could name, who stand much lower in my esteem. I'll not hear a carping word against Nick. It is high time that his worth was fully appreciated.'

Gill curled a lip in scorn. 'Oh, it is, it is. We took his measure this afternoon.'

'What say you?' asked Firethorn.

'Your precious Nicholas Bracewell was at last revealed in his true light. He is not the paragon of virtue you take him for, Lawrence.' Gill was working himself up into a mild rage. 'He not only let us down in our hour of need, he committed the most foul assault on my person.'

'With good reason, I dare swear.'

'He attacked me, Lawrence!'

'I have often thought of doing so myself.'

'Violent hands were laid upon me.'

'How I envy him!'

'Our book holder became a vicious animal.'

'Never!' said Margery. 'Nick is as gentle as a lamb.'

'Your opinion was not sought,' snapped Gill.

'I offered it *gratis.*'

'Please keep out of this discussion.'

'Do not bandy words with my wife, sir!' said Firethorn.

'Then ask her to withdraw from our conference.'

'Will you be assaulted again!' she threatened.

'Desist, woman! You are not a sharer in the company.'

'*I* am,' said Firethorn, leaping off the bed, 'and that gives me the right to box your ears first. Nobody speaks to Margery with so uncivil a tongue and escapes rebuke. Though she is not one of Westfield's Men, she is a sharer in a house and home whose hospitality you dare to abuse.' Still in his nightshirt, he took a step towards the now quaking Gill. 'You have denounced Nick Bracewell, insulted my dear wife and presumed to call in question my role as the manager of the company. Whipping would be too soft a punishment for these trangressions. Mutilation would be too kind. You deserve to be dragged through the streets on a hurdle, then set in the stocks for a fortnight.' He towered over Gill and vented his spleen. 'Get out of my house, you prancing ninny! Take your fine apparel and your false reports away from Shoreditch. Or by the affection that now guides me most, I'll tear you limb from limb and feed your rotten carcass to the pigs. Avaunt! Begone! Away, you sea-green sickness!'

He lunged at his visitor but Barnaby Gill was too quick for him, electing to take to his heels rather than to try to reason with a homicidal maniac. With a cry of fear, he raced down the stairs, flung open the front door and hurtled out into Old Street as if pursued by the Devil himself.

Up in his bedchamber, Lawrence Firethorn roared like an enraged bull and pawed the ground with one foot. Margery surveyed her husband with lascivious admiration.

'That was heroic! My big, strong, wonderful hero!'

Hands on hips, he inflated his chest and basked in the unstinting adoration of his wife. Theirs was a turbulent marriage but it was grounded in deep love and understanding. This enabled them to enjoy to the full the glorious lulls between the recurring marital storms. Firethorn knew that such a lull was now upon them. Then he realised something else and his misshapen face beamed with joy.

'It is gone, Margery. My toothache has abated.'

'You frighted it away, my love!'

'By Jove! I feel as if I am a new man.'

'I see it well. Every muscle about you ripples.'

'I have risen from my bed of pain!' he said with a laugh of sheer relief. 'Let me return to it as to a palace of pleasure. Anger is indeed the surest medicine. It has made my blood boil. Come, Margery. I have been set free. I have come back to you as a doting husband. Is this not a just cause for celebration?'

'Oh, yes!' she said, flinging herself down on the bed with weighty abandon and kicking her legs in the air. 'Yes, yes, yes!'

'You are the best cure for any toothache, my angel.'
'Let my body be your physick.'
'I am whole once more.'
'Take me, Lawrence! Take me!'
The bed creaked happily for half an hour.

Nicholas Bracewell had even more to do than usual in the wake of that afternoon's performance. He had to convey the body of Ben Skeat to a private room at the inn, send for a surgeon, placate the landlord, Alexander Marwood, who was almost demented at the thought of someone actually dying in such a public fashion on his premises, supervise the dismantling of the stage, ensure that all costumes, properties and scenic devices were safely locked away and advise the company when they would next be needed. There was marginal relief in the fact that there would be no performance on the following day because it was the Sabbath. Westfield's Men used a venue within the precincts of the city and were thus debarred from playing on a Sunday. No such regulation hampered their rivals at The Theatre and The Curtain in Shoreditch, or at The Rose in Bankside.

The surgeon confirmed what Nicholas had suspected. Ben Skeat had died by natural means. He suffered a heart attack of such severity that it killed him almost instantly. It was the surgeon's opinion that Skeat may well have had earlier warnings of his failing health but he had evidently kept them to himself. Nicholas believed that he knew why.

'Does he have a family?' asked the surgeon.

'None,' said Nicholas.

'No wife to mourn him?'

'She herself died six months ago. He and Alice had been married for nearly thirty years. That is unusual in this profession. Actors are poor husbands. Few enjoy such a happy marriage as Ben Skeat.' He gave a wistful sigh on his own account, then read the next question in the surgeon's face. 'Three children in all but they were not destined for this harsh world. None of them lived to see a first birthday. It drew Ben and Alice even closer. Two such well-matched souls it would have been hard to find.'

'He must have been cut adrift without her.'

'Half his life was stolen away from him.'

'Did he pine?'

'Ben kept his grief hidden but it was there.'

As Nicholas talked with the surgeon, he recalled other small signs of the strain the actor had been under. Skeat had started to eat larger meals and drink far more ale. He had become more withdrawn from his fellow-actors and brooded in dark corners. Hitherto an almost vain man, he took less care with his attire and appearance. The book holder had offered what solace he could to his old friend but something of the latter's spirit had gone into the grave with his wife. In recommending him for the part of Duke Alonso in the play, Nicholas Bracewell thought to help him out of his despondency. Instead, the additional pressures of such a taxing role may have helped to put an end to his life. It made the book holder feel obscurely responsible.

A sense of guilt stayed with him as he arranged the removal of the body to the morgue before returning to his other duties at the inn. Would his friend have survived longer if he had not had the leading role thrust upon him? Or was he already dwindling quietly towards his coffin? Had Ben Skeat, in a sense, willed his own death so that he could quit his profession as he scaled its highest peak? Was an element of choice involved? Speculation on these and on other issues left Nicholas both sad and perplexed.

He was glad when his chores were finally over and he could repair to the taproom to join his fellows. He felt the need of a drink and a respite before going to Shoreditch to report to Lawrence Firethorn. The taproom was busy when he entered.

Good-humoured banter could be heard on all sides. Nicholas simply wanted to drop on to a stool and call for some ale but he saw that one more chore awaited him. Edmund Hoode was seated at a table, crouched over his tankard in an attitude of despair and oblivious to the reassurance that Owen Elias was trying to pour into his ear.

The Welshman looked up as Nicholas joined them.

'Thank God you've come, Nick. He is deaf to my voice.'

'How much ale has he taken?'

'Far too much. Sorrow is a thirsty comrade.'

'What has Edmund said?'

'Nothing. That is the worry of it. He is struck dumb by circumstance.' He gave Hoode a gentle nudge. 'Nick is here. Will you join us both in a fresh pot of ale?' The playwright remained silent and Elias gave an elaborate shrug. 'It is like talking to a post.'

'The mood will pass,' said Nicholas.

'Have you ever seen the fellow in such a state?'

'Not from this cause, Owen.'

Elias chuckled. 'Ah, well, I take your meaning. If there was a woman in the case, all would be explained. Edmund is a martyr to the fairer sex. Another doomed love affair might plunge him into this misery but that is not so here.' He spoke into Hoode's ear. 'Come back to us, Edmund. We are your friends. Let us help.'

The hurt silence continued. Nicholas ordered ale for himself and Owen Elias, then talked with the latter as if a third person were not present. They discussed the demise of Ben Skeat and the exigencies it forced upon them. Both had high praise for Barnaby Gill's invention onstage and more caustic comment for his behaviour off it. They wondered if a new sharer would be brought into the company and how such an actor would be recruited. Owen Elias was voluble on this topic. Having laboured for so long in the humbler regions of the hired man, he relished the privilege of being accepted as a sharer.

The Welshman eventually came back to the play itself.

'Let us be honest, Nick,' he said, lowering his voice to a whisper. '*The Corrupt Bargain* was not his best play.'

'It was serviceable enough.'

'Too much matter, too little poetry.'

'You are a stern critic, Owen. I liked it.'

'Why, so did I. But less than his other plays.'

'It merely needed more work on it,' said Nicholas.

'New title, new characters, new plot.' Elias grinned. 'Its defects would soon be mended then. It lacked vigour.'

Edmund Hoode murmured his way into the conversation.

'It lacked everything that bears the name of drama.'

'Welcome back to the land of the living,' said Elias. 'Nick and I were just passing judgement on—'

'I heard,' interrupted Hoode. 'Heard and suffered every word that passed between you.'

'Your play had much merit,' said Nicholas.

'Then it was put there by other hands,' confessed the author gloomily. 'Owen was right. It is a time for honesty and honesty compels me to admit that *The Corrupt Bargain* was my worst piece of work. The characters were stiff, the plot would not bend to my purpose, the verse would not soar from the page. My art is moribund, gentlemen. That is why I am so oppressed. I have lost my creative spark.'

'That is not true, Edmund' said Nicholas loyally. '*The Corrupt Bargain* bore all the marks of your talent, but it had no chance to display them in that performance. The finest drama ever penned will not yield up its true essence if it loses its hero in the middle of Act Three.'

'Ben's death was your misfortune,' said Elias.

'No,' said Hoode. 'It was an apt comment on my play. Ben Skeat went to his grave to escape the ignominy of being in such a lame and undeserving tragedy.'

'The rest of us lived to enjoy it,' noted Elias.

'Enjoy!' Edmund Hoode gave a hollow laugh. '*Enjoy!*'

Nicholas Bracewell traded a glance with Owen Elias and the latter rose gratefully to take his leave. The Welshman had tried and failed to raise the spirits of the company's actor-playwright. A more delicate hand was needed and only the book holder could supply that. Elias took his ale off to a more boisterous table and was soon joining in the raucous badinage. Nicholas leaned in closer to his companion.

'Take heart, Edmund. You have had setbacks before.'

'This was no setback, Nick. It was a catastrophe.'

'Not of your making.'

'*The Corrupt Bargain* was a sign.'

'Of what?'

'His end.'

'Whose end?'

'That impostor.'

'You talk in riddles.'

'That cheat, that counterfeit, that mountebank.'

'Who?'

'Edmund Hoode, poet.'

'He sits before me even now.'

'I am merely his ghost.'

'This is foolish talk.'

'No, Nick,' said Hoode with solemn assurance. 'It is a wisdom born of cruel experience. Ben Skeat was not the only poor wretch who died upon that stage this afternoon. *I* did as well. My art finally expired. Give it a decent burial, then find another poet to fashion your new plays.'

'We already have the best in London,' said Nicholas.

'Kind words will not conceal the ugly truth.'

'We *need* you, Edmund.'

Hoode shook his head. 'I have nothing left to give.'

'That is arrant nonsense!'

Nicholas did what he could to lift his friend's morale but it was all to no avail. What made his task more difficult was the fact that there were distinct elements of truth in what Hoode had been saying. *The Corrupt Bargain* fell far short of his best work. Its construction was faulty, its pace uncertain and its promising theme not fully explored. Given a rousing perform-ance—and with Lawrence Firethorn as the exiled Duke of Genoa—the play would have passed muster but not even its greatest admirers would wish to see it given a regular place in the repertoire of Westfield's Men.

While heaping lavish praise on the poet, and struggling to keep a positive note in his voice, Nicholas was all too conscious of the recent deterioration in the latter's work. Edmund Hoode was contracted to write three new plays for the company each year. *The Corrupt Bargain* was the last, and least impressive, of his annual trio but its two predecessors had also been disappointing works, competent rather than inspiring, and wholly deficient in those flashes of brilliance for which the playwright was so renowned.

'The Muse has deserted me, Nick,' concluded Hoode.

'Not so.'

'When did I last create anything of consequence?'

'With this afternoon's play.'

'Shallow stuff. Poorly put together.'

'You heard the spectators. They acclaimed you.'

'They acclaimed my fellows for replacing the vile scenes that *I* gave them with more worthy material of their own. That is what hurt me most. That crude and disfigured version of *The Corrupt Bargain* was better than my original.'

'Never!'

'It was, Nick. I am done.'

'You have still dozens of fine plays left in you.'

'No, let us not delude ourselves.' He put a hand on his companion's arm. 'You know the hideous truth as well as I do, dear friend. My last work of any real quality was *The Merchant of Calais* and that owed much to your help and encouragement. You gave me both plot and theme.'

Nicholas winced slightly. He had also helped to draw the

character of the play's eponymous hero, a merchant from the West Country who bore a closer resemblance to his own father than he had either wished or intended. *The Merchant of Calais* had been a triumph for its author but it carried some rather uncomfortable memories for Nicholas Bracewell. It made him anxious to change the subject.

'No more of that,' he said. 'Sleep is the only true physician here, Edmund. Go home and rest your troubled head. The case will be altered in the morning. A spent man may go to bed this evening but a gifted poet will rise from it.'

Hoode was about to contradict him when an outburst of laughter took their attention to the far end of a taproom. A group that included Owen Elias was clustered around a young man and guffawing appreciatively as he told them a tale. The stranger was young, well favoured and attired like a gallant in doublet and hose of a subtle red hue. His hat was set at a rakish angle and his cloak was thrown back to reveal its silken lining. He mimed the drawing of a dagger and stabbed the air dramatically to produce fresh mirth from his audience.

'Who is he?' asked Hoode.

'A roisterer, by the look of him,' said Nicholas. 'He seems to have fallen in very easily with our fellows.'

'There is something of an actor about him.'

'And rather more of a swaggerer. Every hostelry in London is plagued by such roaring boys. Drunk with ale and the sound of their own voices. Friends of all the world on a moment's acquaintance, ready to dupe and cozen when occasion serve.' Nicholas watched the way the stranger slipped his arms familiarly around two of the group. 'He will pick no fruit from that tree. Owen and the others are too sharp to be gulled by a smooth-faced knave like that.'

'He is a noisy devil,' complained Hoode. 'My ears begin to ache with the very sound of his voice and their jollity.'

'Take yourself home to bed,' said the other.

'Sound advice.' He stood up and swayed violently. 'My head obeys you but my legs rebel.'

'You took more ale than you thought,' said Nicholas with an indulgent smile, getting up to support his friend. 'Come, Edmund. I'll bestow you at your lodging before I make my way to Shoreditch and give my account of this afternoon's escapade to Master Firethorn.'

'Barnaby will already have been to Old Street.'

'That is why *I* must go as well. To correct his version of events, for it will surely be well wide of the truth.'

They shared a laugh as they headed for the door. Hoode was grateful for the steadying arm of Nicholas Bracewell. As they passed the group at the far end of the room, the young man was at his loudest and most expressive, sharing some new jest and reinforcing it with comical gestures. Owen Elias was shaking with glee. The newcomer was patently a soulmate.

It was a pleasant evening as the two friends stepped out into Gracechurch Street to begin their journey. Shadows were lengthening but there was still enough light for them to be able to pick their way easily along. Hoode's lodging was in Silver Street near Cripplegate but he would never have got there without his friend's assistance. Drink and despair had robbed him of his sense of balance.

'Will you give Lawrence the awful tidings?'

'He will already have heard of Ben Skeat's death.'

'I speak of my own demise.'

'That news will keep, I fancy,' said Nicholas tactfully. 'Master Firethorn has already endured severe toothache and a visit from Barnaby Gill. Three calamities in one day are too much for any man to bear.'

'Why does he not have the tooth drawn?'

'He fears the surgeon.'

'Does he expect the pain to go away on its own?'

'His prayers tend in that direction.'

'The only way to cure a diseased tooth is to pull it out by the roots,' said Hoode in maudlin tones as he saw a parallel situation. 'As with Lawrence, so with the company.'

'Company?'

'We have been in pain these many months, Nick. Poor performances of weak plays by dispirited actors. Our reputation has suffered. It wounds me to say this but our rivals wax while we but wane. Banbury's Men hold first place among the companies. We trail far behind them.'

'How does a diseased tooth come into it?'

'He lurches along at your side.'

'You?'

'Who else?' He heaved a deep sigh of regret. 'I did not realise it until this afternoon but *I* am the source of pain in the mouth of the company. *The Corrupt Bargain* was a symbol of our agony. My failure has infected everyone. Until I am plucked from Westfield's Men by a pair of pincers, the rest of you will suffer the torments of the damned.'

'Those torments would be greater still without you.'

'My way is clear. I must quit the theatre.'

'Your contract forbids you.'

'I'll buy myself out of it.'

'But you *love* the stage, Edmund.'

'It no longer loves me.'

'Put these wild thoughts aside,' said Nicholas. 'A true man of the theatre will never desert his calling.'

'You did.'

'That was . . . a mistake that was soon put right.'

'But you did try to escape this verminous occupation.'

'Yes,' conceded the other. 'I did.'

Nicholas fell silent. It was not a happy memory and he tried to erase it from his mind. When a woman whom he loved forced him to choose between her and the theatre, he had turned his back on the latter only to find that his sacrifice had come too late. Restored to the fold, he vowed that he would never try to leave it again. The theatre offered only a precarious living but it was his natural home.

Edmund Hoode burbled on without even realising that he was having a long conversation with himself. His mood of self-pity was gradually eroded by exhaustion and he was virtually hanging on to his friend's shoulder as they came within sight of Silver Street. Nicholas only half listened to the sorrowful outpourings. Another sound had claimed his interest and he had been glancing behind him whenever they came to a bend or a corner. When they finally reached Hoode's lodging, he propped the poet up against the wall and put a hand on the hilt of his sword.

'Do not leave me here, Nick,' begged the other.

'It will not be for long.'

'Take me in. I can never climb those stairs alone.'

'Wait but a moment.'

'Why do we stay here in the street?'

'Because we are followed,' whispered Nicholas

'I see no one.'

'He stays in the shadows.'

'Where?'

'Watch.'

Drawing his weapon, Nicholas swung quickly round and ran diagonally across to the dark alley on the other side of the narrow street. Someone stirred in the darkness and he caught the flash of another blade. Nicholas engaged his man at once and the swords clashed in the gloom.

'Hold, sir! Hold!' called his adversary. 'I seek no quarrel. I am a friend!'

'Why, then, do you fight with me?'

'Merely to defend myself. I pray you, stand off.'

Nicholas took a few steps back but kept his weapon at the ready. The other man stepped forward into the half-light with an apologetic smile. He gave a shrug and sheathed his own sword. Nicholas was startled. It was the young man whom he had seen roistering at the Queen's Head but there was no hint of the latter's inebriation now. The roaring boy had become a gentleman who bore himself with dignity.

'Who are you?' demanded Nicholas.

'Someone who would like to know you better, sir.'

'For what purpose?'

'That can only be divulged in privacy.'

'You followed us!'

'How else could I find out where you went?'

'Why were you carousing with our fellows?'

'So that I could learn more about Nicholas Bracewell.'

'Me?'

'You and Edmund Hoode.' He pointed to the sword. 'We would have easier conference if you were to put that away. I mean you no harm. I will happily surrender my own weapon, if that will reassure you.'

'No need.' Nicholas relaxed slightly and sheathed his sword. 'Now, sir. What is your name?'

'I would rather not speak it in the street.'

'Why have you come to spy on us?'

'Because I need your help,' said the other with obvious sincerity. 'I would not have come else. You and Master Hoode are the only ones whom I could trust.'

'Trust?'

'May we not step inside the house? It is safer there.'

'Safer?'

'For all three of us.'

'Why?'

The young man threw a nervous glance up and down the street before stepping back into the shadows. His rampant joviality had been left behind at the Queen's Head. He had other preoccupations now. There was a polite seriousness about him which compelled respect. He certainly posed no threat to Nicholas.

Edmund Hoode was now barely awake, his back to the wall

of the little half-timbered house, his feet slowly losing their purchase on the cracked paving. He registered the newcomer's appearance without hearing a word of what he said. Secure in the knowledge that Nicholas Bracewell would fend for him, Hoode gave up all pretence of interest in the remainder of the day and drifted off into a welcome sleep. The book holder was just in time to catch him before he slumped to the ground. Crossing to join them, the young man took his share of the playwright's weight.

'One good turn deserves another,' he said.

'Leave him be, sir.'

'Two can carry more easily than one.'

Nicholas spurned the offer. Hoisting the slim body of Edmund Hoode across his shoulders, he took him swiftly into the house before ascending the rickety staircase to his chamber. The room was in darkness but Nicholas knew its geography well enough to negotiate the meagre furniture and lower his cargo gently down on to the bed. Hoode gave a loud yawn of gratitude. After lighting a candle and checking that his friend was lying in a comfortable position, Nicholas went back downstairs and into the street. It seemed to be quite empty but he knew that their visitor would be hiding in the shadows.

'Come forth, sir,' he called.

'Thank you,' said the other, emerging from the darkness.

'I shall want plain speaking if you are admitted.'

'You will get it.'

Nicholas led the way in and shut the front door behind them. When they entered Hoode's chamber, the lodger was still dozing peacefully on the bed. The young man peered down at him with some misgiving.

'He does not look like a famous poet.'

'Appearances can mislead. As you well know.'

'Indeed, Master Bracewell.'

They exchanged a smile. The young man crossed to the window and gazed down into the street for a moment. Only when he was satisfied that there was nobody outside the house did he turn around and nod at Nicholas. The latter appraised him shrewdly.

'Why all this secrecy?' he said.

'I am often watched.'

'By whom?'

'That is the problem. I do not know.'

'Are you in danger?'

'I will be.'

Nicholas waved him to a stool, then moved the candle so that it illumined the visitor's face. Handsome features were set off by a dark beard that was carefully trimmed. A high forehead glistened with intelligence. The large brown eyes sparkled. It was time for some elucidation.

'What is your name?' said Nicholas.

'Simon Chaloner.'

'Who are you?'

'A friend to Westfield's Men.'

'Friend?'

'I bring something of great value,' he said. 'I offer it to you in return for your help.'

'Why?'

'All will became clear in due course.'

Simon Chaloner studied him carefully as if unwilling to go on until a proper scrutiny had been made. Nicholas took in the cut and cost of the man's apparel and noted, for the first time, the bulge in his doublet. He remained calm under the young man's searching gaze. Eventually, his visitor gave a firm nod of approval. Whatever examination he had been subjected to, the book holder seemed to have passed it.

'They all speak well of you.'

'Who?'

'Your fellows. They say that you are the prop that holds up Westfield's Men, its very foundation.'

'They overpraise me,' said Nicholas. 'I am but the book holder. Lawrence Firethorn is our manager.'

'I know his reputation. That is why I came to you.'

'Me?'

'To you and to Edmund Hoode.' He looked over at the sleeping poet. 'Master Firethorn would not listen to me. He is too caught up in himself, too restless a spirit. He is a born actor. Need I say more? You, on the other hand, have more forbearance. Patience.'

'That patience is fast running out, sir.'

'Then I will trespass on it no further.' An urgency came into his voice. 'Briefly, my plea is this. Undertake to read something for me. Ensure that Master Hoode reads it as well for he alone can invest it with real life and purpose. If the piece offends you, return it to me forthwith and no harm will have been done. If it please you—and I dare swear that it will set your curiosity alight—then we may talk further.'

'You wish to offer us a play?'

'A semblance of one, Master Bracewell. It is more an idea for a drama than a finished manuscript, and yet it would not take much to mould it into an acceptable shape.'

'Are you the playwright, Master Chaloner?'

'I was involved in the creation of it.'

'A co-author, then?'

'Not quite, sir.'

'Then what?'

'Read the piece first. It speaks for itself.'

'We are given dozens of new plays every year.'

'Not like this one.'

'Do not raise your expectations too high.'

'They are based on my knowledge of Nicholas Bracewell and Edmund Hoode. The one will give me a fair hearing and the other will be able to repair the many faults in the play. Together, you would be able to persuade Lawrence Firethorn to take an interest in the project.'

'You presume far too much, sir.'

'This is no rash move on my part, I assure you. I have watched Westfield's Men for some time. You have qualities that none of your rivals can offer.' He gave a smile. 'What is more important, you are ready to take appalling risks.'

'Risks?'

'A man died onstage this afternoon. The play went on.'

'You are very perceptive,' conceded Nicholas, 'but that particular risk was thrust unsought upon us.'

'You contended with misfortune and won through. Most of the spectators saw nothing amiss but I did. I applaud your skill without reservation. It is one of the main reasons that I chose your company.'

'What are the others?'

'Read the play, sir. Then I will tell you.'

He undid the fastening on his doublet before putting his hand inside to pull out a thick manuscript. Sheets of yellowing parchment were bound neatly together by a red ribbon. The young man fondled the play for a moment with distant affection before holding it out to Nicholas. The latter felt obliged to issue a warning that he gave to all aspiring authors.

'It will be read in time,' he promised, 'but we can give no guarantee of performance. Most of the work submitted to us either falls below the standard required or is simply not suitable for Westfield's Men. Prepare yourself for disappointment.'

'There is no question of that now that we have met.'

'I have little influence on the choice of plays.'

'You will fight on behalf of this one. Take it, sir.'

He thrust the manuscript into Nicholas's hands, then crossed rapidly to the door. The book holder took a few bewildered steps after him.

'Wait, sir. You have not said where you dwell.'

'That is my business.'

'How, then, do we get in touch?'

'I will come to you.'

'But we need more details than that.'

'Find them in the play.'

Nicholas glanced down at a manuscript that clearly held immense significance for his mysterious visitor. With no small risk to himself, it seemed, Simon Chaloner had gone to great lengths to deliver the play. The veil of secrecy was annoying but it was also intriguing. Not withstanding his suspicions, Nicholas felt his interest quicken.

'What is its title?' he asked.

The Roaring Boy.'

[CHAPTER THREE]

Having feasted with the gods on ambrosia and nectar, Lawrence Firethorn suffered grievously for his over-indulgence. When he opened his eyes once more, he was no longer at a banquet on Mount Olympus, sporting with a compliant young nymph. He was twisted like a convolvulus around the ample frame of his wife and a tiny mole was burrowing its way eagerly through his swollen cheek. Connubial delight was at an end. Toothache reigned supreme. Time thereafter throbbed slowly past.

'Fenugreek,' said Margery later that evening.

'What?'

'Fenugreek. That is what the apothecary recommends.'

'A fig for his recommendations!'

'You are still in agony, Lawrence.'

'I do not need to be told that!' he howled.

'Is not this fenugreek at least worth trying?'

'No!'

'Fill the tooth with it, said the apothecary. Hold it in place with wax. In time, he assured me, the ailing tooth would so loosen that you may pluck it out with your fingers.'

Firethorn bridled. 'I'll pluck the apothecary's stones off with my fingers if he dares inflict that remedy on me! God's tits! The cure is worse than the disease.'

It was only a few hours since they had smothered pain beneath a blanket of passion but it seemed like a century ago. When he tried to bestow a fond smile on her, his face remained locked into a lopsided grimace. Firethorn extended a forlorn hand to his wife and she gave it a sympathetic squeeze. She was about to steal away and leave him alone in the flickering light of the bedchamber when there was a loud knocking at the front door of the house.

'Nick Bracewell, I'll be bound,' she said.

'Where has the rogue been?'

'I'll show him in myself.'

'Chide him for his lateness when you do so.'

'He is always welcome here, whatever the hour.'

Margery went skipping down the stairs with an almost girlish delight and waved away the servant girl who was about to open the door. Nicholas was admitted by the mistress of the house and greeted with an affectionate smile. He doffed his cap politely.

'I am sorry I have been delayed,' he said.

'We knew that you would come when you could.'

She gave him a warm hug and pulled him into the house before closing the door. Her voice became conspiratorial.

'Deal gently with him, Nick.'

'How is he?' whispered the other.

'More comfortable but still in pain.'

'Has a surgeon been sent for yet?'

'He will not consider it.'

Nicholas glanced upwards. 'Is he still awake?'

'Yes!' bellowed Firethorn. 'Still wide awake and able to hear everything the pair of you are muttering. Send him up here, Margery. Make haste, sir. I have waited long enough.'

Nicholas smiled and picked his way up the staircase to the main bedchamber of the house. With a lighted candle either side of him, Lawrence Firethorn was propped up on some pillows in his nightshirt like a potentate worn down by the cares of state. He wagged an admonitory finger.

'What on earth has kept you away for so long?'

'Ben Skeat.'

'That news was an aching tooth in itself.'

'We still reel from the shock of it.'

'Have all the arrangements been made?'

'Yes,' said Nicholas. 'I engaged the services of an undertaker and spoke to the parish clerk of St Leonard's. Ben Skeat will be buried beside his beloved wife.'

'When is the funeral?'

'On Tuesday next at ten.'

'The whole company must be there.'

'They will need no urging on that score.'

'No,' said Firethorn. 'He was loved and respected by all. How many of us can say that? But let us save our tears for his funeral. Now, tell me what happened.'

'Has not someone already played the messenger?'

'Oh, yes. Barnaby came dancing in here to boast of the way that he had rescued the company from extinction. The villain crowed over me like a very Chanticleer. But when he spoke out of turn to Margery, and told her—would you believe?—to hold her peace, I sent him dancing out again with his ears aflame.'

'He may not have given you the full story.'

'It was a pack of lies from start to finish. He forgot that the apprentices live under my roof. When they got home this evening, their version quarrelled with Barnaby's in every particular.' He gave a quiet chuckle. 'Dick Honeydew was the most trustworthy. The lad was still shaking like an aspen at the horror of it all. Dick says that you were magnificent.'

'I did only what was needful.'

'You stopped them bolting like frightened horses.'

'The play had to go on. Ben would have wanted that.'

Nicholas Bracewell gave a succinct account of the trials endured by Westfield's Men during their performance. He explained that he had helped Edmund Hoode back to his lodgings but made no mention of the poet's determination to write no more. Nor was it the moment to discuss the strange encounter with Simon Chaloner. The actor-manager was in need of comfort rather than anxiety and Nicholas was seasoned in the art of keeping unsettling news from his employer.

'How do you feel now?' he asked solicitously.

'The worst is over, Nick. I'll be back on Monday.'

'*Vincentio's Revenge* is a demanding piece.'

'I can play it in my sleep.'

'You are sure that you will be fully recovered?'

'Doubly sure.' Firethorn beckoned him closer. 'But tell me what neither Barnaby nor the apprentices could. How bad a play was *The Corrupt Bargain?*'

'It would be unfair to judge it on that showing.'

'Come, come, man. Put tact aside for once. Beshrew your love for Edmund. Speak honestly about his work.'

'He has written finer plays.'

'Has he ever penned anything worse?'

Nicholas hesitated. 'Possibly not.'

'His talent has been drying up steadily all year.'

'That is unkind.'

"Unkind but not inaccurate.'

Lawrence Firethorn was sometimes mistakenly regarded as a monster of selfishness whose only interest was in his own performances. It was true that he had the vanity common to his trade and that it sometimes tipped over into an unseemly arrogance, but he had none of the bickering narcissism of a Barnaby Gill or the combative exuberance of an Owen Elias. Firethorn was a proven master of his craft with the confidence to tackle any role and the dedication to strive ever harder for perfection.

Proud of his own achievements, he did not ignore those of

other people. Players were helpless without good plays and he had learned how to coax the best work out of his resident author. Performances were doomed without strict discipline, which was why he set such a high value on the stage management of Nicholas Bracewell. Firethorn might be the central pillar of Westfield's Men but he never forgot that each member of the company made his own contribution. When that contribution was satisfactory, he had nothing but praise. If anyone was giving less than his best, he upbraided him without mercy.

'I will have to speak to Edmund,' he warned.

'Stay your hand a little while.'

'You cannot protect him forever, Nick. Someone has to tell him the truth. He is letting us down. Most of all, he is letting *himself* down.'

'That has not evaded his notice.'

'Then why does he not do something about it?' He warmed to his theme. 'His last two plays barely caused a ripple of excitement. This new one—by all accounts—was dying on its feet until a real death put some life into it. Edmund Hoode is in decline and it must be stopped.'

'I am confident that it will be,' said Nicholas with far more conviction than he felt. He thought of the jaded friend he had left asleep in Silver Street, a man so out of love with his craft that he talked of abandoning it. The book holder had been concealing the truth about Edmund Hoode's condition from Lawrence Firethorn. He would now have to hide the actor-manager's frank criticism from the playwright. 'Edmund has been through a difficult time of late,' he said, 'but he is emerging from it now. His next play will surely vindicate his reputation. Give him time.'

Firethorn sighed. 'Do you know what was worst, Nick?'

'Worst?'

'When I was lying here alone this afternoon.'

'Missing the opportunity to play Duke Alonso?'

'No, not that.'

'Suffering such intense pain from your tooth?'

'Nor that.'

'Being clucked over afterwards by Barnaby Gill?'

'Nor even that,' said Firethorn. 'It was the noise.'

'Noise?'

'From Holywell Lane. Heaven knows, I created a din myself but only to drown out that horrible sound from The Curtain.' He gave a shudder. 'Applause, Nick. Long and loud applause for Giles Randolph and Banbury's Men. While I lay stricken here, he and his company were fêted. At the expense of Lawrence Firethorn. It was unendurable. Topcliffe himself could not have devised a more exquisite torture for me.'

Nicholas gave a wry smile. Richard Topcliffe was the notorious interrogator of suspected Roman Catholics, a man whose name was synonymous with cruelty and who was so dedicated to his grisly work that he had built a private torture chamber in his own house at Westminster.

Firethorn writhed in anguish for a moment.

'Giles Randolph *was* Topcliffe this afternoon.'

'He is only a good actor where you are a great one.'

'A good actor in a good play,' corrected the other. 'And that is far better than a great actor in a bad one. I need powerful weapons to battle against Randolph and my other rivals. Edmund has left me unarmed.'

'He is not our only author.'

'But he remains our touchstone.'

Nicholas could not deny it. Firethorn was only saying what Edmund Hoode himself had admitted. Westfield's Men were having to rely more and more on staple dramas from their repertoire. Other companies were attracting the best and most consistent playwrights. Nicholas looked down at the manuscript that was still tucked under his arm. Though he had told Simon Chaloner that they received a steady flow of new plays, this was the first to be offered to the company in months. It would doubtless meet the same fate as the vast majority of its predecessors. The book holder's instinct told him that *The Roaring Boy* would amount to no more than the scribble of a floundering amateur.

'He must be *told*, Nick.'

'Let me broach the topic with him.'

'Very well,' said Firethorn, 'but do not let sentiment stand in the way of the harsh truth. Edmund must shake off this lethargy and learn to write small masterpieces once more. Otherwise—much as it would grieve me—we will have to dispense with his services as a playwright and replace him with a more durable talent. Make that clear to him!'

Simon Chaloner was a fine horseman who knew how to pace his mount. After the meeting in Silver Street, he retraced his steps to the Queen's Head and collected the animal he had stabled there. With night starting to wrap its warm cloak around the capital, he went over London Bridge at a rising trot, kicked the horse into a steady canter and headed east along the old Roman thoroughfare of Watling Street. It was the road which pilgrims had taken for centuries to the shrine of St Thomas Becket in Canterbury and it could not be more apposite for him. Chaloner rode with the anticipatory thrill of a man on the way to meet a saint.

The moon was a kindly lantern that splashed his route with subdued light. It was highly dangerous for a lone horseman to venture so far by day. Night brought additional hazards but he paid them no heed. Speed and a sense of purpose were protection enough for Simon Chaloner. When jeopardy loomed up ahead of him, he met it up cold disdain. Two men, armed with daggers, lying in wait for travellers a mile or so from Deptford, jumped out into his path as he approached and waved a ragged cloak in the air to startle the horse into throwing its rider.

They chose the wrong victim. Chaloner's heels dug into the animal's flank and it surged into a gallop to knock the two men flying. One went rolling over helplessly on the hard ground while the other was hurled with force against a stout elm. The highwaymen were still counting their bruises and cursing their luck as the sound of the pummelling hooves faded away in the distance. Nothing was going to stop this particular traveller.

The horse slowed down to clatter over the bridge at Deptford Creek, then resumed its canter for the last leg of the journey. Chaloner's destination was only a mile away now and it was not long before he caught his first glimpse of guttering light. Torches were burning at Greenwich Palace to define its elegant bulk and to throw shifting patterns upon the river that fronted it. Seen in silhouette, it had an almost fairy tale quality about it. Chaloner goaded his mount into one last spurt as the village itself came hazily into view with its houses, churches and civic buildings in a haphazard cluster. A community with strong naval associations, it was surrounded on three sides by a scatter of imposing manors, tenanted farms and market gardens.

In recent years, the popularity of Greenwich had continued to grow. It was close enough to London to allow comfortable access by boat or horse, and far enough away to escape its seething crowds, its abiding stink and its frequent outbreaks of plague. There was an air of prosperity about the place, set in a loop of the Thames and surrounded by lush green fields. Ships lay at anchor in front of the palace and sheep grazed safely on the pasture. Even at night, Greenwich exuded a quiet pride in itself.

Simon Chaloner reached a large house in the main street and went to the stables at the rear. An ostler came running to take the reins from him as he dropped down from the saddle, and he tossed a word of thanks to the man before hurrying away. A maidservant admitted him to the house itself and conducted him without delay to the parlour.

A pale young woman was pacing the room anxiously with lips pursed and hands clasped tightly together. She looked up with trepidation as she heard the door open but gave a gasp of relief when she saw who it was. She ran to him on tiptoe.

'Simon!'

'Did you think I would never come?'

'I am so glad to see you safe returned!'

He removed his hat and gave a mock bow, then took her hand to place a soft kiss on it. The maidservant was lingering in the doorway to see if she would be needed further but her mistress waved her away. When they were left alone, the young woman stood in front of her visitor with trembling impatience.

'Well?' she demanded.

'Let me first get my breath back, Emilia.'

'Did you watch the play?' He nodded and removed a glove to dab at the specks of perspiration on his brow. 'And were you satisfied?'

'Satisfied and even amused.'

Her face clouded. 'Amused?'

'I will explain in a moment,' he promised. 'But only when you calm down and stop badgering me, my sweet. Take a seat so that I may look at you properly. I have ridden such a long way for this pleasure and I surely deserve my reward.' When she still hesitated, he sounded a warning note. 'If you would hear my report, you must humour me.'

Emilia gave a wan smile and lowered herself into one of the carved oak chairs. Tallow candles had been set on the table and on the low cupboards. Simon Chaloner chose a seat which enabled him to see her encircled by light. Short, slim and graceful, she had a face that remained enchanting even when it was marked, as now, with signs of acute distress. She wore a plain dress of a dark blue material but it was the robe of a saint to him. This was his shrine and his eyes worshipped gratefully.

His love was frank and unashamed but her feelings for him were held in check by an inner sadness that pushed everything else out to the margins. Chaloner understood this only too well and made allowances for her fitful impulses of affection towards

him and her wavering concentration. Emilia had more immediate concerns than their relationship.

'You went to the Queen's Head,' she said. 'What, then?'

'I enjoyed the performance.'

'What, then? What, then?

'I mingled with the players to win their confidence so that I
could sound them out on certain matters. Though I say so
myself, I gave an excellent performance in my role.'

'Was your opinion of Westfield's Men confirmed?'

'Whole-heartedly, Emilia.'

'You spoke with their manager?'

'Lawrence Firethorn was indisposed.'

'With whom, then?'

'Nicholas Bracewell.'

'One of the sharers?'

'The book holder.'

Emilia was jolted. 'A book holder!' she exclaimed. 'You
entrusted something as important as this to a book holder?'

'There is no more able or discreet fellow in the entire company,' said Chaloner seriously. 'He holds them all together. I
tell you, Emilia, without his boldness, that play would have
fallen to pieces this afternoon.'

'Why?'

'They suffered a mishap both tragic and amusing.'

He recounted the story of the performance and praised the
way that Westfield's Men had overcome adversity, albeit with
some moments of incidental comedy that had not been devised
by the author. Emilia hung on his words and was much reas-
sured by what she heard of Nicholas Bracewell. The narrative
wended its way to Silver Street.

'He accepted the play?' she said.

'Without obligation.'

'I hope you insisted that he take great care of it.'

'No need. Plays are like gold to them. The book holder will
guard it with his life and he is not a man to yield that up lightly.

I would hate to meet Nicholas Bracewell in a brawl. He is someone to have as friend and not foe.'

'But discreet, you say?'

'Discreet and influential. His word is respected.'

'How much did you tell him?'

'Little beyond the title of the play.'

'When will it be read?' she said, rising from her seat. 'How soon can we have an answer? Who will make the decision?'

'Do not alarm yourself, Emilia,' he soothed, crossing to ease her back down into the chair. 'I have delivered the manuscript to the right person, of that there is no doubt. It may take some time to get a verdict. Be patient.'

'I have been so for many months.'

'This is a delicate enterprise. It may not be rushed.'

'Pray God they see its merit.'

'They will be blind else.'

'And their playwright?'

'Edmund Hoode? I talked with him as well, more or less.'

'More or less?'

'He was present at our discussion.'

Simon Chaloner tailored the truth to fit more snugly over her apprehension. There was no point in telling her that the resident poet of Westfield's Men had been too drunk even to stay awake, let alone to take part in an intelligent conversation. Chaloner put his faith in Nicholas Bracewell.

'What happens next, Simon?'

'We wait and watch.'

'And if they do show an interest in *The Roaring Boy?*'

'I will conduct the negotiations.'

She squeezed his arm gratefully. 'You have done so much already,' she said. 'I will be forever in your debt.'

'You'll find me a doting creditor.'

'A cautious one, too, I trust.'

'Do not fret about me.'

'You put yourself in a perilous situation.'

'Every man who falls in love does that.'

She gave him another wan smile and released his arm. Simon Chaloner moved away and glanced around the room. It was spacious and well furnished with a tapestry adorning one wall and rich hangings at the windows. The floor was lightly strewn with rushes mixed with sweet-smelling lavender and rosemary clippings. For all its hints of luxury, however, the parlour had a curious emptiness to it. Flushed with his exertions, he nevertheless felt a cold shiver.

'When it is all over, I will take you away from here.'

'Why?' she said.

'This house has too many bitter memories.'

'They are balanced by fond recollection.'

He blinked in surprise. 'How, in God's name, can you speak of fondness, Emilia? You are surrounded by ghosts here. They haunt you dreadfully. They rob you of your peace of mind. It was within these self-same walls that—'

'Say no more!' she protested.

'We must build a new life together.'

'I do not even wish to think about it yet.'

'But that is what drives us on, is it not? That is why we have entered this battle. To win some happiness.'

'Happiness and justice.'

'The one flows from the other.'

He went quickly back to her and knelt beside the chair but she was in no mood for impassioned declarations. She stilled his mouth with the tips of her fingers, then brushed his lips with the merest whisper of a kiss. He was content. The patience which he had recommended to her must be his own watchword. A long struggle lay ahead and it was fraught with unknown danger. Only when that struggle was resolved could he come to claim her as his own. Only then would she yield herself completely to him. Pilgrim and saint would be at last be united in marriage.

'When will you go back to London?' she asked.

'Soon, my love.'
'And if they reject the play?'
He grinned bravely. 'They will not *dare!*'

Edmund Hoode fell headfirst into a bottomless pit and spi-
ralled his way down through eternity until he met an unexpected obstacle. What he thought was the first circle in hell
turned out to be the floor of his chamber in Silver Street and
its hard surface buffeted him straight out of his nightmare and
back into the waking world. One bleary glance at it told him he
would prefer the bottomless pit. At least there had been no pain
during his leaf-like fall through a perpetual autumn. Plucked
untimely from his deep slumber, he discovered that his head
was now pounding, his back felt as if it had been flayed and his
stomach was so queasy that it was about to stage an armed
mutiny against its owner.

He crawled to the chamber pot just in time and lowered his
face below the rim. The steaming vomit gushed out of him and
left a foul taste in his mouth. When he dared to raise his head,
he vowed that he would never again drink so much ale so fast
in a tavern. Why had he done such a reckless thing and who
had helped him back to his lodging?

Through fluttering eyelids, he looked across at the window
and saw that dawn was slowly pushing the dark clouds apart
like curtains. Supporting himself against a wall, he made a
supreme effort and dragged himself upright before making his
way to the casement. The feat was impressive but the result was
not encouraging. His head pounded harder, his back smarted
more and his stomach began to consider a second revolt. What
worried him most was that his eyes seemed to take on indepen-
dent lives, one watering while the other burned, each giving
him conflicting pictures of the murky London to which he had
been reluctantly dragged back.

As he looked through the window, one eye told him that a

familiar figure was turning the corner of his street but the other identified only a dog. Which intelligence should he trust? He closed both lids and felt his way back to the bed before lowering himself on to it as gingerly as he could. Once horizontal again, he resolved to stay there until his various organs proved capable of at least a degree of co-operation.

He was just starting to drift off to sleep when a fist banged on the front door below. Hoode felt as if someone were knocking directly on his forehead. It made both eyes water. The front door was locked and bolted overnight so it took a moment for the servant to open it. Voices joined in the briefest of conversation, then heavy footsteps came up the staircase. The tap on his door was soft and considerate.

'Edmund?'

'What?' he groaned.

'May I come in?'

'Who is it?'

'Nicholas.'

'At this time of the morning?'

'I have been up all night.'

'Why?'

Nicholas opened the door and took a tentative step into the room. The sight that confronted him was daunting, the smell even more so. He crossed immediately to the small window and flung it back on its hinges to admit a draught of air. Edmund Hoode propped himself up on his elbows and found that his eyes had at last come to an amicable agreement with each other. Pleased to see his friend, he was embarrassed to be caught in such a disgusting condition.

'Up all night, you say?'

'With advantage, Edmund.'

'That means there is a lady in the case.'

'I found a more exciting bedfellow.'

'Indeed.'

'This.' Nicholas held up the manuscript. 'A play.'

Hoode gaped. 'You stayed awake to read *that?*'

'Twice over.'

'Have you run mad?'

'Only with joy. I had to bring it to you.'

'Take it away, Nick. I am done with plays. I never want to see, write or act in one again.' Hoode was now sitting upright without undue calamity and his head was actually beginning to clear. Curiosity stirred. 'What is it called?'

'*The Roaring Boy.*'

'Who wrote it?'

'I have no idea.'

'Where did it come from?'

'A stranger.'

'What is its theme?'

'Murder.'

'That's a stale plot.'

'None could be fresher, Edmund.'

'Why?'

'Read it for yourself.'

'Never!'

'Be ruled by me and you will live to be grateful.'

'Grateful?' moaned Hoode. 'To be woken at dawn for no better reason than to have a scurvy play waved in front of me? You expect thanks for this ordeal? I lie abed, man. What I need beside me is a gentle girl not a roaring boy.'

'You will soon change your mind,' said Nicholas as he dropped the manuscript into the other's lap. 'Take care of it. I am giving you the most precious gift of all.'

'What is that?'

'Salvation in five acts.'

The Parish Church of St Leonard's was a medieval foundation which dated back to the time when Shoreditch was no more than a straggle of houses near a crossroads. It was now partly hemmed in by other buildings but its nave was long and its graveyard accommodating. Several actors lived or lodged in the district, attracted by its suburban charms and its two theatres. Some—including Lawrence Firethorn—were known to worship at St Leonard's. Others only visited the church with regularity when they were laid to rest there.

Ben Skeat had always had a close relationship with St Leonard's. He had been married before its altar and attended services there on most Sundays with a gladsome mind. It was also the place where he had buried his three children. His wife had joined them in time and Skeat—having travelled on without her until he found the journey too onerous—elected to follow her into the grave. Westfield's Men were all there to bid farewell to a cherished colleague. What was even more touching was the fact that so many actors from other companies came to pay their respects. Skeat had been a presence on the London stage. Even his rivals admired him.

'Why does the fool not shut up?' asked Firethorn.

'He is almost done,' said Nicholas.

'I'll have none of this dribbling vicar when *I* die.'

'He speaks well of Ben.'

'We come to mourn, not to hear an hour's sermon.'

Seated in the church beside his employer, Nicholas Bracewell was more tolerant. Traditionally, the parson of St Leonard's was always the archdeacon of London but the mundane round of baptisms, services of holy matrimony and funerals was left to the vicar. Advanced in age himself, the vicar had known Skeat for decades and took his congregation through an accumulation of pleasant memories. Firethorn grew weary of the address but his wife, Margery, seated on the other side of him, was moved to tears. Nicholas was held by the well-meaning benevolence of the vicar's words.

They adjourned to the churchyard for the burial. A sad occasion was made more depressing by a steady drizzle. Skeat had only a few distant relatives to witness his descent into the good earth. The acting fraternity dominated and one or two of them used the occasion to attract undue attention. Barnaby Gill was the most blatant offender, attired in black and given to sudden fits of weeping over a man to whom he had never been more than polite in the past. Firethorn gave a snort of disapproval at the performance but was powerless to prevent it. In any case, he had to mollify his colleague rather than take him to task.

'Stay, Barnaby,' he said. 'A word in your ear.'

'My thoughts lie in the coffin with Ben Skeat.'

'He is beyond our help now.'

'You were not beside him when he died—*I* was.'

The funeral was over and the congregation dispersed. As no performance was scheduled for that afternoon, most of the company headed in the direction of Bishopsgate so that they could ease their sorrows at the Queen's Head and exchange reminiscences of the dear departed. Lawrence Firethorn had another funeral to attend. He somehow had to bury the violent quarrel he had in his house with Barnaby Gill.

Since that moment of conflict, the two had hardly spoken a word to each other. Firethorn's toothache had faded to a dull ache that allowed him to give an adequate—if rather muted— account of the title role in *Vincentio's Revenge* on the previous afternoon. Gill had played opposite him with his customary brio but sulked in silence when he came offstage. The rift in the lute had to be mended.

Nicholas Bracewell undertook to begin the repairs.

'We need your advice on a most pressing matter.'

'Can I not be left to mourn in peace?' said Gill.

'You will not be detained long.'

'Save it until the morrow.'

'It may be too late, Master Gill.'

'For what?'

'The decision.'

'Lawrence makes all the decisions. Talk to him.'

'This one requires your approval, Barnaby,' said Firethorn with an appeasing smile. 'Return to my house with us and partake of some refreshment.'

'You wish to feed me this time before you evict me?'

'I mean to apologise to you.'

Gill thawed visibly at the mention of an apology and Nicholas stepped in again to secure an advantage. By alternately praising Gill's work with the company and emphasizing the importance of his opinion, the book holder managed to escort him all the way to the house in Old Street before the actor really noticed. When he took stock of his surroundings again, Gill found himself in the very house from which he had been expelled so rudely on Saturday.

Margery Firethorn had been schooled in her part.

'Welcome, Barnaby!' she said with open arms. 'It is a joy to have you beneath our humble roof once more. But I intrude here. Woman's work is in the kitchen.' She beamed at the three men. 'I will leave you alone, sirs.'

She went out of the parlour and shut the latch door behind her. Before Gill could pass any comment, his host thrust a cup of Canary wine into his hand and passed another to Nicholas Bracewell. All three drank a toast to the memory of Ben Skeat, then settled down on upright chairs.

Barnaby Gill was still morose and defensive.

'I was outraged on my last visit to this house.'

'It will not happen again,' Firethorn assured him.

'Toothache sometimes has bad manners,' said Nicholas.

'Those, I accept,' said Gill. 'Violence, I abhor.'

Firethorn grasped the nettle. 'I apologise, Barnaby.'

'You admit you were in the wrong?'

'There were faults on both sides.'

'I was unjustly set upon!'

'Through a misunderstanding,' said Nicholas. 'Let us put that aside and turn to the matter in hand. It is a cause for mild celebration though it is not without its qualms.'

Gill turned to Firethorn. 'What is he talking about?'

'Nick will tell you himself. It is his tale.'

'I hope it be shorter than the vicar's narrative.'

'Hear him, Barnaby.'

Nicholas cleared his throat and gave a brief account of how *The Roaring Boy* had come into his hands. He found it exhilarating and gave it to Edmund Hoode. The playwright thought it inspiring and passed it on to Lawrence Firethorn. The actor-manager considered it immensely promising as it had a powerful role for him. All three were keen to give the work the accolade of a performance by Westfield's Men.

Gill flew at once into a state of apostasy.

'I refuse to countenance this folly!'

'But you have not even seen the play,' said Nicholas.

'That is exactly why I object to it. Since when have I been forced to take my turn behind a book holder and a poet? I should have been the first to study any new work.'

'After me, that is,' reminded Firethorn.

'Does it matter in what order it is read?' reasoned Nicholas. 'I gave it to Edmund Hoode because the play needs him to give it shape and direction. Without his help, we would not be able to proceed.'

'Could not the author improve it himself?' said Gill.

'We do not know who he is.'

'An anonymous play?'

'The author has a reason for concealing his name.'

'Is he then ashamed of his work?'

'He has every right to be proud.'

'It is a somewhat makeshift affair at the moment,' said Firethorn, 'but the faults lie only in construction. Those are soon mended. The piece has great spirit, Barnaby. If we can make it work, Westfield's Men will take London by storm.'

Gill remained sceptical but he agreed to let Nicholas Bracewell outline the plot of *The Roaring Boy*. It was a domestic drama based on a murder case whose reverberations were still being felt in the capital. Thomas Brinklow was a highly successful mathematician and marine engineer from Greenwich. When he married a young wife, Cecily, he did not realise that she was still in love with the steward of her former household, Walter Dunne. Wife and lover conspired to have Brinklow murdered in order that they could be together and inherit his wealth.

Two villains, Maggs and Freshwell, were engaged to do the deed. When Thomas Brinklow was butchered to death, the plot was uncovered and three of the malefactors were arrested. Freshwell went to the gallows with Cecily Brinklow and Walter Dunne. The other killer, Maggs, eluded capture and was still at large. So brutal was the actual slaughter that it even shocked a city where murder was a daily event. London was still buzzing about the grotesque treatment accorded to Brinklow of Greenwich.

'I remember the case well,' said Gill airily. 'Who does not? But there is no call to show this heinous crime upon a stage. The murder was solved and the guilty hanged.'

'But they may not have been guilty,' said Nicholas.

'Aye,' noted Firethorn. 'There's the rub.'

'Not guilty!' Gill laughed derisively. 'Why, that scheming steward was actually taken *in flagrante* with the slippery wife. What more proof of guilt do you need?'

'That only confirms their adultery,' said Nicholas. 'They admitted that in court. Complicity in the murder was denied. They protested their innocence to the end.'

Gill was unconvinced. 'Which murderer does not? The wretches tried to throw all the blame on to their two accomplices. Did not this Freshwell confess all? They paid him and his vile comrade to hack poor Brinklow to death.'

'Supposing that they did not?' said Firethorn.

'Is that what the play suggests?'

'Suggests and proves, in my estimation,' said Nicholas. *The Roaring Boy* is about a miscarriage of justice. If its argument be true—and we will take pains to verify that—then we have something which will do more than merely entertain our spectators. It will have a moral purpose.'

'It will clear the name of innocent people,' added Firethorn with an expansive gesture. 'The whole city will flock to see us. Murder is always good business but we offer intrigue and wrongful arrest as well. Westfield's Men do not just have a duty to stage the play. It must be our mission!'

Barnaby Gill threw up a dozen serious objections to the idea but Nicholas Bracewell had a plausible answer for each one. The book holder admitted that there were still a few obstacles to overcome—not least the corroboration of the facts that lay at the heart of the drama—but he was certain that *The Roaring Boy* was a play that answered all requirements. It would cause great controversy, redeem Edmund Hoode from his depression, enhance the reputation of Westfield's Men, tell a cautionary tale and help to right a terrible injustice.

When he could find no more faults, Gill capitulated. High tragedy and rumbustious comedy were the hallmarks of Westfield's Men and they had hitherto held aloof from the presentation of dramas based on such sensational material from the annals of crime. But *The Roaring Boy* was obviously a special case and it was perverse to miss an extraordinary opportunity. Similar plays had always had immense, if short-lived, popularity. There was an added bonus of topicality with *The Roaring Boy*. Its gory appeal was fresh in the public mind. Gill conceded all this. Only one question was now pertinent.

'Does the play have a suitable part for *me?*'

Orlando Reeve spread his bulk on a cushioned bench in the upper gallery and gazed down into the yard of the Queen's Head with an amalgam of envy and disdain. He was impressed by the size of the audience that was filling every available inch of space but contemptuous of their manifest lack of quality. The one-penny standees included students, discharged soldiers, tradesmen of the lower sort, apprentices who had sneaked away from their work and rough countrymen in search of entertainment. The yard was also salted with wives, women and punks, bold thieves and sly pickpockets, and every manner of rogue and trickster. Orlando Reeve wrinkled his nose in disgust at the stink that rose up at him and inhaled the aromatic herbs in the silver pomander which hung from a chain around his neck.

It was the day after Skeat's funeral and Westfield's Men were back in harness, but Reeve had not come to watch them in *A New Way to Please A Woman*. Its very title offended his sensibilities and its rustic humour could not even provoke the ghost of a smile from him. He was appalled at the ease with which the rest of spectators were amused. To his left was a tall silkweaver, who giggled inanely throughout: to his right, a merchant from Ulm released a series of long, low chuckles at all the wit and word-play even though his grasp of English was so uncertain that he understood no more than one word in five. The gallants and their ladies loved *A New Way to Please A Woman*. Everyone seated in the galleries gave the piece their warmest approval. Attended by his usual fawning entourage, the company's patron, Lord Westfield, was shaking with glee at the antics below him on the stage.

Orlando Reeve closed his eyes and relied solely on his ears. He was at least able to savour something. No play at the Queen's Head was complete without vocal and instrumental music. While the players' histrionics only bored Reeve, their songs delighted him throughout. Voices were clear and true. The consort was well-balanced and rehearsed to a high standard but Reeve had expected no less from its leader. Peter Digby, conductor and musician, was an old friend of his and still as expert on the bass viol as he had always been. Orlando Reeve wallowed in the glorious sound that Digby and his consort were producing from their instruments, then he writhed in horror when the music was submerged beneath braying laughter at the latest piece of vulgarity onstage.

When the play was over, and the yard cleared of what he regarded as its offal, Reeve made his way to the taproom of the Queen's Head to renew his acquaintance with Peter Digby. The contrast between the two could not have been greater. Peter Digby was a thin, ascetic man whose grey hair was slowly migrating to the farthest reaches of his skull and whose forehead was striped by long years of anxiety. His shoulders were hunched, his legs bowed, his whole appearance suggesting decline and neglect.

Sleek, fat and oozing self-importance, Orlando Reeve looked fifteen years younger than a man who was virtually the same age as himself. Pink, flabby cheeks wobbled in a round face into which a pair of twinkling eyes had been set close together. There was enough material in his expensive white satin doublet to make three whole suits for Peter Digby and still leave a remnant behind. The latter was at once pleased but embarrassed to meet Orlando Reeve again.

'Well-met, Peter!'

'I did not think to see you here.'

'Even Court musicians are permitted some leisure.'

'You were never wont to spend it at a play.'

'I came to listen to you,' said Reeve. His voice was a study in affectation and almost eunuchoid in its high pitch. 'You are still the complete master of your instrument.'

'Praise indeed, coming from you!'

'Your music made the play bearable.'

'Did you not care for *A New Way to Please a Woman?*'

'Its theme was tiresome.' He exposed tiny, pointed teeth in a razor grin. 'I have no time for women. Still less for strutting men. Music and musicians fill my world. Who needs anything more?'

'On that argument, we may readily agree.' He remembered something and clutched at his purse. 'Let me offer you a cup of wine, Orlando. This chance meeting calls for celebration.'

'Unhappily, I may not stay. We play this evening.'

'At Whitehall?'

'Yes. Her Majesty has returned from Greenwich. We have been there this past month, filling its corridors with song and gracing its banquets with dance. I received the personal commendation of no less than three visiting ambassadors.'

'It was deserved,' said Digby.

Orlando Reeve had his faults but nobody could question his musicianship. He was one of the finest keyboard-players in London, equally adept on virginals, clavichord and chamber organ. His recitals took place before royalty or in packed cathedrals. Peter Digby, once a colleague of his, performed in the humbler arena of the Queen's Head, stationed in a part of the balcony above the stage that had been curtained off to give the consort some protection from the wind. Court musicians had countless prerogatives but, as he looked up into the beaming self-satisfaction of his friend, Digby was strangely relieved that he had chosen another path.

'How much of the music did you compose?' said Reeve.

'All of it.'

'Even the songs?'

'We have to work for our wage in the theatre, Orlando.'

'I am pleased to see you so busy.'

'There is no rest for me when Westfield's Men take to the stage.' He gave a shrug. 'And far too much rest when the plague drives them out of London. We perform on occasion at the Inns of Court and elsewhere, but the theatre is our life-blood. Take that away and we wilt.'

'So I see,' said Reeve, running a censorious eye over him and observing the tear in his sleeve and the stain on his ruff. 'You are like to have a good season this year if the weather is kind to you. Have you any new plays to lift your company above its rivals?'

'One or two.'

'May I know what they are?'

'I do not even have their names myself, Orlando.'

'Come, come. You are part-author of everything that West-field's Men perform. Your music gives beauty to even the most beastly drama, and there has been a plentiful supply of that in this innyard, from what I hear.'

Digby became defensive. 'We are still without compare.'

'Only if the plays reach the standard of your music.'

'Our repertoire is acclaimed.'

'But old and musty. You must bake fresh bread.'

'We do,' said Digby. 'We will please every palate.'

'With what?'

'Our next new offering.'

'And that is?' He raised his pomander to his nostrils and sniffed hard to ward off the dark odours of the taproom. 'You may tell me, Peter,' he continued as he released the chain again. 'We are good friends, are we not? I will not betray you. The secret will be locked securely between the tongue and the lips. Nobody will ever know.'

'I am bound by my loyalty to the company.'

'Do I ask you to break it?'

'Our rivals lurk on every side to bring us down.'

'They will get no help from me.' He put a podgy hand on Digby's shoulder and massaged it. 'Your new play?'

'It is only a rumour.'

'Tell me and it dies inside my ear.'

'Master Firethorn warned me he would need many songs.'

'In what, Peter?'

'And music low and sombre, if we proceed with it.'

'With what?'

Peter Digby weakened. He was feeling completely overawed by a companion who was prospering so well in the higher reaches of his calling. Orlando Reeve was a visible boast of success. Something was needed to match that boast and to elevate Digby's drooping self-esteem.

'The play could be the most popular we ever staged,' he said. 'I was given no details and can tell you little beyond the terms of the plot but that alone will fire the imagination.' He lowered his voice to a whisper. 'It is a play about a most lamentable murder.'

'We have enough of those to vex us,' said Reeve.

'This one puts most of them to shame.'

'How so?'

'Brinklow of Greenwich. You remember the case?'

'Clearly, Peter. The poor fool of a mathematician wed a young wife whose affections were placed elsewhere. She and her lover—Dunne, was he called?—plotted to kill her husband. The pair of them were hanged for the crime.'

'They were hanged certainly but were they guilty?'

'What does your play decide?'

Peter Digby shook his head. He knew nothing more. The oily smile on Orlando Reeve's face congealed to a frosty grimace. He had heard what he had been sent to find out. Patting Digby on the shoulder in farewell, he waddled out of the tap-room and headed for the stables. It had been a long and trying afternoon for him but it had yielded its bounty.

He would earn his reward.

The transformation in Edmund Hoode's attitude and appearance was remarkable. Gone was the melancholy poet who was ready to lay down his pen for good. In his place was an eager and dedicated craftsman, who wanted to spend every waking hour at his table. *The Roaring Boy* imbued him with an elation he had not known since the night when he had climbed into bed with Mistress Jane Diamond during her husband's convenient absence. That joy had, in fact, stopped short of consummation but this latest one would not. Written entirely in prose, the play was pitted with the faults of the novice and strung together too loosely to have full impact. But its passion was overwhelming. It was a cry from the heart that Hoode could not resist.

The faults could easily be remedied, the construction just as swiftly improved. What the playwright had been given was something far more precious even than Jane Diamond's virtue. *The Roaring Boy* was a dramatic gem that needed to be cut, polished and placed in the correct setting. When that was done, the play would out-dazzle anything on the London stage.

'Let me come with you, Nick,' he begged.

'The message was sent to me alone.'

'But I must meet this Simon Chaloner. How else can I rewrite the play unless I have the true facts at my fingers? He and I must work jointly on the venture.'

'You have made progress enough without him so far,' said Nicholas Bracewell, glancing down at sheets of parchment on the table. 'This play obsesses you night and day. We had to drag you away to bear your part in this afternoon's perform-ance. Stay here in your lodgings and work on, Edmund.'

'I need more help.'

'You will get it through me.'

'Why does the fellow behave so strangely?'

'I hope to find out.'

'Where did he get all this evidence of duplicity?'

'That subject, too, will be pursued.'

It was evening and the friends were back at Silver Street. The chamber was now clean, tidy and a fit place in which a play-wright could labour for long hours. Fresh rushes had taken away the stench. Nicholas had called to tell his friend that word had at last come from the roaring boy who had first burst into their life at the Queen's Head. A letter summoned the book holder to a tavern in Eastcheap. He had been warned to come alone.

Hoode was persistent. 'Why do I not go with you and stand privily where I may overhear the conversation?'

'He has expressly forbidden your presence.'

'But I am slaving over his play!'

'Not his, Edmund. Not anyone's as yet. Simon Chaloner has

set the rules and we must play by them.' Hoode was crestfallen. 'Take heart,' said Nicholas. 'I will hasten straight back here to report to you.'

'Be quick or I'll have torn the manuscript to shreds!'

'Then you'd throw away a pearl out of spite.'

Hoode nodded and tried to contain his frustration. He was still shamed by the fact that he slept drunkenly through his first meeting with Simon Chaloner, and hoped that a second encounter would give him the chance to make amends for his conduct. It was not to be. Nicholas Bracewell was the chosen interlocutor. He must be left to divine the reason why the young man courted the shadows.

Nicholas took his leave. He was sorry to disappoint his friend but certain that he would elicit more from Simon Chaloner on his own. Having read the play, he understood why it had been given to them in such a covert way. If its allegations were true, it would cause tremors in legal circles and uproar among the common people. It might also help to bring the real malefactor to justice. The imperative was to establish the play's authorship. Edmund Hoode felt that it was the work of one man but Nicholas wondered if it might not be the product of many hands. One of them, he suspected, belonged to Simon Chaloner.

The Eagle and Serpent was a large, sprawling tavern in an area famed for its boisterous inns and ordinaries. As Nicholas entered the taproom, he was hit by a wall of tobacco smoke and noise. It was an unpropitious meeting-place for two people who wanted a peaceful conversation. Nicholas was still trying to peer through the fug when a plump serving-wench came over to him.

'What is your pleasure, sir?' she said.

'I have arranged to meet someone here.'

'Then you are the gentleman I was told about.'

'By whom?'

'Follow me, sir.'

The girl bobbed across the room and Nicholas ducked under the sagging beams as he went after her. Evidently, a private room had been hired for the occasion and that was reassuring. He and Chaloner would be able to talk without interruption. The serving-wench took him up the dimly lit staircase with sure-footed confidence. She escorted him along a dark passageway on the second floor and paused at a door to turn to him.

'You are to wait within, sir.'

'Thank you.'

'The door is stiff. Let me help you.'

She knocked on the stout oak and gave it a firm shove with her bare shoulder. The door creaked open and she stood aside to let him enter. Candles burned to afford him a glimpse of a small, featureless chamber with little more than a table and a few chairs in it. He was given no chance to take a proper inventory. As he stepped into the room, something hard and purposeful struck him across the base of his skull with chilling force. Knocked senseless, Nicholas Bracewell slumped to the floor. He did not even feel the cruel feet that kicked repeatedly at him.

[CHAPTER FOUR]

As dark shadows rubbed the last of the colour from the lawns and the flowers, Valentine dismissed his two assistants and shambled out of the garden. He was a big, ungainly, middle-aged man, who had worked at the house in Greenwich since he was a boy. Few people liked him and most were repulsed by his appearance. Straggly hair, blotchy skin, two large warts and a wispy beard combined to give his face a sinister look. The broken nose had been caused by a fall from an apple tree in the orchard but the harelip was a defect of birth. In a vain bid to hide the latter handicap, his blackened teeth were forever bared in an ingratiating grin that made him even more unsightly. A conscientious gardener, Valentine wrapped his ugliness in the beauties of nature.

He shuffled to the rear door of the house and rang the bell. The maidservant deliberately kept him waiting and was brusque when she deigned to answer his summons.

'Yes?'

'I must speak to the mistress,' he said.

'She is not at your beck and call.'

'Tell her I am here.'

'Can your business not wait until tomorrow?'

'No, Agnes.' He gave her a knowing leer that so clearly affronted her that he snatched off his cap in apology. 'Let us not fall out, my dear. Call the mistress and I will be be very thankful.'

'Speak to her in the morning.'

'My question will not wait.'

'Then tell it me and I'll convey the message.'

'I must see her myself,' said Valentine, replacing his cap and rubbing his huge, gnarled hands up and down his coarse jerkin. 'She gave order for it.'

'Are you sure?'

'The mistress was most particular. She has instructions for me.' The harelip rose higher above the hideous teeth. 'Will I step inside while you fetch her to me?'

'No,' she said. 'Wait here.'

The maidservant shut the door in his face. She was a short, stout, motherly woman in her thirties with a normally pleasant manner. Confronted by the egregious Valentine, she became curt and irritable. The fact that he tried to show some fumbling affection towards her made him even more grotesque. Agnes went first to the parlour and then to the dining room. Finding her mistress in neither place, she went upstairs to the main bedchamber. That, too, was empty.

Only one place was left. Agnes went bustling along the landing and descended by the kitchen stairs. They took her down to a buttery and she sensed that her mistress was in the room beyond. It had been added to the back of the property several years earlier at considerable expense and meticulous care had been taken with its design and construction. Long, high and commodious, it had large windows along three of its walls to admit maximum light.

None of those windows had survived. As Agnes tapped on the door and opened it, she stepped into a veritable wilderness.

A room which had once been filled with tasteful furniture and costly equipment was virtually razed to the ground. Little of the walls still stood and only one crossbeam remained in place to suggest that there had once been a ceiling. Open to the elements, the room had been invaded by weeds and become a prey to vermin.

'You have a visitor, mistress.'

'What?'

'The gardener is asking to see you.'

'Why?'

'He says that you sent for him.'

Emilia was sitting in the middle of the room on the charred remains of a chair. She looked lonely and cheerless but oddly at home in the bleak surroundings. Agnes moved towards her to take her by the arm.

'Come back into the house,' she said kindly.

'I like to sit out here.'

'It will be dark soon.'

'Will it? I had not noticed.'

'Valentine is eager to speak with you?'

'Valentine?' Emilia spoke the name as if she had heard it for the first time, then she came out of her reverie and composed herself. 'Oh, yes. The gardener. There is no need for me to see him myself. Simply tell him this. I want all the weeds cleared out of here.'

'Do you want the stone and timber removed as well?'

'No, Agnes. He is to touch nothing else.'

'Would it not be better to clear it all away?'

'Better?'

'It might help to put the matter from your mind.'

Emilia's eyes flashed. 'I do not want it put from my mind, Agnes,' she snapped. 'I want my orders obeyed and that swiftly. Do not presume to give me advice about what I may do and may not do in my own house. Nothing is to be touched in here except the weeds. Is that understood?'

'Yes, mistress.' A submissive curtsey.

'Tell the gardener to begin tomorrow. Tell him I want every dock, dandelion and blade of grass pulled out by the roots. Tell him that I want this room completely tidied up.'

Agnes was about to leave when a voice interrupted them.

'No need,' said Valentine. 'I heard everything.'

He stepped out from behind one of the vestigial walls and gave them a servile grin.

As Nicholas Bracewell slowly regained consciousness, he became aware of the pain and discomfort. His whole body was aching and he could feel a trickle down his forehead. The back of his head was on fire, though something cold and wet was trying to smother the flames. He stifled a groan. An arm was put around his shoulders to help him up, then a cup was held to his lips. The aqua vitae was bitter but restorative. He revived enough to be able to open his eyes. Blinking in the light of the candle, he saw a figure bending over him.

'How do you feel?' asked Simon Chaloner.

'Drowsy . . . Where am I?'

'Alive. More or less.'

'Still at the tavern?'

'Yes. But quite safe now.'

Nicholas touched his head. 'Someone hit me.'

'Hard, by the look of it.'

'Who was it?'

'Let us worry about that in a moment,' said Chaloner.

He dipped a wet cloth into the bowl of water on the floor and squeezed it out before dabbing at Nicholas's temple. The latter winced slightly. They were in the room where the attack had taken place, and the boards were splashed with red where Nicholas's head had lain.

'It is not a deep gash,' said Chaloner. 'Hold this to your head until the bleeding stops. Can you do that?'

'Yes.' Nicholas lifted an arm and felt its soreness. His palm held the cloth in place. 'What happened?'

'You were beaten and kicked.'

'For what reason?'

'It was a warning.'

'Of what?'

'The danger we face.'

Nicholas had regained his wits now and was anxious to get to his feet but Chaloner counselled him to rest until he had a clearer idea of the extent of his injuries. There was a throbbing lump on the back of his head where he had been struck and the gash had been collected as his temple grazed the rough floor-boards, but there were other random abrasions as well. His body and legs were a mass of bruises and he could feel a swelling beneath one eye. His fair beard was flecked with blood, his neck was stiff and difficult to move without a shooting pain. Clearly, the warning had been delivered with thoroughness.

No bones had been broken, however, and the loss of blood was relatively minor. Simon Chaloner had arrived in time to disturb the attackers but they had fled from the premises before he could confront them.

'How many were there?' asked Nicholas.

'Two of the rogues.'

'It feels as if there were a dozen,' he said, hauling himself upright and finding new sources of grief in his thighs and shoulder. 'You saved me from worse punishment. I thank you for that.'

'You should be blaming me.'

'Why?'

'For getting you so soundly beaten.'

'It was not your doing.'

'I fear me that it was.'

'Why?'

'The warning was not for you.'

'Then for whom?'

'Me.' There was a noise outside the door and Nicholas tensed for a moment. 'They will not come back, I promise you. Those ruffians will only attack one man by surprise. They would never dare take on two who are ready for them.'

He flicked his cloak back over his shoulder to reveal weapons at his waist. Nicholas took a closer look at him and saw that Simon Chaloner was in much more sober garb than at their previous meeting. Instead of the garish apparel of a roaring boy, he was now wearing a doublet and hose that would not have been out of place on a lawyer. Nobody at the Inns of Court, however, would have been as well-armed as Chaloner. In addition to a sword and dagger, he had a ball-butted pistol in a holster attached to his belt.

The younger man looked at the injured face and sighed.

'I offer you a thousand apologies, Nicholas, if I may call you that. In trying to protect you from danger, I seem unwittingly to have led you into it.'

'It was not your fault,' said Nicholas, attempting to piece together the sequence of events. 'I was caught off guard. When I entered the tavern, a serving-wench was waiting for me. She brought me up here and led me into the trap.'

'But only because of me.'

'How so?'

'I called here earlier to hire a room. Obviously, I was followed and my business learned from the landlord. The serving-wench was party to the ambush. I will swear that she is not employed at the Eagle and Serpent.'

Nicholas walked a few paces but found his legs heavy and unsure of themselves. Chaloner helped him to a stool before sitting opposite him at the table. Raucous laughter filtered up from far below. Other revellers could be heard in the street. The atmosphere in the room was noisome but at least they had a measure of privacy. Nicholas kept both elbows on the table for support.

'The case is altered, I think,' said Chaloner sadly.

'Case?'

'You came here this evening to tell me that Westfield's Men would stage *The Roaring Boy*. Had you not, you would have brought the manuscript with you to return it. Had you or Edmund Hoode despised the play as a vile concoction, you would not even have bothered to answer my summons.'

'That is true.'

'But your offer will now be withdrawn, alas.'

'Why?'

'Because of the beating you took. Every scratch and bruise about you was put there by *The Roaring Boy*. It is, as you see, a perilous enterprise. Now that you know the risks we take here, you will run headlong from the project.'

'Westfield's Men are not so easily frightened, sir,' said Nicholas. 'You were right to think the play found favour. Lawrence Firethorn and Edmund Hoode judged it a remarkable piece of drama—when it is made fit for the stage by a more practised hand. If they commit themselves to something, they are not easily deflected.'

'Nor are you, I suspect.'

'The Eagle and Serpent has given me a personal stake in this business,' said Nicholas, lowering the wet cloth to examine the bloodstains on it. 'I have a score to settle with the two men who set upon me here this evening. And with the person who hired them. The only way I can do that is if we perform *The Roaring Boy*. That will bring them back.'

'Unhappily, it will.'

Nicholas felt another trickle down his forehead and folded the cloth before applying it to the gash once more. The lump on the back of his head continued to pound away. He appraised his companion for a moment and took especial note of his weaponry.

'You have served in the army, I think,' he said.

Chaloner was surprised. 'Why, yes.'

'And saw service in Germany?'

'Holland. I was at Zutphen when our dear commander, Sir Philip Sidney died. How on earth did you guess that?'

'You have something of the stamp of a military man,' said Nicholas. 'And you have a soldier's bravery, certainly. You would not else have undertaken such a dangerous business. You carry those weapons like a man who knows how to use them.' Nicholas gave longer attention to the stock of the pistol, which protruded from the other's holster. 'I would say that fought in the cavalry.'

'Even so! By what sorcery did you divine that?'

'Your pistol. May I see it?'

Chaloner handed it over at once. 'Here, 'tis yours.'

'It is of German design,' said Nicholas, 'its stock inlaid with engraved staghorn. A wheel-lock. Such weapons are highly expensive and not to be wasted on common foot-soldiers, where the risk of damage would be great. This is a German cavalry pistol.'

'Indeed, it is,' agreed Chaloner with a grin. 'I borrowed it from its owner when he had no more use for it. The villain had the gall to discharge it at me. When our swords clashed, I cut him down and took it as a souvenir. You name him aright, Nicholas. He was a German mercenary.' He took the pistol back and returned it to his holster. 'How does a book holder with a theatre company come to know so much about firearms?'

'It is all part of my trade, sir. We use pistols and muskets in our plays as well as swords and daggers. Nathan Curtis, our stage carpenter, fashioned a caliver out of wood but two weeks ago. Before that, an arquebus. Painted replicas but made with great skill.'

'And a ball-butted German cavalry wheel-lock?'

'No,' said Nicholas, 'that is beyond his art and our needs. But he works from a book of firearms that I keep and study for pleasure. It contains a drawing of your pistol. It is very distinctive.' He leaned forward and his voice hardened. 'So you see,

Master Chaloner. I already know more about you than you intended. Do not put me to the trouble of finding out who you really are. Enough of all this mystery and evasion. If you wish to proceed in this affair, we must have more honesty between us.'

'There is only so much that I may tell you, Nicholas.'

'Then we might as well part company now.'

'Do not mistake me,' said Chaloner, easing the other back on to his stool as he tried to rise. 'I will answer any question you put to me. Some of those answers, I must insist, are for your ears only and I rely on your discretion to perceive what they might be. But my own knowledge is far from complete. On many things, I am still in the dark.'

'Let us begin then where light can be shed.'

'Please do.'

'How did they know I was coming to this tavern?' said Nicholas. 'When you hired the room here, did you tell the landlord my name?'

'The devil I did! He did not even get my own.'

'Then why was I expected at the Eagle and Serpent?'

'I can only guess, Nicholas.'

'Well?'

'Someone learned of my business with Westfield's Men,' decided Chaloner. 'Not from me. I am as close as the grave. And only one other person on my side knew of our meeting. Someone at the Queen's Head must have let slip our plans.'

'Only three people know them apart from myself.'

'Word got out somehow. It shows how subtly they work.'

'They?'

'The people who ordered the death of Thomas Brinklow. Who sent his wife and her lover—guilty of sin, but innocent of murder—to the gallows. The people whom the play sets out to expose and call to account.'

'But what are their names?' pressed Nicholas.

Chaloner hesitated. 'I am not certain.'

'You are lying.'

'More evidence yet is needed.'

'You *know* who they are.'

'I believe I know who *he* is but not his confederates.'

'Name the man,' demanded Nicholas. *The Roaring Boy* is a tasty loaf indeed but only half baked if we exonerate the innocent without pointing a finger at the malefactor.'

Chaloner shrugged. 'It is not as easy as that.'

'Very well, sir. Let us come at it another way.'

'As you wish.'

'Did you know Thomas Brinklow of Greenwich?'

'Extremely well.'

'Was he a friend or a relative?'

'He was like to have been both,' said the other. 'I am betrothed to his sister, Emilia. Had he lived, Thomas would have been my brother-in-law by now.'

'You are still betrothed to the lady?'

'We will be fast married as soon as this business is finally over.' Chaloner's glib charm was replaced by a warm compassion. 'Emilia has suffered deeply over this. She lost a brother whom she adored and a sister-in-law whom she liked in spite of Cecily's failings. Emilia was as anxious as anyone to see Thomas's death answered on the gallows but not when it meant the execution of two innocent people. She is desperate for the real murderer to be convicted. As am I.'

'That is only natural,' said Nicholas. 'Emilia Brinklow is that one other person of whom you spoke just now?'

'Yes. She alone is in my confidence.'

'What of the author?'

'The author is . . . no longer involved in the project.'

'Why?'

'Because he has gone away, Nicholas. Far away.'

'Without waiting to see his work performed?'

'The play was written out of love for Thomas Brinklow and

given to us. I took upon myself the task of trying to get it staged by one of our leading companies.'

'On Saturday last, you told me that you were involved in the creation of the piece.'

'That is so.'

'What form did that involvement take?'

'I provided the facts of the case,' said Chaloner, 'the author supplied the art. To put it another way, Nicholas, I made the bricks and he built the house.'

'You have worked hard.'

'With good cause.'

'How many of your facts are true?'

'All of them!' said the other with sudden vehemence. 'I can vouch for each and every one of them. Do you think I would spend all that time and money in pursuit of something so important and let it elude my grasp? Consider what we are up against here. You have only been yoked to *The Roaring Boy* for a matter of days and it has cost you a beating. Imagine the dire threats *I* have received these past few months. I have to look over my shoulder wherever I go. Were I not so well-trained in the arts of war and able to take care of myself, Emilia would be mourning another loved one. That devil has sent his men after me a dozen times.'

'What is his name?' insisted Nicholas.

'Speak it to nobody else, I charge you.'

'Who is he?'

A long pause. 'Sir John Tarker.'

'You are certain?'

'As certain as any man can be.'

'Sir John Tarker that excels in the tournaments?'

'The same.'

'Was he acquainted with Thomas Brinklow?'

'He was,' said Chaloner. 'Sir John spends much time at Greenwich Palace. Thomas was often a guest there.'

'For what reason did he want Master Brinklow killed?'

'Dislike, envy of his wealth.'

'Murder needs a stronger warrant than that.'

'Thomas and he had quarrelled. Sir John is a bellicose man who bears a grudge against any who gainsay him. His ire festered. When Thomas crossed him again, the testy knight hired ruffians to cut him down.'

'There is something you are not telling me.'

'They quarrelled. I would swear an oath on that.'

'About what?' said Nicholas.

'Does it matter? They fell out. That is enough.'

'Not for me,' said Nicholas. 'What was the cause?'

'Some foolish disagreement.'

'Is folly to be paid for with a life?'

'They simply could not abide each other.'

'The reason?'

'Hold off, Nicholas,' said Chaloner, turning away. 'You have heard the truth about Sir John Tarker. You have read the play. It says all. What else do you need to know?'

'Why you are shielding Mistress Emilia Brinklow.'

Chaloner reached involuntarily for his dagger but Nicholas was too quick for him, grabbing his arm in a grip of steel and holding it tight while he stared deep into the other man's eyes. They were locked in a battle of wills for a long while before Nicholas finally prevailed. Chaloner's wrath subsided and he gave a resigned nod of acceptance. Nicholas released his hold. A memory made the young man shake with muted fury.

'Sir John Tarker made unwelcome advances to Emilia.'

'Her brother intervened?'

'Most strongly. Thomas was a mild man but he could be a lion when roused. Sir John was more or less thrown out of the house in Greenwich, an insult that he would nor bear lightly.' An angry scowl descended. 'He was fortunate. That scurvy knight was very fortunate. Had I been there, I would have used something more damaging than harsh words.'

'Where were you at the time?'

'In Holland. I came back within the month.

'To be told this sorry tale.'

Chaloner's head dropped. 'No, Nicholas. They kept it from me. My own dear Emilia was all but molested by that foul lecher and they hid it from me lest I run wild. I did not learn the truth of it until after Thomas's death. When it was too late.' He looked up with haunted eyes. 'Can you see now why I am obsessed with this affair? Thomas was killed because he defended my bethrothed. I'll not rest until Sir John Tarker is arrested for the crime.'

Nicholas gave him time to recover from what had been a harrowing confession. It had robbed Chaloner of his poise and left his face ashen, but it had thrown a whole new light on *The Roaring Boy*. Nicholas brought the cloth away from his head and felt the wound with tentative fingers. It had stopped bleeding. He put the cloth aside and resumed the conversation. Something had struck him forcibly.

'His sister is not mentioned in the play.'

'Nor can she be. Emilia insists on that.'

'But she is an element in the story.'

'It is one that she prefers to forget,' said Chaloner. 'The fact of Sir John's guilt is more important than its causes. He has been given reason enough in the play to murder Thomas, has he not? Why add more?'

'Because we go in the pursuit of truth.'

'Truth has to be tempered with consideration.'

'I must speak with the lady.'

'That, too, is impossible.'

'Then we waste time here. Your play is not for us.'

'Nicholas—'

'Good night, sir,' he said, rising to his feet. 'I will not stay to be misled any further.'

'You ask too much of me.'

'And you ask too much of us!' retorted Nicholas with a show

of spirit. He snatched up a candle and held it to his face. 'I have taken a beating for you and this play. That entitles me to know everything there is to know about it and I cannot do that unless I speak with the lady. If she will not meet my request, I'll advise Master Firethorn to put the piece aside. That path has much appeal for me, I assure you.'

Their eyes met again in another contest of strength but it was soon over. *The Roaring Boy* was doomed without the help of Westfield's Men. No other company would have the bravado to stage it and the skill to do it to bring the best out of it. Simon Chaloner was being forced to make the one concession he hated most but he had no choice.

'I will speak to Emilia and arrange a meeting.'

'We will try not to intrude too long upon her grief.'

Chaloner stiffened. 'We?'

'Edmund Hoode and I.'

'Can you not conduct the interview alone, Nicholas? She has been almost a recluse since her brother's death. One person will be distressing enough for Emilia to accommodate. Two will throw her into a state of profound dismay.'

'Master Hoode must be there,' argued Nicholas. 'If he is to make your play fit for the stage, he must know every detail that appertains to it. Have no fears on his part. He is the gentlest soul and will pose no threat to the lady.'

Chaloner sighed. 'Very well. I will bring Emilia to London and the four of us will meet secretly.'

'Why not in Greenwich? That is the obvious place.'

'I'd welcome the excuse to get her away from there.'

'Then find it on some other pretext,' said Nicholas. 'Edmund Hoode will not only wish to meet the sister of Thomas Brinklow. He will want to see the house where the man lived and the place where he was murdered. It will all help to make *The Roaring Boy* a richer and more accurate play in the end. That, surely, is our common goal.'

'Let me talk with Emilia. This may require persuasion.' He

got to his feet. 'May I tell her, then, that the play will be performed if she agrees to help?'

'Yes,' said Nicholas. 'You may also tell her that we will offer five pounds for the privilege. Westfield's Men always pay the price of a good play.

'We want no money, Nicholas. Only justice.'

'The author might wish for payment.'

'He has been well paid already.' He crossed to the door and paused. 'I will send word to you at the Queen's Head. Until then . . . '

'Not so fast. I have one last question.'

'What is it?'

'The world believes that Thomas Brinklow was cruelly butchered by two men hired by his wife and her lover. How can we persuade everyone to think otherwise?'

'The play tells you. That is why it is called *The Roaring Boy*. Freshwell was one of the killers and he was a notorious swaggerer. When he goes to the scaffold at the end of Act Five, he makes a speech denouncing the true villain.'

'It did not happen quite that way,' reminded Nicholas. 'It was Freshwell's testimony which confirmed the guilt of those who suborned him. He made full confession.'

'Did anyone *see* that confession?' said Chaloner. 'It was extracted under torture and a man will say anything to escape further agony. I am certain that Freshwell did not drag the names of Cecily Brinklow and Walter Dunne into the reckoning. He did not even know them. For what reason should he bear false witness? Freshwell was liar, rogue and black-hearted murderer but he must certainly be absolved of perjury.'

'Why do you say that?'

'Because I was *there*, Nicholas. At his execution.'

'Did Freshwell not make a final speech, repenting of his wickedness and asking for God's mercy?'

'No. He roared so loud, they had to gag his mouth.'

Nicholas was unconvinced. 'Men often behave so at their

execution. It is a last act of defiance. They roar to show that scorn for the majesty of the law. There is yet another reason why they rave so at the last. Those wild cries are often a means to disguise their terror.'

'That was not so in Freshwell's case,' explained the other. 'Had he been allowed to speak, I believe that he would have named the man who hired him to do his filthy work. If Freshwell had but an ounce of conscience, he would also have pleaded for Cecily and Walter Dunne to be released.'

'Why did he not do so instead of roaring in anger?'

'The executioner's assistant explained that.'

'His assistant?'

'He pinioned Freshwell in his cell before bringing him to the scaffold, so he got as close to him as anyone. The hangman himself would not even speak to me but his assistant took my bribe willingly enough. He told me why the roaring boy went to his death so noisily.'

'And?'

'Freshwell was no longer able to denounce anybody.'

'Why not?'

'They had cut out his tongue.'

A new resolution coursed through Nicholas Bracewell.

'We will stage this play,' he promised.

Heavy rain turned the streets and lanes of London into miry runnels of mud. People dived for cover under the eaves of houses or huddled in doorways or filled church porches with impromptu congregations. Cats and dogs scurried wildly to the nearest shelter. Horses churned up the slime and spattered the walls with indiscriminate force. Unrelenting water explored every leaking roof, splintered door, cracked paving slab and broken window in the city. The vast, noisome, accumulated filth of the capital became a voracious quagmire, which tried to swallow up each leg, paw or hoof foolish enough to tread on it.

In the space of a few minutes, a hitherto mild night was transformed into sodden torment.

Sir John Tarker missed the worst of the downpour but that did not still his high temper. While the city itself was feeling the first drops of damnation, he spurred his horse out through Ludgate and galloped along Fleet Street until it became the wide and well-paved Strand. Here were some of the most palatial dwellings in the kingdom, fit only for those from the higher reaches of the nobility or the clergy, built along the line of the River Thames and linking the city with the architectural wonder of Westminster. The Strand was one long strip of wealth and privilege.

As the rain began to pelt down in earnest, Sir John Tarker turned his horse in through the gates of Avenell Court and clattered to a halt on the slippery cobbles. Dismounting with practised ease, he yelled for an ostler and cursed his delay in coming. When the man finally did emerge from the stables, he earned himself a stern rebuke and a vicious blow to the head. Even in clement weather, the guest was not someone to be kept waiting. He spat his contempt at the heavens before hurrying into the building.

Avenell Court was a large, looming, battlemented house of Kentish ragstone with a dry ditch by way of a moat and an army of tall chimneys patrolling its steep roof. The hint of a castle was replicated in its interior as well. Corridors were long, cold and lined with suits of armour. Swords and shields decorated the walls of all the rooms on the ground floor. The main hall had a display of weaponry—from many nations—which could rival that at the Tower of London. Banners, pennants and coats-of-arms further enriched an exhibition which had been put together with considerable care and at immense cost. There was even a life-size statue of a warhorse in gleam- bronze.

In such a setting, it was difficult not to hear th' battle but the figure who reclined in the high' beside the huge fireplace managed the feat without undue effort. Instead of the din of armed conflict, he was listening to the sombre strains of a pavan as played with exquisite touch by Orlando Reeve. Head down, eyes closed in concentration, shoulders hunched, the corpulent musician was perched on a stool, his bulk almost hiding the instrument that stood before him on the dais at the end of the hall. Podgy hands seemed to flutter over the keyboard to draw the most affecting tone from the virginals. Orlando Reeve had composed the dance himself in the Italian style and given it a slow and bewitching dignity.

When he finished the piece, he inhaled deeply before expelling the air through his nostrils. He opened a hopeful eye to search for the approval of his audience. The man in the chair mimed applause with his hands, then flicked a palm upwards to call for something more lively. Orlando Reeve obliged at once with a sprightly galliard that soon had his lone spectator tapping a foot in accompaniment as the little instrument all but filled the hall with its tinkling harmony. The musician was so engrossed in the dance that he did not observe the guest who was conducted in by a servant.

Divested of his wet cloak and hat, Sir John Tarker strode across the marble floor with a haughty familiarity. He was a tall man with broad shoulders and a full chest that tapered down to a narrow waist. The swarthy face was framed by long black hair and a neatly barbered beard. Dressed as a courtier, he had the arrogant swagger of a soldier and the natural impatience of a man of action. He accorded Orlando Reeve no more than a derisive snort as he approached his host. Sir John Tarker had not come to listen to music.

Before he could speak, however, the visitor was waved into silence by the man in the chair. Shorter, slimmer and ten years older than his guest, Sir Godfrey Avenell was a striking figure of middle years, wearing doublet and hose of the latest and most expensive fashion below an elaborate lawn ruff that set off his sallow countenance. Silver hair and beard gave him a distinction that was reinforced by the upward tilt of his chin and the piercing blue eyes. The habit of command sat easily on Sir Godfrey Avenell and elicited a grudging respect from his visitor.

As the galliard continued, the foot kept in time on the marble. Its owner looked up with a contented smile.

'Is this music not sublime?' he said.

'I am not in the mood for it, Sir Godfrey.'

'Come, come, man. Does it not make you wish to dance?'

Tarker was politely emphatic. 'No.'

'I love the virginals,' said the other, savouring each note. 'Did I never tell you of the occasion when I heard the Queen herself at the keyboard? I dined one time with my dear friend, Lord Hunsdon, who drew me up to a quiet gallery where I might listen to Her Majesty upon the virginals. She played excellently well. Since her back was towards me, I ventured to draw back the tapestry and enter the chamber so that I could hear the more clearly. Her Majesty sensed my presence at once and stopped forthwith, turning to see me and rising from her seat to chide me. "I play not before men," she said, "but only when I am solitary, to shun melancholy." I have always remembered that phrase—to shun melancholy. Such is the soothing power of music. What better way to keep black thoughts at bay?'

'With a willing wench on a bed of silk.'

'Your taste needs schooling.'

'A man is entitled to his desires.'

'Not when they are as coarse as yours sometimes are.'

The galliard stopped and Orlando Reeve looked up for further endorsement. He was always glad to be invited to give a private recital at Avenell Court. His host was a most cultured and generous patron of music. The instruments which had been collected at the house were of the highest quality. Reeve was able to practice and entertain at the same time.

Praise was not immediately forthcoming. The musician was

forced to wait while Sir Godfrey Avenell stood up to give his guest a proper welcome. The older man clapped his friend on the shoulder, then spoke in a low whisper.

'Well?'

'It is done,' said Tarker.

'Then our information was sound?'

'Very sound.'

'Good.'

Sir Godfrey Avenell threw a shrewd glance at Orlando Reeve, then softened it with a benign smile. Strolling across to the dais, he took a purse from his belt and tossed it into the eager palms of the musician. The weight of the purse told Reeve the value of its contents.

'Thank you, Sir Godfrey,' he said obsequiously.

'You played well for me.'

'I am rewarded beyond my deserts.'

'The gold is not only for your music, Orlando.'

Reeve understood and nodded obediently. He gathered a scowl from Sir John Tarker and a dismissive nod from his host before stepping down from the platform and scuttling out of the hall. Avenell turned back to his guest.

'You do not like Orlando, I think?'

'He is a fat fool.'

'Even so, yet he can play like an angel.'

'I hate those fawning musicians.'

'He has his uses,' said Avenell, moving to stand in front of the ornamental chimney-piece which climbed halfway up the wall. 'We have had proof of that this very day. That fat fool was cunning enough to insinuate himself into the counsels of Westfield's Men and we must be grateful to him for that. It has enabled us to nip disturbance in the bud.' His smile faded. 'At least, I trust that this is so.'

'Have no fears on that account.'

'Then reassure me straight.'

'Everything went according to plan.'

'I seem to have heard that boast before.'

'The best men were chosen.'

'That, too,' said Avenell with hissing sarcasm. 'The best men come at the highest price. When you saved a few pence on the hiring last time, you bought us unlooked-for trouble. I do not wish to encounter further unpleasantness in this matter. It puts me to choler. Convince me that it is over and done with.'

'You have my word on it.'

'The play has been destroyed?'

'To all intents.'

'Explain.'

'A member of the company was beaten senseless.'

'Will they heed the warning?'

'They must,' insisted Tarker. 'My men know their trade. Their orders were clear. The intercessory was to be all but killed. No sane creature would proceed in a business that is fraught with such danger.'

'Sanity is not a normal property of the theatre.'

'We struck at their chief prop.'

'Lawrence Firethorn?'

'A man called Nicholas Bracewell. He is but the book holder with the company but carries the whole enterprise on his shoulders. Without his strength and resource, they would be in a sorry state. Maim him and they all limp. There is no question but that we seized the right prey.'

'And left him for dead, you say?'

Sir John Tarker nodded and gave a grim smile.

'We will hear no more of Westfield's Men.'

Nicholas Bracewell and Edmund Hoode travelled to Greenwich by means of the river. Since no performance was being given by Westfield's Men that afternoon, they were released for the whole day. The long journey from London Bridge gave them ample time to rehearse the many pertinent questions that needed to be put. The promised meeting with Emilia Brinklow had been arranged by Simon Chaloner on the condition that he himself would be present to advise and assist her. For their part, the book holder and the playwright agreed to be tactful and considerate in their enquiries. Evidently, Chaloner felt that his betrothed required protection even from putative friends.

It was a fine morning with a stiff breeze blowing upstream. Craft of all sizes were gliding along on the broad back of the Thames. Seated in the stern of their boat, the two friends felt the refreshing tug of the wind and conversed to the creak of oars and the plash of blades dipping into the dark water. The watermen were too immersed in their strenuous work to pay any attention to their passengers. It was a few days since Nicholas had been attacked at the Eagle and Serpent but he still bore the marks of the assault. His face was covered in bruises and the head wound beneath his cap still had a dressing. Appraising him now, Hoode began to have second thoughts.

'It is not too late to abandon this folly,' he said.

'I have given my word, Edmund.'

'What if there is another beating?'

'Then I will administer it instead of receiving it. They will not take me unawares a second time. Besides,' said Nicholas with a grin, 'I have a bodyguard. Now that you have moved into my lodging to watch over me, I am quite safe.'

Hoode blenched. 'But I thought *you* were looking after *me!* That is why Lawrence wanted me out of Silver Street. So that I might have your strong arm to shield me.'

'A wise precaution. When they realise that we are determined to press on with this venture, they may try to wreck the play itself.'

'Along with its author!'

'His identity, alas, remains concealed.'

'Mine does not,' said Hoode. 'Everyone in London knows that I hold the pen for Westfield's Men, whether in the writing of new dramas, the cobbling of old ones or the wet-nursing of novice playwrights. *The Roaring Boy* may be the work of another hand but the signature of Edmund Hoode is also scrawled across it.'

'You should be proud of that fact.'

'Indeed, I am, Nick. Very proud—but very fearful.'

'Stay close by me and banish all apprehension.'

'I will try.'

Edmund Hoode and Lawrence Firethorn had been highly alarmed to learn of the beating taken by their book holder but their reaction had been positive. Both had their faith in the play reaffirmed, believing that the violence proved its veracity. Indeed, the actor-manager announced that they now had a mission as well as a duty to stage *The Roaring Boy* and Hoode was momentarily carried along by Firethorn's rhetoric. As the playwright was rowed ever closer to the scene of the crime, however, his resolve began to vaccilate.

'We take the most dreadful risks, Nick.'

'That is why we work in the theatre.'

'This is a matter of life and death.'

'Yes,' said Nicholas. 'The life of Emilia Brinklow and the cruel death of her brother. If we can sweeten the one by uncovering the truth about the other, we will have done noble service. We may also have cleared the names of two innocent people wrongly convicted of the murder.'

'But we are up against such powerful men.'

'All the more reason to bring them down.'

'That is a task for the law, not for mere players.'

'When the law fails, we must seek retribution ourselves.' He put a comforting arm around his sagging colleague. 'Take heart, Edmund. This will be one of the most fateful pieces that ever issued from your teeming brain. You will give pleasure to your audience and dispense justice at one and the same time. Hold fast to that thought and the dangers that haunt you will fade to distant shadows.'

'You are right,' decided Hoode. 'I must be brave.'

'We are too far in to turn back now.'

Nicholas spent the next ten minutes in bolstering his friend's sense of purpose. Hoode's commitment was pivotal. They could expect wild protest from Barnaby Gill but he could usually be overruled by Lawrence Firethorn. If the comedian persevered with his objections, they could even present the play without him. Edmund Hoode, however, was quite indispensable. It was for this reason that Nicholas had been appointed as his keeper. He sensed that it would be a difficult assignment.

When he next looked out across the water, Nicholas saw that they were approaching the royal dockyards at Deptford. The jumble of storehouses, slipways, sawpits, masthouses and cranes brought a mixture of nostalgia and regret. It was a long time since he sailed with Drake on the circumnavigation of the globe but the experience was tattooed on his soul. A first glimpse of *The Golden Hind* provoked a flurry of memories. It stood on the foreshore in a dry dock for people to gape at, its hull now hacked by a thousand knives in search of a piece of history. Looking at the vessel—still trim and well fitted out—Nicholas found it impossible to believe that so many men had been crammed into such a small space for such an interminable period of time.

Reflection on his past brought a surge of confidence in the future. Drake and his mariners had met with recurring horrors during their three years at sea yet they somehow survived. What kept them going was an indomitable spirit. So it must be with *The Roaring Boy*. It involved a much shorter voyage, albeit over uncharted water, but it would bring its share of tempests. They had to be withstood at all costs. Nicholas must regard the attack at the Eagle and Serpent as simply the first squall. It was vital for Westfield's Men to combat hostile elements and keep the ship on course until they could bring it into port.

Simon Chaloner was waiting at Greenwich to escort them to the house and to prepare them for their meeting with Emilia Brinklow. They walked together along the main street.

'I beg you to show all due care,' he said.

'Is the lady unwell?' asked Hoode.

'In mind but not in body. She grieves. Be gentle.'

'We shall,' said Nicholas. 'But there are some personal matters which we must broach with her. Issues on which even you have been unable to satisfy us.'

'All I ask is that you proceed with caution.'

Nicholas Bracewell wondered what sort of fragile woman Emilia Brinklow must be to require such delicate handling. Simon Chaloner was patently a robust young man with an extrovert streak in his nature. Could he really be drawn to the frail being that his description of Emilia had conjured up? Had she been told of the perils that attended *The Roaring Boy?* Or was he deliberately keeping her ignorant of them?

When they reached the house, they paused to look up at its facade. Edmund Hoode was frankly impressed.

'It is beautiful,' he said. 'So neat, so symmetrical.'

'Thomas took a hand in its design,' explained Chaloner. 'First and foremost, he was a mathematician. All that you see around you will be geometrically exact.'

'A remarkable building,' said Hoode, marvelling at the size and scope of the place. 'I had no idea that there was so much money in mathematics.'

'Thomas was a genius.'

'A renowned engineer, too, I believe,' said Nicholas. 'Did he not design naval equipment for the royal dockyards?'

'Yes,' said Chaloner. 'There was no limit to his abilities. He worked with distinction in many fields. You will catch something of his personality here. The imprint of Thomas Brinklow is on every part of the house and garden.' He remembered something and became brisk. 'Come, gentlemen. Emilia is waiting in the arbour to meet you. Please bear in mind what I told you.'

They followed him to a side-gate and went around the house to the long, rectangular garden at the rear. It was laid out with mathematical precision and kept in immaculate condition. Straight paths bisected well-groomed lawns. Flowers and shrubs grew in orderly beds. Every tree seemed to have been put in the perfect location. Wide stone steps led up to an arbour at the far end of the garden that was screened off from the house by a series of concentric hedges. The pattern envisaged by Thomas Brinklow had been brought scrupulously to life.

Emilia was seated on a bench in the arbour, talking to the maidservant. As soon as she heard the visitors, Agnes turned to give them a polite curtsey before hurrying back in the direction of the house. Simon Chaloner placed a gentle kiss on Emilia's hand, then raised her to her feet to perform the introductions. She was poised but taciturn, bestowing wan smiles of welcome on the two men before resuming her seat. Chaloner indicated that the visitors should sit down before lowering himself on to the bench beside Emilia. Nicholas Bracewell and Edmund Hoode had no choice but to take up a position diametrically opposite. Mathematics quashed even the slightest rebellion against order.

'It is kind of you to invite us here,' said Nicholas politely, 'and we do appreciate it. We will not take up any more of your time than is necessary.'

'Thank you,' she replied.

Hoode tried to speak but his lips betrayed him. So struck was he by the pallid loveliness of Emilia Brinklow that he was bereft of words. The playwright was no stranger to beauty. Having dedicated much of his life to the futile pursuit of feminine charms, he felt that it was a subject in which he had acquired some painful expertise but here was someone who broke through the boundaries even of his wide experience. Emilia Brinklow was wholly enchanting. Dressed in a dark green satin that blended with the lawns, she wore blue hat and gloves to complement the tiny blue shoes that peeped out below the hem of her skirt. A single piece of jewellery—a pendant ruby—

sparkled against the divine whiteness of her neck. Edmund Hoode was instantly vanquished.

Nicholas Bracewell was as much interested in her manner as her appearance. She was composed and watchful. Though her fiancé sat beside her by way of defence, she did not look as if she was in need of his assistance. Hoode might find her demure but Nicholas detected a quiet self-possession. Emilia Brinklow was by no means the shrinking violet of report.

She weighed the two of them up for a few moments, then spoke with soft urgency.

'The play will be performed, will it not?'

'They have sworn that it will, my dear,' said Chaloner.

'Let me hear it from them.'

'Westfield's Men will present it,' croaked Hoode.

'When it is ready for the stage,' said Nicholas. 'And that can only be when we have plumbed its full depth. There is still much that we do not understand.'

She met his gaze. 'I will help you in any way I can.'

'Within reason,' said Chaloner. 'Let us begin.'

Nicholas turned to Hoode. 'Edmund is our playwright. He it is who must put words into the mouths of the characters and flesh on the bones of the plot. Hear him speak first.'

Hoode's voice faltered as he gazed on Emilia Brinklow.

'*The Roaring Boy* is an uncommonly good play.'

'Your high opinion is very gratifying,' she said.

'Who wrote the piece?'

'A friend.'

'May we know his name?'

'He prefers to hand over his work to Westfield's Men.'

'And take no credit?'

'None, sir.'

'Then he is a most peculiar author.'

'These are most peculiar circumstances.'

'In what way?'

'I have explained all this to Nicholas,' said Chaloner with some asperity. 'We do not have to go over old ground again. I gathered the material from which the playwright wove the fabric of *The Roaring Boy*. Neither of us seeks public acknowledgement. Take the piece and make it work.'

'It is not a simple as that,' observed Hoode. 'I can match the style of any author when I am acquainted with him. If he is anonymous, my task is far more difficult. Tell me at least something about my co-athor. Is this, for instance, a first play or has he written others for the stage?'

'A first play,' said Emilia crisply.

'A worthy effort indeed for any novice.'

'He has always loved the theatre,' said Chaloner, 'and has sat on the benches at the Queen's Head many a time.'

'Then why miss the performance of his own play?'

'He has his reasons.'

Hoode turned back to Emilia. 'He knew your brother?'

'As well as anyone alive,' she said.

'That play was written by someone who admired him.'

'Admired and loved him.'

'Everyone loved Thomas Brinklow,' said Chaloner, cutting in once more. 'He was the most civilised and personable man on God's earth. Kindness itself to those fortunate enough to be his friends. It was impossible not to love him.' His face darkened. 'Yet he inspired hatred in someone and it cost him his life. That is what has brought all of us here today.'

Nicholas Bracewell disagreed. The murder had bonded them together but it was Simon Chaloner himself who had organised the interview with Emilia Brinklow in Greenwich and who was presiding over it with such vigilance. Nicholas waited patiently as Edmund Hoode tried to prise further information out of her but the interrogation was woefully half-hearted. The playwright was so manifestly in awe of Emilia that he was quite unable to pursue any line of questioning with the polite tenacity required. Whenever Hoode did ask something of real importance, Simon Chaloner jumped in to deflect him.

It was a skilful performance but it did not deceive Nicholas Bracewell. He recognised stage management. As long as Chaloner was at her side, there was no hope of gaining vital new facts from Emilia Brinklow. Nicholas somehow had to speak with her alone. He, too, was acutely aware of her charms, noting with surprise how the deep sadness in her eyes only served to enhance her beauty. Though Chaloner's love for her was open, she was too locked up in her distress to show him any real affection. Behind her quiet dignity, however, Nicholas saw flashes of a keen intelligence.

Conscious of his scrutiny, she responded with a smile.

'You are strangely silent, sir.'

'Edmund speaks for both of us.'

'Do you have nothing to say for yourself?'

'Nicholas has already questioned me a dozen times,' said Chaloner with a laugh. 'Do not unleash him on us again, Emilia. 'He is a terrier for the truth.'

'What does he wish to ask?' she wondered.

'How word of this play leaked out to others,' said Nicholas. 'You and Master Chaloner are patently discreet and we have been careful to divulge nothing of our association with *The Roaring Boy*. Yet the secrecy has been breached. How?'

Her face clouded. 'In all honesty, we do not know.'

'But it is one of the reasons that we have met out here in this arbour,' said Chaloner. 'Walls have ears. The house itself listens to all that we say.'

'You have a spy in the camp?' said Nicholas.

'No!' denied Emilia hotly. 'I will not conceive of such an idea. The entire household is loyal. Thomas engaged most of the staff himself. They would not betray us.'

'Someone did,' noted Chaloner, 'and that enforces the utmost caution on our part. At least, we are safe out here. Nobody will be able to eavesdrop on us in this isolated part of the garden.'

A mere six yards away, Valentine laughed silently to himself. He had merged his ugliness with floral abundance to become part of nature itself. Deep in his lair, the gardener could hear every word that they spoke. He was intrigued.

[CHAPTER FIVE]

After lying dormant for some days, the raging toothache awoke to turn breakfast at the Firethorn household into an ordeal for everyone concerned. Apart from his wife and children, the four apprentices from Westfield's Men also lived with the actor-manager so they, too, sat around the table as mute witnesses to his suffering, deprived of any appetite themselves by his blood-curdling howls of anguish. Lawrence Firethorn's bad tooth was a burden that they all shared. Margery once again advocated extraction but her husband would not even countenance the notion, preferring to endure intermittent torture rather than submit himself to the pincers of a surgeon. When she pressed him hard on the matter, he insisted that he suddenly felt much better and that his mouth would even permit the introduction of a little moistened food. The first bite had him roaring louder than ever.

At the Queen's Head later that day, Firethorn wisely restricted himself to a cup of Canary wine. It soothed his swollen gum and calmed his throbbing tooth. Owen Elias was on hand to activate the pain in both once more.

'A lighted candle,' he recalled.

'Candle?' repeated Firethorn.

'He held the palm of my hand over it.'

'Who did?'

'The surgeon.'

'Why?'

'So that he burned my skin.'

'You went to a surgeon to be set alight?'

'No, Lawrence,' said the Welshman with a chuckle. 'I needed to have a bad tooth pulled. That rogue of a surgeon distracted my attention. I was so taken up with the injury to my hand that I hardly noticed him pulling out the tooth until it was too late. One sharp pain disguised another.'

Firethorn's mouth felt as if a hundred candles had just been lit inside it to be carried in procession by a choir of chanting surgeons. A sip of Canary wine only seemed to make the flames burn brighter. It was at this point, when the actor-manager most needed sympathy and succour, that Barnaby Gill joined his colleagues at their table in the taproom. Lowering himself on to the settle, he dispensed with the civilities and came straight to the point.

'I will not act in this lunatic venture,' he said.

'We do not expect you to act, Barnaby,' teased Owen Elias. 'Simply stand there as usual and say what few lines you can remember. *We* act in the play—you merely appear.'

'Cease this levity. I speak in earnest.'

'Lower your voice, man.'

'Why?'

'Out of respect for the dead.'

Gill started. 'Another of our company has died?'

'Lawrence's tooth. It will pass away any minute.'

'Not if you keep prodding at it, you torturer!' yelled Firethorn. 'We are here to discuss business, not to talk of surgeons with lighted candles. God's blood! If my tooth were sound, I'd use it to bite off your mocking face! No more of it, Owen. Let us hear Barnaby out before we answer him.'

'You have heard all,' said Gill. 'I say nay.'

'When you have not even read the play?'

'I do not need to, Lawrence. It spells disaster.'

'Yes,' said Elias. 'For our rivals. If *The Roaring Boy* is but half the success it deserves to be, Westfield's Men will rise head and shoulders above the other companies.'

'We already do that,' argued Firethorn.

'This play will let us eclipse them completely.'

'It is the road to Bedlam,' said Gill. 'When I consider its subject, every part about me quivers.'

'That is only fitting,' said Firethorn. 'It should make you quiver with excitement, Barnaby.'

'I shake with fear.'

'You should glow with pride.'

'I shudder with disgust.'

'This play is the sword of justice.'

'It will cut down the lot of us.'

'Not if we wield it ourselves,' said Owen Elias. 'Westfield's Men will hold the slicing edge of death.'

Lawrence Firethorn did not regret taking the Welshman into their confidence. The attack on Nicholas Bracewell was a grim warning. Apart from the book holder himself, nobody had such skill in arms as Owen Elias. His belligerence could be trying at times but it was a source of comfort now. The victor in a score of tavern brawls, he lent strength as well as experience to Westfield's Men. For this reason, it was wise to keep him informed of every development relating to *The Roaring Boy*. Like the actor-manager, Elias was outraged by the injuries sustained by his beloved friend and longed for the opportunity to avenge each blow struck at Nicholas. He would be a most effective guard dog.

Barnaby Gill, by contrast, had no stomach for a fight.

'We court unnecessary peril,' he bleated.

'Think of the prize that awaits us,' said Firethorn.

'Violent assault.'

'Righting a grave wrong.'

'Yes,' said Elias. 'Bringing a villain to the scaffold. Publishing his wickedness to the whole world.'

'He will not stand idly by while we do that.'

'Of course not,' conceded Firethorn. 'We will be hounded and harrassed at every turn but we must not give in. Our safety lies in our unity. Hold fast together and we can withstand the onslaught of the Devil himself.'

'I want nothing whatsoever to do with the play,' said Gill impetuously. 'I wash my hands of it forthwith.'

'A Pontius Pilate in our ranks!'

Owen Elias grunted.' A Judas, more like!'

'Very well,' said Firethorn with uncharacteristic calm. 'Withdraw into your ivory tower, Barnaby. Shun your fellows. Spurn this heaven-sent chance to turn Westfield's Men into agents of the law. You can be spared, sir. Indeed, your decision brings relief. If truth be told, I was not certain in my mind that you were equal to the task before us.'

'I am equal to anything!' retorted the other.

'This role was beyond even your scope, Barnaby.'

'Falsehood! Every part is within my compass.'

'Even that of a hapless mathematician, who is foully murdered by hired villains? No, it is too heavy a load for you to bear. Stay with your clowning and your comical jigs. They place no great strain on your art.'

'What are you telling me, Lawrence?'

'That you release us from vexation,' said Firethorn. 'Had you played in *The Roaring Boy,* the leading part would have fallen to you.'

'Thomas Brinklow?'

'The same.'

'Would not you have seized upon the role?'

'Indeed not. I am satisfied with Freshwell, the roaring boy himself. He lords it in the title of the play but Brinklow carries the piece. Edmund spoke strongly on your behalf but I was not minded to accept his judgement. You have rescued me from that dilemma. Stand aside.'

'Not so fast, Lawrence.'

'Does that mean *I* am Thomas Brinklow,' asked Elias.

'You were my choice at the start, Owen.'

'The matter is not yet settled,' said Gill quickly.

'But you deserted us even now,' said Firethorn. 'You are frighted out of the project. I heard you say as much. So did Owen here.' He gave the Welshman a sly wink to ensure his complicity. 'What was it that he said?'

'That he will not act in this lunatic venture.'

'Nor will I,' said Gill, folding his arms in a posture of indifference. After a moment's reflection, however, he weakened visibly. 'Unless certain conditions are met.'

'You have surrendered the role,' said Firethorn, working on the other's pride. 'It goes to Owen. He needs to impose no conditions on the company.' He heaved a sigh. 'Had old Ben Skeat still been with us, I would have offered the part to him. Ben would have been a noble Thomas Brinklow.'

'Why, so will I,' asserted Gill.

'He had the authority. The dignity.'

'So do I, so do I.'

'Ben Skeat would have anchored the play securely.'

'He did not anchor *The Corrupt Bargain* securely,' said Gill with a rueful glare. 'Had we relied on him, we would have drifted on to the rocks. It was I, who saved the day. I, who proved my mettle. I, who led the company. Where was Ben Skeat then? Beyond recall!' He rose to his feet. 'Thomas Brinklow must first be offered to me. I have all the qualities of the man. If Edmund can but find me a song or two in the role, I will consider it afresh. Good day, sirs. That is all the parlay that I will permit.'

It was enough. Barnaby Gill was caught in their net. Owen Elias expressed token disappointment at the loss of a part he had never expected to play and Firethorn feigned reluctance but the two men had achieved their objective. Barnaby Gill would act in *The Roaring Boy*. When the comedian strutted out of the taproom, Lawrence Firethorn turned to his companion with a whoop of delight.

'It worked, Owen!'

'We played him like a fish on a line.'

'I talk of the lighted candle.'

'When that surgeon burned my hand?'

'One agony drove out another,' said Firethorn. 'The pain of dealing with Barnaby's vanity has quite taken away my tooth- ache. He was the flame that distracted me. It is a blessing. I am recovered to give my full attention to the challenge of *The Roaring Boy*.

'All we need now is the play itself,' said Owen.

Firethorn emptied his cup. 'Put trust in our fellows. Edmund Hoode is no inquisitor but Nick Bracewell will dig out the truth. Our book holder will not leave Greenwich until he has sifted every detail of this endeavour.'

Nicholas Bracewell became increasingly fascinated with Emilia Brinklow. His first impression of her was slowly ratified. The sedate figure on the bench opposite was patently still mourning the loss of her brother but she was not prostrated by grief. There was an air of cool detachment about her and she was evidently in control of her situation. When Agnes brought refreshment for the visitors, Emilia thanked the maidservant and gave her crisp new instructions. When the assistant garden- ers strayed too close to the arbour, she despatched them with a glance. Thomas Brinklow had died but his sister was more than able to run the establishment in his stead. House and garden were being maintained in the way that he himself had designated.

Having exhausted enquiries about the play, and the facts underlying it, Edmund Hoode stared at her with open-mouthed infatuation. His commitment to the project was now complete. Two hours in the garden with Emilia Brinklow had turned *The Roaring Boy* into the most exhilarating work of his career. Simon Chaloner manoeuvred them around to more neutral topics, believing that he had safely brought her through what could have been a harrowing encounter for her. He was still congratulating himself on his adroit management of the interview when Emilia herself supplanted him.

She turned a searching gaze upon Nicholas Bracewell.

'You are not happy, I think.'

'Our visit has been a most pleasant event,' he said.

'Yet it has left you feeling disappointed.'

'No!' said Hoode gallantly. 'There is no disappointment on my side. I was never more content in my life.'

Her eyes never left Nicholas. 'Your friend does not share your contentment, I fear. Do you, sir?'

Nicholas felt oddly discomfited by her inspection. He wished that his face were not so bruised and found himself wanting to appear before her at his best rather than in such a battered condition. At the same time, he noted an interest on her part that went beyond mere curiosity. She was sitting with one man who loved her and another who adored her on sight yet her attention was fixed solely on Nicholas.

'Something is puzzling you, is it not?' she said.

'No, Emilia,' said Chaloner, trying to seize the initiative once more. 'We have been through every aspect of the case. There is nothing left to discuss. Let me show our visitors the spot where the hideous deed took place, then they can make their way back to London.'

'Do not rush our guests away so fast, Simon.'

'But Edmund is eager to resume work on the play.'

'Indeed, I am,' said Hoode willingly.

'We must not detain them, Emilia.'

'Something must first be resolved,' she said, her gaze still on Nicholas. 'I still await your answer.'

'You are right,' he said. 'Many things puzzle me.'

'Tell me what they are.' Her hand shot up as Chaloner sought to intervene. 'Leave this to me, Simon. I do not need your protection. I have nothing to hide.'

'Why do you not appear in the play?' said Nicholas.

'Because I was not involved in the murder.'

'Indirectly, you were. Through Sir John Tarker.'

'That was a distressing episode that I have tried to forget. My brother was not killed because of me. Other reasons prompted his death. If the play brings the real villain to light, we shall learn what those reasons were.'

'Emilia Brinklow should still be a character in the action,' insisted Nicholas. 'Thomas would then have someone in whom he could confide his worries about his wife. I am sure that Edmund could write some touching scenes between brother and sister.'

'It would be an honour!' said the playwright.

'But it would also confuse the audience,' rejoined Emilia. 'Their sympathy must be wholly with Thomas. He must command the stage. If I am dragged into the story, I will draw away attention that rightly belongs to my brother. They will feel sorry for me when they should be saving all their pity and compassion for Thomas.'

Hoode purred with admiration. 'A sound reason!'

'And one that I accept,' said Nicholas graciously, not wishing to pursue an argument he could never win. 'We will keep Emilia Brinklow in our minds but out of the play.'

'Thank you.' She got to her feet. 'Come with me.'

'Where are you going, Emilia?' said Chaloner anxiously.

'To show him something.'

'I can conduct them both to the place.'

'We will go alone. I wish for private conference.'

Chaloner was bewildered by her decision but he did not contest it further. Seeing his distress, she put a consoling hand on his shoulder before leading Nicholas up the garden in the direction of the house.

'Simon watches over me too closely,' she explained.

'Why?'

'He fears for my safety.' She turned to look up into his face. 'You have seen for yourself how dangerous is our situation. I am truly sorry that you suffered a beating.' Her voice faltered slightly. 'You have such a kind face. It reminds me of Thomas. I hate to see such injuries on it.'

'You know of the attack, then?'

'Simon tells me everything. He has spoken well of you and holds you in high esteem. That is a compliment.'

'I am duly flattered by it,' said Nicholas, 'and even more so by your trust in me. Master Chaloner is indeed fortunate to be betrothed to such a lady.'

She gave him an enigmatic smile, then led him along the path through the trees. They came around the angle of a hawthorn hedge and were confronted by the rear of the house. Nicholas stopped in surprise when he saw the fire damage.

'What was that building?'

'My brother's laboratory and workshop. Thomas virtually lived there. There never was a man so wedded to his work.'

'When was it burned down?'

'The same night that he was killed.'

'Who started the fire?'

'We do not know,' she said. 'The villains who murdered him, we believe. His life's work was in that laboratory. It was destroyed as cruelly as he himself.'

'Why?'

'They were vindictive men.'

'Then why not burn down the whole house?'

'We can only guess.'

Nicholas looked down at her and inhaled her fragrance. Seated in the arbour, she was handsome and composed. Seen in close proximity, however, her beauty was far more striking. He felt a distant envy of Simon Chaloner. There was something about Emilia Brinklow which set her apart from the common run and he could not quite decide what it was. All he knew was that it made her infinitely appealing. When he had parted company with his beloved Anne Hendrik, he feared that he would never meet her like again yet Emilia Brinklow had many of Anne's qualities, allied to features that were all her own. Both of them, he reflected, had been devastated by the loss of a loved one and forced to rebuild their lives. It gave Emilia the same subdued but steely resolve.

Determination made her eyes glint and her jaw tighten.

'This play gives purpose to my life,' she said. 'Simon is a dear man but he is only involved because of his devotion to me. I am the moving spirit here. *The Roaring Boy* has become my obsession. Can you understand that?'

'I think so.'

Her voice took on a new intensity. 'I lost a brother and a sister-in-law in this business. One was murdered by hired killers, the other by judicial process. Cecily was no saint, it is true, but neither was she a murderer. In her own way, I believe, she cared for Thomas.'

'But it was an unhappy marriage.'

'They were simply not suited.'

'Why, then, did they wed?'

Emilia shrugged. 'It seemed the natural thing to do. Cecily was fond of him and Thomas had great respect for her. Other people kept saying that they were an ideal couple.'

'Marriage needs more than fondness and respect.'

'Yes,' she said sadly. 'You have a wife yourself?'

'Alas, no.'

'Thomas was a kind husband but Cecily loved another.'

'Walter Dunne. They paid dearly for their passion.' He looked at the debris in front of him. 'What sort of work did your brother do in his laboratory?'

'Anything and everything,' she said proudly. 'Thomas loved all the sciences but his abiding interest was in mathematics. That workshop was his private sanctum. His finest inventions were conceived within those walls.'

'Inventions?'

'Thomas had a questing mind. He was always looking for new solutions to old problems. When he was retained by the royal dockyards at Deptford, he designed a compass that was far more reliable than any of its predecessors. An astrolabe, too, if you know what that is.'

'Most certainly,' said Nicholas. 'I sailed with Drake around the world, so I learned all there is to learn about navigation. An astrolabe is an instrument for measuring the altitude of heavenly bodies, from which latitude and time may be calculated. Your brother invented one, you say?'

'The best of its kind.'

'I would dearly like to see that.'

'His own version perished in the fire with the rest.'

'A tragedy.'

'Vindictiveness.'

A look of sudden helplessness came into her eyes.

'Why did you wish to speak to me alone?' he asked.

'Because I feel I can trust you.'

'Nobody is more trustworthy than Edmund Hoode.'

She shook her head. 'He can be trusted to refashion the play but you are the only one who can be relied upon to see it staged. Simon is an excellent judge of character and he singles you out.' A smile danced around her lips. 'We are not ignorant provincials in Greenwich, sir. When Thomas was alive, we often came to London to see a play. I love the theatre and my brother indulged my taste. Westfield's Men were always my favourite company.'

'I'll tell that to Master Firethorn.'

'Beg him to present *The Roaring Boy*.'

'He will implore you to give us that privilege.'

'Whatever setbacks, whatever dangers . . .'

'It will be staged. I give you my word on it.'

She touched his arm. 'I knew that I could trust you.'

Voices approached and she stepped back involuntarily. Simon Chaloner came up with Edmund Hoode and the latter reacted with horror to the destruction of the laboratory. Thomas Brinklow had not just been killed. His life's work had been obliterated. Emilia soon took her leave of them, giving Hoode a smile of gratitude that would keep him happy for days but reserving a more meaningful glance for Nicholas.

Chaloner now took them into the house to view the actual scene of the crime. It was near the foot of the main staircase, a shadowy area even by day. Thomas Brinklow had returned at night to be ambushed in his own home.

'How did the villains get in here?' said Nicholas.

'They must have picked the lock,' replied Chaloner.

'Or had a confederate inside the building.'

'Emilia will not hear of such an idea.'

'What is your opinion?'

He looked around to make sure that Emilia was not within earshot. 'This house was well-protected with locks and bolts. Thomas saw to that. They were either given a key or let in.'

'Did no one hear the commotion?' asked Nicholas.

'Agnes, the maidservant. She was awakened by cries and raised the alarm. Not soon enough, alas. Before anyone got downstairs, the killers had made good their escape.'

'After first setting fire to the laboratory?'

'No,' said Chaloner. 'That happened much later in the night. They must have returned to wreak further havoc.'

'Was the fire not part of Freshwell's confession?'

'He admitted the murder. That was enough to hang him.'

Nicholas walked up and down the hallway and tried all the

doors to see which was the most likely mode of entry and exit for the two villains.

'Was Thomas Brinklow a big man?'

'Big and strong, Nicholas. Something of your build.'

'He would have fought his attackers?'

'No question of that.'

It made surprise a vital element in the ambush and that confirmed Nicholas's feeling that the killers had concealed themselves beneath the staircase. As Thomas Brinklow tried to mount the steps, they must have leapt out and hacked him down from behind. Edmund Hoode stared ghoulishly at the spot where the mathematician fell but Nicholas was concerned to analyse the murder in great detail. He also made a mental note of the setting of the crime for use in the performance of the play itself. Only when he had explored every possibility in the location did he announce that it was time to go.

The visit to Greenwich had been a revelation and his few minutes alone with Emilia Brinklow were invaluable. He and Hoode would have much to debate on their return journey. As he looked around the sumptuous house with its costly furnishings and its air of formal luxury, one question kept nagging away at him. He turned to Simon Chaloner.

'When did he realise that his marriage was a mistake?'

'Too late, I fear. Far, far too late.'

'How did he meet his wife?'

'At Greenwich Palace. They were introduced by a mutual friend, who often stayed there.'

'And who might that be?'

'Sir Godfrey Avenell.'

'The Master of the Armoury?'

'No less.'

'How did Thomas Brinklow come to know such a man?'

'He had many friends in high places,' said Chaloner. 'His circle of acquaintances was very wide. He dined with Sir Godfrey at the Palace one day when Cecily was also a guest. She warmed to Thomas and showed a keen interest in his work. That is rare among women.'

'How soon did they marry?'

'Less than a year after that first meeting. Sir Godfrey was delighted to have played Cupid. At their wedding, he showered them with the most generous gifts. He had a real investment in that marriage.'

'It gave him a miserable dividend.'

'Yes,' agreed Chaloner. 'He was mortified. Sir Godfrey Avenell must wish that he never brought them together.'

Greenwich Palace was a magnificent structure built around three quadrangles. Faced in red brick and ornamented with pillars, it lay on the bank of the Thames like a giant alligator basking in the sun. A long pier gave access to the river at all states of the tide. The main entrance was through a massive gatehouse which led to the central court. Successive members of the Tudor dynasty had lavished money and affection unstintingly upon their favoured residence and Queen Elizabeth was no exception. Having herself been born in the riverside palace, she always had a special fondness for it and liked nothing more than to spend her summers there, holding court, entertaining foreign dignitaries or watching plays, masques and musical concerts.

She particularly enjoyed the regular tournaments that were held at Greenwich Palace, glittering occasions that would find her seated amid her retinue in the permanent gallery above the tiltyard. Tournaments were immensely popular but exclusively reserved for the elite. Only the rich could afford to take part in an event which imposed enormous costs upon them. Only the very rich could finance such a contest. The Queen's own father, Henry VIII, once spent £4000 on the Westminster tournament, almost double the cost of his huge warship, *The Great Elizabeth*. The Tudor monarchy took jousting very seriously.

A lone figure sat in the permanent gallery and surveyed the busy tiltyard. Sir Godfrey Avenell had much to divert him. Greenwich was an ideal place for would-be knights to practice their horsemanship and to hone their technique with the lance. The tilt itself was a permanent wooden fence some one hundred and fifty yards long, gaily painted and defining the nature of combat. It prevented any collision when jousting knights thundered towards each other on horseback on either side of the fixture. It also obliged them to attack an opponent from an angle. Several pairs of knights were in action, some fighting on foot but most taking their turn in the saddle.

Sir Godfrey Avenell watched it all with an imperious air. Dressed in his finery, he cast an expert eye over the proceedings. He had been a keen jouster in his day and still took part in the occasional practice but he left competition in the prestigious Court tournaments to younger and stronger riders. One such man, Sir John Tarker, rode into the tiltyard below and Avenell's interest quickened. He had good reason for such bias towards the newcomer. The splendid armour worn by Tarker was commissioned and paid for by his friend. Sir Godfrey Avenell was scrutinising his own money.

The Office of the Armoury was based at the Tower of London. As its Master, he operated largely from that base but made frequent visits to Greenwich because the finest armour was made in its workshops. The Green Gallery and the Great Chamber at the palace housed a display of supreme examples of the armourer's art and Avenell never saw them without wishing that he could take some of the pieces away for his own collection. There was something about their design and craftsmanship that he found truly inspiring.

Leaning forward in his seat, he examined Sir John Tarker's new suit of armour with meticulous care until he was satisfied that his money had been well spent. The gleaming breastplate was decorated with white and gilt bands into which the Tarker coat-of-arms had been inscribed. The helmet had similar decoration and a latticed visor which protected its owner's face completely while giving him a fair degree of visibility. The leg armour was beautifully tailored to allow easy movement. Even from that distance, the Master of the Armoury could see that the gauntlets were masterpieces of construction, the left one a manifer or bridle gauntlet, designed to cover hand and lower arm on the exposed side of the jouster.

Sir John Tarker's destrier was also arrayed. Its shaffron, a superbly moulded piece of armour that covered its forehead, cheeks and nose, allowed clear vision through the flanged eye-holes. A spike projected from the centre of the forehead to give it the appearance of a steel unicorn. The horse also wore a patterned crinet, a section of armour that was attached to the shaffron in order to guard the animal's neck and mane. During a tournament itself, the destrier would also wear armour plate to protect its chest, crupper and flank but Tarker had dispensed with that during the practice in the interests of speed. Other knights would have baulked at exposing their mounts to un-necessary danger in this way but Tarker was confident that his skill in jousting was a sufficient safeguard for the animal.

Sir Godfrey Avenell was suitably impressed. His man cut a fine figure in the saddle. When he fought in the Accession Day Tournament in November, Sir John Tarker would need to call on his friend for some additional expenditure. Much prepara-tion went into such an illustrious event. A knight had to decide on a theme for his entry into the tiltyard and choose the cos-tumes for himself, his pages, his servants, his lance bearers, his grooms, his trumpeters and any other musicians he hired for extra effect. His horse, too, would require a caparison to match the costumes. Sir Godfrey Avenell had already laid out well over £400 on the suit of armour and its garniture. He was quite happy to meet further exorbitant costs in order to attain the best results.

Sir John Tarker trotted across to him and dipped his lance in acknowledgement. Avenell took a closer inventory.

'How does the armour feel?' he said.

'It fits me like the supplest of leather.'

'Weight?'

'Heavy enough to protect, light enough for movement.'

'Decoration?'

'Exactly as prescribed.'

'Total cost?'

'Murderous!' They shared a laugh. 'I am eternally in your debt. Shall I put it to the test?'

'That is why I am here.'

'Then watch.'

Sir John Tarker wheeled his horse and spurred it into a canter that took it to the far end of the tiltyard. Reining it in, he swung round once more to face his opponent, a burly knight in dark armour, sitting astride a powerful black destrier that was drumming the turf with its hooves. Tarker's reputation frightened away many combatants but this man clearly had courage enough for the encounter and confidence enough in his own ability. He adjusted his shield, lifted his lance and made ready.

The preliminaries were soon over. When the signal was given, the two riders jabbed their horses into action and pounded towards each other on either side of the tilt. Sir Godfrey Avenell respected the challenger's skill but knew it would be unequal to the task. Sir John Tarker was a masterly jouster. His mount was steered at the right pace, his lance and shield held at the correct angles. The long pummelling approach ended in a momentary clash of metal. Tarker's shield deflected the oncoming lance while his own weapon found a tiny gap in the defence and struck his adversary full in the chest. Since the lance was rebated, its blunt end did not damage the breastplate but the man was promptly unseated and Sir Godfrey Avenell rocked with appreciative laughter.

Tarker reined in his horse again and trotted back to the

fallen rider with token concern. Pages were already running to the latter's assistance.

'Are you hurt?'

'No, Sir John,' said the other breathlessly, as they helped him up. 'My pride only has been wounded.'

'Will you remount and engage me a second time?'

'I will not. Find some other fool to challenge you.'

Tarker grinned behind his visor. 'They are frighted.'

'Who can blame them? You have no peer as a jouster. A man with your skills could look to be Queen's Champion.'

'I do, believe me. I do.'

Pleased with his performance and wanting approbation from the source he respected most, Tarker took his horse across to the gallery once more. He flicked up his visor so that he could see Sir Godfrey Avenell more clearly and enjoy the latter's praise. His friend, however, was no longer beaming down at the tiltyard. He was reading a letter, which had just been handed to him by a servant. The frown of alarm became a scowl of anger as he scrunched up the missive in his hand. Rising to his feet, he fixed Tarker with a venomous glare and pointed an accusatory finger.

'You failed me again!' he snarled.

'How?'

'You swore the matter was dead and buried.'

'What matter?' He realised the subject of the letter and spluttered. 'It is. We may forget the whole thing.'

'*We* may but Westfield's Men will not.'

'Westfield's Men?'

'Two of their number visited a house in Greenwich but yesterday,' said Avenell. 'One was their playwright and the other was this Nicholas Bracewell whom your men, you assured me, had beaten into submission.'

'They did!' asserted Tarker. 'On my honour, they did!'

'You failed.'

'That is not so!'

'You failed miserably,' said Avenell with scorn. 'I give you a simple task and you let me down. Does such an imbecile deserve the brightest armour from the workshops? Has such a bungler any call on my friendship?'

'I did but as you urged me,' said Tarker hurriedly. 'If there is some fault, it is not of my making. Blame the fools I hired. They promised me they had all but finished this Nicholas Bracewell. They lied to me, the rogues. I'll have the hide off their backs for this.'

'I'll have the armour off yours!' snarled Avenell. 'If you do not wipe up this mess you have made—and that with all celerity—I'll turn Sir John Tarker into the poorest knight in Christendom. You'll be jousting at the Accession Tournament in fustian on the back of a donkey. The Queen's Champion indeed! They will hail you as the Queen's Champion jester!'

Westfield's Men were steeped in affliction and seasoned by regular crisis but the next ten days brought pressures of an intensity that even they had not known before. The whole company was in a state of muted desperation. Stimulated to a fever pitch of creation by his visit to Greenwich, Edmund Hoode worked tirelessly on *The Roaring Boy,* wholly convinced of its importance and buttressed by thoughts of winning the approval of Emilia Brinklow. He still acted in the current offerings at the Queen's Head but no longer stayed for a celebratory drink after a performance. Within half an hour of quitting the stage, he was back at his post in the lodging he shared with Nicholas Bracewell.

The book holder himself rarely left Hoode's side. He helped him, advised him and guaranteed his safety. Given the proper space in which to work, the playwright blossomed. Owen Elias was a second line of defence, watching over his friends from a distance and ready to ward off any attack. The rest of the company were also schooled in the basic elements of security.

Convinced that Westfield's Men might be ambushed at any moment, Lawrence Firethorn counselled them to stay in groups at all times and to remain alert.

But the expected assault never came. *The Roaring Boy* was allowed to grow from a halting drama into a full-fledged play. The actors did not, however, relax. They felt that they had merely been given a stay of execution and that the axe would fall on them in time. Nicholas Bracewell wondered if its enemies planned to scupper the play in a more bloodless fashion. Every new work had first to be read by the Master of the Revels before it was licensed for performance. If Sir John Tarker had some influence at court, he might well use it to have the play banned. To guard against that eventuality, Nicholas suggested a counteraction.

'It must be twofold,' he told Firethorn.

'Speak on, Nick.'

'*The Roaring Boy* must not mention Sir John Tarker by name or that will invite censorship for sure. Edmund will devise a suitable disguise for the character. Nobody will hear the name of Tarker but everyone will recognise it.'

'What is your other strategy?'

'We make use of our patron, Lord Westfield.'

'In what way?'

'He is a personal friend of the Master of the Revels.'

'True. He and Sir Edmund Tilney often dine together.'

'We must ask Lord Westfield to submit *The Roaring Boy* on our behalf,' said Nicholas. 'A word from him in the ear of a boon companion may get the piece read and licensed much sooner than would otherwise be the case.'

'Your advice as ever is sound.'

Nicholas took the opportunity to grasp another nettle. 'Let me add more of a personal nature.'

'Personal?'

'Have your tooth pulled by a surgeon,' said Nicholas. 'A little pain now will spare you a lot of agony in the future. You claim that the discomfort has gone but that swelling in your cheek argues the contrary case.'

'Leave my tooth alone. It is not relevant here.'

'It is if it keeps you off the stage again.'

'It will not!' snapped Firethorn, feeling a menacing tingle in his gum. 'Simply forget my toothache and it will go away. Stoke up the fire with constant carping about it and my mouth is an inferno. You mean well, Nick, I know that. But your concern is unfounded. Trust me, dear heart. A dozen bad teeth will not keep me away from *The Roaring Boy*. They will simply make Freshwell roar all the louder.'

Nicholas Bracewell accepted the promise and backed off.

His strategy with regard to the Master of the Revels was a shrewd one. It was the book holder's job to take each new drama to Sir Edmund Tilney's office and pay the fee to have it read. Delays were normal and often very lengthy. Since *The Roaring Boy* relied on its topicality, it was essential to bring it into the light of day as quickly as possible. Lord Westfield served his players well. A tactful word to his friend and a troublesome play was granted an immediate licence with hardly a line of the work altered.

Edmund Hoode took much of the credit for its apparent harmlessness. Sir John Tarker was featured as The Stranger and accused by inference rather than name. The real power of *The Roaring Boy* lay not in the lines that were spoken but in the action that went on between them. Hoode had contrived to damn Sir John Tarker in the most visible way possible. There was a cunning reference to the latter's jousting skills and many other hidden clues that would be instantly recognised by those who knew the knight. His identity would be trumpeted to the skies.

While performances continued to be given at the Queen's Head in the afternoons, the leading members of the company rehearsed the new play secretly in the evenings. Hired men were not brought into the venture at this point. Their parts

were too small to be of significance and Nicholas argued that
the fewer people who knew the true substance of *The Roaring
Boy*, the less chance there was of any details of its contents
falling into the wrong hands.

Hard work, punishing hours and the constant strain of being
on guard inevitably took their toll and frayed tempers occasionally rocked a rehearsal. Barnaby Gill exploded like a powder keg
at regular intervals, torn between delight at the leading role he
had been assigned and trepidation at the consequences of playing it. But he was always calmed by the others and equilibrium
was soon re-established. *The Roaring Boy* took on real shape and
was ready for its premiere well ahead of the original schedule. It
was inserted into the company's programme at once. Lawrence
Firethorn supervised the printing of the playbills himself. In
sonorous tones, he read one of them out to his fellows.

THE ROARING BOY

*Being the Lamentable and True Tragedy
of M. Brinklow of Greenwich
Most wickedly murdered by foul means
Supposedly at the behest of a wanton wife*

It was enough to ignite great interest without giving too
much away. Whatever else might happen at the performance
of the play, Westfield's Men could rely on getting a large and
excitable audience. A savage murder involving an adulterous
wife was a cautionary tale that none could resist.

Orlando Reeve was less than pleased to be sent back to the
Queen's Head to sit on a crowded bench and endure the stench
of horse manure and the stink of the commonalty that rose up
in equal parts from a packed courtyard. What increased his
dismay was the fact that his paymaster this time was not the

bounteous Sir Godfrey Avenell but the tight-fisted Sir John Tarker. While the former loved music, the latter was openly contemptuous of musicians and treated Reeve with a disdain which he found quite intolerable. Tarker's command could not be ignored, however, so the second ordeal had to be faced.

The play on offer that afternoon was *Mirth and Madness* but Orlando Reeve was untouched by either. A rumbustious comedy sent the audience into an almost continuous spasm of laughter but the adipose musician remained stony-faced. Only the work of Peter Digby and his consort brought any relief to a grim afternoon for him. When the performance was over, he cornered his old friend in the taproom. Digby was astounded to see him again and wondered why Reeve was so eager to buy him a cup of wine and talk about former times. Not wishing to stay in the noisy tavern any longer than he had to, the visitor swiftly guided the conversation around to *The Roaring Boy.*

'I see that you play the murder of Thomas Brinklow.'

'On Saturday next.'

'A warning to all men foolish enough to marry.'

'His wife may not be the villain that you imagine.'

'Indeed?'

'She was the victim of a plot conceived by another.'

'Tell me more of this, Peter.'

'I may not,' said Digby, remembering the dire warnings issued by Lawrence Firethorn. 'I am sworn to secrecy. We have enemies all around us and have built a wall of silence to keep them at bay. But this I may tell you. *The Roaring Boy* will blaze across the stage. Westfield's Men have not had such a play in years.'

'Does it have songs and dances?'

'All our work contains those, Orlando.'

'And incidental music between scenes?'

'I have composed it all.'

'What yet remains to exercise your talents?'

'A tuneful setting for the ballad.'

'Ballad?'

'It begins the play,' said Digby, 'and tells what lies ahead. It is a simple enough task to match it to music but I have not yet found the trick of it. I am too bound up with composition of a more serious kind to master the ballad-maker's art.'

'Perhaps I may help,' volunteered the oleaginous Reeve.

'It is beneath the dignity of a Court musician.'

'Not so. I turned my hand to ballads in younger days. Give me but the first verse, then hum your tunes for me. I'll help you choose the one most apt.' He poured the hesitating Digby another cup of wine and gave him a flabby grin. 'Come, Peter. One verse will break no solemn vow of secrecy. I come to you as a fellow-musician. Sing it in my ear.'

Saturday finally dawned and brought with it the prospect of release from the appalling tensions that had built up within the company. The stage was set up in the yard of the Queen's Head and an attenuated rehearsal held that morning. Lawrence Firethorn did not wish to reveal anything to prying eyes. He simply walked his cast through the play to familiarise them with their movement around the boards and to acquaint them with the scenic devices that would be used. Hired men were slotted into minor parts for the first time. It was such a fraught occasion that they were grateful to Barnaby Gill when his spectacular fit helped to clear the air.

Forearmed against danger from without, Nicholas Bracewell also had to cope with a hazard from within. Alexander Marwood, the landlord of the Queen's Head, enjoyed a nervous relationship with Westfield's Men, believing that actors were little better than wild goats and that he never ought to place either his tavern or his nubile daughter within their lustful reach. He was a small, ageing, restless man with hollow cheek and haunted eyes. A few last strands of greasy hair still remained, not knowing whether to cling to the lost cause of his mottled skull or to fling themselves into the void after their fellows.

When Marwood scurried across his yard, his face was simultaneously twitching in three distinct areas. With an unerring instinct for misfortune, he could smell calamity in the air. His arms gesticulated wildly.

'You bring trouble into my yard, Master Bracewell.'

'We bring the biggest audience we have had for many a week and thereby put extra money in your purse.'

'*The Roaring Boy* alarms me.'

'Why?'

'I do not know but I feel it in my bones.'

'We cannot choose our plays to appease your anatomy.'

'More's the pity!' said Marwood, as the three separate twitches met in the middle of his face to make his nose tremble violently. 'I had this same presentiment before *The Devil's Ride Through London* and what happened, sir? You all but burned my tavern to the ground.'

'No fire is used in this play. You are safe.'

'From conflagration, maybe. But what of the fire in the play's subject? May not that flare up and scorch us?'

Nicholas calmed him with a mixture of argument and assurance but the book holder was by no means as confident as he sounded. The landlord, for once, had scented danger where it genuinely existed. Once it started, *The Roaring Boy* would be walking a tightrope between hope and terror.

The atmosphere in the tiring-house was as taut as a bowstring. As the hour of performance edged nearer, the whole company fell prey to niggling anxiety. Barnaby Gill gave way to bitter recrimination, Edmund Hoode flew into a sudden panic at the thought that Emilia Brinklow would be among the spectators to judge both him and his work, Owen Elias grew more pugnacious than ever and Lawrence Firethorn—intending to rally them with a high-flown speech that stressed the significance of the event before them—only succeeded in disseminating more unease. It was left to Nicholas Bracewell to lead by example with the quiet efficiency which had become his hallmark.

'Stand by, my lads!' said Firethorn. 'We are there!'

The bell in the nearby clocktower chimed twice and the performance began. As the consort played the introductory music, the spectators gave a concerted cheer. Packed into the yard and crammed into the benches, they positively buzzed with anticipation. The murder of such a decent and upright man as Thomas Brinklow was an emotive subject and their passions were already stirred. *The Roaring Boy* had no need to warm up an audience already simmering in the sunshine.

Simon Chaloner sat in the lower gallery beside Emilia Brinklow. He scanned the benches all around him for signs of danger but her attention never left the stage. This was the moment of truth for her. When Simon felt her tremble, he took her hand in his and found the little palm moist. Grateful for his love and support, Emilia tossed him a little smile, then watched the stage with beating heart.

Instead of the expected Prologue, the penitent figure of Cecily Brinklow stepped out from behind the arras. Richard Honeydew wore the plain dress, in which he would later go to his death, and an auburn wig. With cosmetic aid, the young apprentice was a most attractive and convincing wife. As a lute played in the gallery above him, he sang his ballad with a tearful simplicity that all but hushed the audience.

> *Ah me, vile wretch, that ever I was born,*
> *Making myself unto the world a scorn;*
> *And to my friends and kindred all a shame,*
> *Blotting their blood by my unhappy name.*
>
> *Unto a gentlemen of wealth and fame,*
> *(One Master Brinklow, he was called by name)*

I wedded was to this man of great renown,
Living at Greenwich, close to London town.

This husband dear, my heart he fully won,
Until I met again with Walter Dunne,
Whose sugared tongue, good shape and lovely look,
Soon stole my heart, and Brinklow's love forsook.

The remorseful wife was not alone on stage for long. As each new character was mentioned in the plaintive song, he or she stepped out to take up position in a carefully arranged tableau. Spectators soon recovered their voices. Thomas Brinklow set off a ripple of sympathy and Walter Dunne was greeted with a hiss of anger, but it was the murderers themselves who provoked the loudest response. When Lawrence Firethorn and Owen Elias skulked on to the stage as Freshwell and Maggs, respectively, they were met with concerted abuse. Pictures of wickedness in their ragged garb, the two actors played on the spectators with roars of defiance and increased the general ire by making obscene gestures at them. Here were no wretched penitents. They were villains who clearly revelled in their villainy.

Cecily Brinklow waited for the uproar to abate before she sung verses that offered a whole new perspective on tragic events in a house in Greenwich.

The world reviles for e'er my hated name,
With Walter Dunne, I bear eternal blame.
But though we sinned together through the night,
To murder did we nobody incite.

Another hand unleashed these evil scrags
(The one called Freshwell, and the other Maggs)
This cruel man had Thomas killed stone dead
But Walter Dunne and I hanged in his stead.

Who this foul demon is, our play will tell,
He dwells in London here but comes from hell.
Call him The Stranger until his face you espy.
Send him to the gallows to hang up high.

There was a gasp of disbelief as Edmund Hoode strode on to the stage in a long black cloak with a hat pulled down over his eyes. For the vast majority of those present, The Stranger was a sensational new element in the story. Could the law really have hanged Cecily Brinklow and Walter Dunne for a crime they did not commit? Was the play going to offer fresh evidence that would exonerate them and incriminate the dark figure on the stage? Who was the Stranger and why would he wish to have Thomas Brinklow so viciously killed?

Simon Chaloner was chilled by the sinister entrance of the newcomer. Emilia Brinklow stifled a cry with the back of her hand. Both of them marvelled at Edmund Hoode's skill as an actor. The moon-faced playwright had been turned into a stealthy figure of doom. What neither of them realised was that the Stranger himself was sitting above them in the upper gallery, lurking in a shadowed corner and already smarting with discomfort. Sir John Tarker watched it all with growing frenzy.

With the ballad over, the play unfolded in a series of short but effective scenes. Thomas Brinklow was first seen at home with his wife, bestowing rich gifts upon her as a token of his undying love. Barnaby Gill floated joyously on the waves of sympathy that came rolling towards him. The first meeting between Cecily and Walter Dunne aroused fresh hisses of disgust but the adulterous couple were no longer condemned out of hand. In the light of the ballad, the audience was at least now ready to suspend judgement for a while.

The Stranger came to the house in Greenwich as a friend but departed as a sworn enemy. What caused the intemperate row with Thomas Brinklow was not made clear but the Stranger's vile threats left nobody in any doubt about his intentions. When he engaged the services of Freshwell and Maggs, all three of them were subjected to the most ear-splitting denigration from the onlookers. Lawrence Firethorn had to use the full force of his voice to rise above it.

Murder was to be followed by malicious deceit. Having instigated the killing, the Stranger plotted the arrest and conviction of Cecily Brinklow and Walter Dunne. It was when he explained that they would be caught *in flagrante* that the real explosion came. Sir John Tarker could endure no more. He gave the signal to his confederates and they acted with promptness. Freshwell was in the middle of a drunken speech of praise for the Stranger when a member of the audience clambered up on to the stage to wave a club at him. One roaring boy was suddenly confronted by another.

The standees bayed at the interloper but they soon had a more immediate problem of their own. A fight broke out in the very middle of the yard between two of Tarker's men. It quickly spread until several dozen people were involved. When a second affray erupted in the lower gallery, the whole audience was in turmoil. Nicholas Bracewell rushed out to overpower the man with the club but his intervention was too late. The performance was ruined. Spectators who had been absorbed in the drama only minutes before now joined in the brawl or fought their way to the exits. Simon Chaloner had to use all his strength to protect Emilia from the busy elbows and bruising shoulders all around them. His howled attempts to calm down the mob went unheard.

Sir John Tarker presided over it all with malignant satisfaction. Having been upbraided so roundly by Sir Godfrey Avenell, he was anxious to redeem himself in the most dramatic way. Instead of launching a second attack on any of Westfield's Men, therefore, he bided his time to give them the illusion that they were safe. The moment to strike was when he could inflict maximum damage on the company and on the play that they were daring to present. As he viewed the seething chaos below, he was content. *The Roaring Boy* was now no more than a fading memory in the minds of brawling spectators.

Lawrence Firethorn was livid, Barnaby Gill was aghast and Edmund Hoode was utterly destroyed. Owen Elias was belabouring the man who had first jumped on the stage and Nicholas was trying to save the structure itself from collapse. Alexander Marwood was in an ecstasy of hysteria, running around in circles like a headless chicken as each new surge of violence inflicted more damage on his property and holding his hands over his ears to keep out the deafening clamour of combat.

It was a long time before even a semblance of order was restored. Nicholas Bracewell stood on the wrecked stage with Firethorn and Hoode. The yard was littered with wounded bodies, the galleries were cluttered with broken benches, the balustrades were stained with blood or draped with abandoned articles of apparel. An air of complete desolation hung over the tavern. As they surveyed the carnage in front of them, the actor-manager tempted fate with an unconsidered remark.

'This has been our Armageddon,' he said with a sweep of his arm. 'But one consolation remains. The worst is now over.'

A sheriff and two constables arrived on cue. Forcing their way through the remnants of the crowd with brute unconcern, they stood at the edge of the stage and looked up at the three men. The sheriff was brusque and peremptory.

'We seek one Edmund Hoode,' he said.

'I am he,' volunteered the playwright.

'You are under arrest, sir.'

'On what charge, pray?'

'Seditious libel. Seize him.'

[CHAPTER SIX]

Valentine heard the sound of horses in the stable-yard and rested his wheelbarrow on the lawn. He pricked his ears and caught the murmur of distant conversation. It was enough to tell him that the mistress of the house had returned. The voices died when a door opened and shut. Evidently, they had gone into the building. Valentine lifted the handles of his wheelbarrow and pushed it with unhurried gait towards the shrubs that grew outside the parlour. It was a warm evening and the windows were still open. Bending to scoop up some of the grass he had mown earlier, the gardener slowly inched himself towards the room until he was within earshot, his ugly face animated with curiosity as he listened to the hurt tones from within. His success was short-lived.

'What are you doing there?' said a sharp voice.

'Picking up this grass,' he said.

'Move away from that window.'

'I have my work to do.'

'Do it somewhere else.'

Agnes stood there with her hands on her hips and a look of

deep suspicion on her face. She hated Valentine enough to have asked for his dismissal more than once but he did his job conscientiously and Emilia Brinklow was reluctant to part with any of the staff who had been engaged by her brother. His furtive manner showed that she had caught him out. Removing his cap with a clumsy attempt at courtesy, he aimed his repulsive grin at the maidservant and shrugged his apologies.

'I've no wish to upset a woman like you, Agnes.'

'Then keep out of my sight.'

'Be friends with me, I beg.'

'You are paid to work here and that is all.'

'Why, so are you. Can we not lighten the load by sharing it a little? A smile and a kind word is all that I seek.'

'You will get neither from me. Away with you!'

Her homely face was a mask of cold anger. Valentine replaced his cap and wiped the back of his hand across his harelip. Wilting under the maidservant's stern gaze, he took his wheelbarrow off down the garden and disappeared behind the fountain. He would have to content himself with the few words he had managed to pick up through the open window.

Unaware of the exchange outside the parlour, Emilia Brinklow and Simon Chaloner continued their urgent conversation within it. The riotous behaviour at the Queen's Head that afternoon had shocked both of them into silence and the long ride back to Greenwich had been a mute ordeal. Back at the house, they were able to give vent to their wounded feelings. White-faced and despondent, Emilia sat on an upright chair while Simon Chaloner circled the room with restless strides.

'I should not have taken you there,' he said.

'It was my own decision to go, Simon.'

'The danger was too great. It was madness.'

'You could not expect me to miss the performance.'

'What performance?' he said ruefully. 'Act Two had scarcely begun when those villains wreaked their havoc. We were lucky to escape injury.' His hand went to his sword. 'Had you not been with me, my love, I'd have hacked the rogues down one by one and sent their stinking carcasses to Sir John Tarker. They were plainly his creatures, hired to start that affray and chase *The Roaring Boy* from the stage.'

'How can we prove that?'

'We do not need to, Emilia.'

'What do you mean?'

'I shall do what honour prompted me to do at the very start,' he said, standing before her. 'Go straight to Tarker and cut out his black heart.'

'Simon, no!' she protested, rising to clutch at him.

'It is the only way to end this business.'

'By throwing away your own life?'

'Tarker is a monster!'

'Then he must answer to the law,' she pleaded. 'If you lay hands upon him, *you* will be the felon. There has to be another way to bring him to justice.'

'Yes, Emilia. We tried it in vain this afternoon.'

'The situation may yet be retrieved.'

'With my sword!'

'No, Simon!' she implored. 'Dear God in heaven—no!'

She held him so tightly that his righteous indignation eventually gave way to concern for her. He stroked her hair and calmed her down with whispered condolences. Lowering her on to the chair again, he knelt down in front of her so that he could look up into her face. He used a gentle finger to brush away a tear that trickled down her cheek.

'Take heart, my love,' he said.

'We were so close, Simon—then all was lost.'

'Only our folly persuaded us that we could win. Tarker set his ambush well. He had *The Roaring Boy* stabbed to death just as callously as Thomas.' He lifted her hand to kiss it, then shook his head with philosophical resignation. 'This morning was so rich in hope but the afternoon has left me poor indeed.'

'Poor?'

'I was doubly robbed at the Queen's Head.'

'How so?'

'I lost both a play and a dearest partner in life.'

Emilia squeezed his hand. 'That is not so.'

'It is,' he said resignedly. 'You will not marry me until this business is concluded and what chance is there of that now? My joy is further away from me than ever.' He stood up again and moved across the room. 'I have worked so sedulously on your behalf, Emilia. I have waited so long and tried so very hard. There is nothing more that I could have done save lay down my life.'

'I know,' she said, 'and I love you for it.'

'But not enough, I fear.'

'Why do you say that?'

'Because you will not be mine,' he said. 'You will not wed me now so that we can join forces to renew this fight together. You will not put me first in line of affection for once. Your love is on condition only.'

She crossed quickly to him. 'It *has* to be, Simon.'

'Why?'

'I have explained it to you a thousand times.'

'And I believed you, Emilia. Until today. Now I begin to wonder if your explanation truly answers me.'

'I will not rest until the murder is resolved.'

'Thomas is dead. Vengeance will not bring him back.'

'It will give me peace of mind.'

'Then—at last—you may pay heed to *my* existence.'

'I do, Simon,' she said with feeling. 'On my honour, I do. But I am not able to open my heart fully to you until this dreadful burden has been lifted from it. That burden only took on extra weight this afternoon, for now I am oppressed by guilt as well as grief.'

'Guilt?'

'At the damage we have inflicted on Westfield's Men.'

'It was not deliberate, Emilia.'

'That does not still my conscience. They risked their lives and their reputation for us. To what end? Their inn-yard playhouse was wrecked, their work dismembered and Edmund Hoode carted off to prison. And all because of me.' She walked across to the window. 'They must hate the very name of Brinklow. It has brought them nothing but trouble.'

'I am to blame for that. I gave them the play.'

'Only at my behest.'

'You charged me to the find the fittest company,' he said, 'and I did that when I met Nick Bracewell. I knew that he would be steadfast enough to hold his company together and put *The Roaring Boy* on the stage. He must regret that he ever got involved with this venture.'

'I regret it, too,' she said soulfully. 'Nicholas was a kind and courageous man. I would not hurt him for the world. I hope his fellows do not turn against him for this.'

A pall of misery hung over the house in Shoreditch. Not even the warm resilience of a Margery Firethorn could lift it. When she served refreshment, only one of the guests, Nicholas Bracewell, had voice enough to give her proper thanks. The others hardly stirred out of their melancholy. Barnaby Gill was morose, Owen Elias stared gloomily at the empty fireplace and Lawrence Firethorn himself was in the grip of a pain deeper even than his toothache. When Margery left them alone again in the parlour, Nicholas Bracewell tried to rouse the others into action.

He slapped a table. 'What are we to do?' he said.

'*You* have done enough already, sir,' accused Gill. 'It is all your doing that we are in this quandary. Had they listened to me, instead of to you, we would not have touched this leprous play. It has infected the whole company. You have much to answer for, Nicholas.'

'Not so!' exclaimed Owen Elias, jumping to the defence of

his friend. 'But for Nick, we would never have had the chance to present such a vital piece of theatre.'

'Too vital!' moaned Firethorn.

'We were not to know the play would be waylaid.'

'It was always a possibility, Owen,' said Nicholas, 'but there was a limit to the precautions we could take. I warned the gatherers to look for any ruffians who sought admission to the play. I stationed extra men to curb any disturbance but they could not be everywhere. The brawl was too sudden and well-planned. We lost control.'

'Control!' snarled Gill. 'If that indeed were all. We have lost more than control, sir. Our occupation's gone!'

'For the time being only,' said Nicholas.

'Forever. Face the truth—forever!'

Gill's voice was like a death knell and nobody tried to interrupt its fearsome echo. *The Roaring Boy* had been an engine of destruction. It not only blackened a record of good audience behaviour at the inn, it caused several injuries, inflicted indiscriminate damage on their venue and led to the arrest of their playwright. Alexander Marwood's furious vow that they would never set foot again in the Queen's Head for once had legal reinforcement. The sheriff, whose men so roughly dragged Edmund Hoode away, also served the company with a writ. An injunction had been taken out forbidding them to perform any play at the Queen's Head until further notice.

'We are voices from the past,' said Gill at his most lugubrious. 'Mere phantoms. *The Roaring Boy* has silenced our art in perpetuity.'

'No great loss where *you* are concerned, Barnaby,' said Firethorn pointedly. 'Bonfires will be lit in celebration. But we will live to act on.'

'Where?' sneered the comedian. 'How?'

'With distinction, sir!'

'There has to be a way out for us,' said Elias.

'There is, Owen,' agreed Firethorn. 'Westfield's Men have

faced adversity before—plague, fire, the machinations of our rivals—and we have always survived. We can do so again at this time of trial.' His bluster became a tentative query for the book holder. 'Is that not so, Nick? Stiffen our spirits. Teach us the road to salvation.'

'But he is the author of our misfortune!' said Gill.

'We all share the blame for that,' retorted Elias. 'Only one man can rescue us and here he sits. Well, Nick? Your counsel is always sage. What must we do?'

Nicholas Bracewell weighed his words before speaking.

'First, we must secure Edmund's release,' he said. 'We may bewail our own lot but at least we still enjoy our freedom. Edmund languishes in the Marshalsea on a most serious charge. We must restore his liberty.'

'How may we do that?' asked Firethorn.

'By calling on our patron once more. He can speak into ears that we are powerless to reach. Request Lord Westfield to find out how Edmund came to be incarcerated.'

'We know that already,' said Elias. 'Seditious libel.'

'Against whom?'

'Sir John Tarker.'

'I am not so certain of that, Owen,' said Nicholas. 'Sir John Tarker has a worthy reputation as a tournament jouster but he is also a notorious gambler and always in debt. He has neither the money nor the position at Court to bring about this action. We wrestle with a higher authority here.'

Firethorn nodded. 'He must have influential friends.'

'We need to know who they are. Only when we identify our enemies can we hope to prevail against them. Then there is another point.' He scratched his beard in contemplation for a moment. 'The play was interrupted well before Sir John Tarker was unmasked. How could Edmund be accused of libel when none took place? Do you follow me here, gentlemen?'

'No,' admitted Firethorn.

'I do not even bother to listen,' said Gill.

'Well, we do, Nick,' said Elias. 'Attentively. Continue.'

'*The Roaring Boy* was swept from the scaffold because a certain person knew that he would be revealed as a partner in the murder of Thomas Brinklow. What we believe is naked truth, he describes as libel. In other words, he must have had fore-knowledge of the rest of the play. Why else attack it?' Nicholas looked around at his three companions. 'How did he find out? We closed ranks against all enquiry. We lived on top of each other to ensure our mutual safety. Yet he *knew*. Who taught him the innermost workings of the company? To speak more plain—who betrayed us?'

The question produced a flurry of speculation from Lawrence Firethorn and Owen Elias along with a vigorous self-defence from Barnaby Gill, who was sensitive to any charge of indiscretion. Nicholas soon interrupted them.

'The fault may not be ours,' he pointed out. 'Before the play came into our hands, it was housed at Greenwich. Someone there may have gained improper access to it and been warned of its contents. On the other hand, no plans for any perform-ance had then been made. The manuscript was harmless until it came alive on a stage. For that reason, I suspect a member of the company is involved.'

'I'll tear him apart limb by limb!' vowed Firethorn.

'Let us find him first.'

'That will be my office,' volunteered Elias.

'No, Owen,' said Nicholas, 'I have more taxing work than that. You must track a more difficult prey with me.'

'Say but his name and I'll run him to earth.'

'Maggs.'

'My part in the play?'

'The same. Freshwell was hanged but Maggs escaped.'

'The law could not find him, how shall we?'

'By searching more assiduously,' said Nicholas. 'The law had scapegoats enough in Cecily Brinklow and Walter Dunne.

With Freshwell to dance at the end of a rope beside them, they could spare Maggs. We may not.'

'How do we know he is still alive?'

'If he was cunning enough to evade capture, he will have the wit to survive. Find out where he is, Owen. The two of us will then have conference with him. There are hidden facts about this case that only Maggs knows.'

Elias chuckled. 'One Maggs will hunt another.'

'While you are about that,' said Firethorn, 'I'll engage the services of Lord Westfield on our behalf. We'll see if he can find the key to Edmund's cell.'

'And what must *I* do,' asked the peevish Gill.

'Nothing,' said Elias. 'That's contribution enough.'

Nicholas reviewed the situation and reached a decision.

'I'll to Greenwich tomorrow at first light,' he said. 'This latest business may force a more complete story from Master Chaloner. I fear that something was held back from us and I will pursue him until I learn why.'

Action dispersed anxiety. Instead of bemoaning their fate, they could now take positive steps to amend it. Barnaby Gill still wallowed in pessimism but the others were eager to vindicate the name of Westfield's Men, and that could be done only if they found out the full details surrounding the murder of Thomas Brinklow. Since *The Roaring Boy* could not prosecute their case, they had to marshal their evidence in a different way. After further lengthy discussion, Nicholas Bracewell and Owen Elias bade farewell to their hosts and set off down the street.

They did not get very far. Someone waited at a corner ahead of them and leapt out into their path with a sheepish smile. Peter Digby was trembling with embarrassment.

'I must speak with you, Nicholas,' he said.

'Is the matter so urgent?'

'I fear that it may be.'

'Then it touches on this afternoon's affair?' Digby nodded

and threw an anxious glance at the Welshman. 'Speak freely in front of Owen,' said Nicholas. 'Though he is famed for babbling tongue, he knows when to hold it.'

'Would that I did!' said the musician.

He took the two friends down a quiet lane so that their conversation could be neither witnessed nor overheard. Peter Digby was so conscious-stricken that perspiration broke out on his forehead. He gave a shamefaced grin of apology.

'What ails you, Peter?' said Nicholas. 'Tell us.'

'I may be wrong,' said the other. 'Pray God that I am! I would never forgive myself if I was lured into treachery. The company is my life. Westfield's Men are my family.'

'They will always remain so,' assured Elias.

'Not after today.'

'Why, man? What have you done?'

'Nothing with intent to cause harm.'

Nicholas put an arm around the musician's shoulders. With the exception of the much-maligned George Dart, there was not a more decent and innocuous member of the troupe than Peter Digby. Any damage or inconvenience he had caused his fellows must be inadvert.

'Do not tell Master Firethorn,' pleaded Digby.

'We will not,' promised Nicholas.

'He would expel me straight.'

'The matter begins and ends here, Peter.'

'Then hear the worst.' He licked his lips and glanced nervously around. 'When the play went into rehearsal, we were all enjoined to reveal nothing of its substance to anyone outside the company. Nor did I, Nicholas. Not wittingly, I swear. But an old friend came to see *Mirth and Madness*. One Orlando Reeve with whom I once studied.'

'Was his visit unusual?'

'Most unusual. Orlando looks down upon the theatre. Yet this was his second appearance at the Queen's Head in weeks.'

'Second appearance?'

'Yes,' said Digby. 'On the first, he bought me wine and teased me about a falling off in our work. He mocked us so much that I had to defend Westfield's Men. I told him that we would assert ourselves with a wonderful new play.'

Nicholas sighed. *'The Roaring Boy?'*

'Even so.'

'What did you disclose of its contents?'

'Little beyond its characters and theme.'

'And this second unexpected visit?'

'Orlando bought me more wine,' confessed Digby. 'He flattered me and wriggled inside my guard. Playbills had been posted up for *The Roaring Boy* and he affected interest. Before I knew it, I was singing him snatches of the ballad.' The old face was contorted with apprehension. 'Tell me that I did no harm, Nicholas. Assure me that I could not possibly have betrayed my fellows in such a foolish way.'

'You did well to confide in me,' said Nicholas. 'This Orlando Reeve is a musician, you say?'

'A virtuoso of the keyboard.'

'For whom does he play?'

'Her Majesty. Orlando is a Court musician.'

'Where does he dwell? Here in London?'

'Sometimes,' said Digby. 'But he also owns a house which is the merest walk from the palace. Much of his time is spent there when Her Majesty is in residence.'

'Which palace?' asked Nicholas.

'Greenwich.'

Sir Godfrey Avenell was a genial host. He ate supper in his apartment at Greenwich Palace with Sir John Tarker and listened with amusement to the latter's account of the commotion at the Queen's Head that afternoon. Tarker soon won back the good opinion of his friend and patron.

'I congratulate you,' said Avenell with a smirk. 'You contrived the perfect ending for *The Roaring Boy*. I like to see revenge spiced with a modicum of wit.'

'The play was wiped clean off the stage.'

'It should never have got there in the first place,' reminded the other. 'Had you snuffed out its flame at an earlier point, there would have been no need for your own theatricals.' The smirk returned. 'But this afternoon's delights do please my palate and I am grateful to you for that. You showed cunning and imagination.'

'I placed my men where they could see my signal.'

'Their money was well-earned.'

'And my new suit of armour . . . ?'

The question hung in the air for a moment while Avenell poured himself another cup of wine. He was still irritated by his companion's earlier failures but his memory of them was dulled by Tarker's patent success at the Queen's Head. The latter might after all have justified the huge expenditure on him.

'I will think it over,' said Avenell.

'You will not have cause to chide me again.'

'Ensure that I do not.'

'I am your man, Sir Godfrey. Help me to prove myself.'

'The armour did sit well upon you.'

'When I put it on, I felt inspired.'

'That inspiration comes at a very high price.' He sipped the wine and kept the other waiting. 'We shall see. Today, you have recaptured my interest. Tomorrow, you may find your way back into my coffers. Who knows? We shall see.'

Sir John Tarker was content. He knew that his career in the saddle would now continue. Avenell's wealth would once more support Tarker's jousts. In spite of differences in outlook and temperament, the two men made a formidable team when they acted in concert. One rejoiced in amassing and spending money: the other sought his pleasures elsewhere. But they were bonded together at a deep level in a private conspiracy.

'One thing only persists.'

'What is that, Sir Godfrey?'

'This play itself. *The Roaring Boy.*'

'It was impounded by the sheriff and his men.'

'That is not enough.'

'I will have it delivered to you, if you wish.'

'Not the manuscript.'

'Then what?'

'The head of its author.'

'It lies on a board at the Marshalsea Prison.'

'I speak not of Edmund Hoode,' said Avenell. 'He is but the cobbler who put new soles on the piece so that it could walk across the stage. What I want, alive or dead, is the man who first drafted this pernicious drama.'

'His name is unknown.'

'Find it, Sir John.'

'We have tried many times.'

Avenell's voice congealed. 'Find it and that soon.'

'Leave the matter in my hands.'

'I feel that I may safely do that now. Your splendid work this day has armoured me against disappointment.' They traded a smile. 'Hoode is in the Marshalsea, then?'

'Fighting off the rats and praying for deliverance.'

'Let him rot there until my pleasure is served.'

'Will he ever see the light of day again?'

'Not while I live.'

They laughed harshly and attacked their food once more.

The Marshalsea was a grim fortress in a squalid corner of Southwark. Infested with crime of all sorts, the city had well over a dozen prisons into which to fling its never-ending supply of malefactors. Debtors, vagrants, drunkards and those guilty of disorderly conduct were also liable to incarceration, so the prison population was always large and varied. Disease, brutality and starvation were rife in all institutions and many who went in for minor of fences never came out alive. Corruption was the order of the day among prison wardens, sergeants, keepers and tipstaffs. Within the dark walls of their respective gaols, they exploited their positions in the most unscrupulous way and inflicted all manner of horrors on those who sought to obstruct or deny them.

Second only to the Tower in importance, the Marshalsea shared all the hideous faults of the other prisons. It was mainly used for debtors but it also housed a number of religious dissidents and those accused of maritime offences. Another category of prisoners was steadily growing. People who sought to ridicule authority by slanderous or libelous means often found themselves inhaling the fetid atmosphere of the Marshalsea so that they might reflect at leisure on the rashness of their behaviour. Like the other institutions of its kind, it was a seething pit of filth into which its unfortunate inmates were dropped without mercy.

Edmund Hoode sat on the stone floor of his cell and shivered with cold. The room was barely six feet square and its dank walls gave off the most noisome vapour. A sodden mattress lay on the flagstones but it was too foul and lumpy to invite any guest. High in one wall, a tiny barred window admitted a thin sliver of light that pointed down at Hoode like the finger of doom. Night in the Marshalsea had been a descent into Hades. Fear, cold and discomfort had kept him awake. Dreadful cries and piteous moans from other parts of the establishment were punctuated by the snuffling of a rat in the pile of straw and excrement that lay in a corner.

'What have I done to deserve *this!* he wailed.

He was still asking the question when morning came. Hoode took no consolation from the fact that many authors had seen the inside of a prison in the course of their precarious careers. It was a recognised hazard of their calling. Plays that contained scurrilous or defamatory matter relating to eminent persons often introduced the playwright to the terrors of confinement. Drama that was entirely free from satire could sometimes cause offence and lead to the arrest of an innocent author. Those who lived by the pen walked in the shadow of the prison cell.

The most disturbing aspect of it all for Hoode was the fact that he was locked up entirely alone. It rescued him from assault by other prisoners but it also argued the severity of his alleged crime. Most offenders were hurled indiscriminately into one of the larger and noisier cells with a frightening assortment of humanity. If Hoode was set apart, it could only mean that some special treatment was reserved for him. Seditious libel was a heinous offence. If he were convicted, the punishment was unimaginable.

Hoode shuddered once more and wrapped his arms around his body. It was galling to be held responsible for a play that he had not himself written. All that he had done was to make it fit for the stage. *The Roaring Boy* had entailed substantial re-working but he had changed nothing of its main thrust and argument. Those were the creation of another hand. A different playwright should be enduring the mean hospitality of the Marshalsea.

The misery of his own condition was compounded by the suffering inflicted on Westfield's Men. In the course of one afternoon, they lost their playwright, their venue and their right to perform. They were homeless exiles. Some might find work with other companies but most would struggle or starve. It was even possible that a few of them would join him in the Marshalsea when they fell headlong into debt.

Further agony came when he considered Emilia Brinklow. The failure of *The Roaring Boy* to achieve retribution was a shattering blow to her and he longed to be able to reach out to embrace her with consoling arms. His love for Emilia had fuelled his belief in the play. Disaster had once again marked a foray into matters of the heart. His plight would at least arouse her sympathy and that brought some comfort. Even in her own distress, she would have compassion for him. Simply to be in her thoughts was a blessed relief.

Heavy footsteps brought him out of his cheerless meditation. As he heard a key being inserted into the lock of his door, he hauled himself to his feet and tried to compose himself. Every bone and muscle ached. The weight of his fatigue was like a boulder across his shoulders. When the door swung back on its hinges, a short, squat man in a studded leather jerkin thrust breakfast at him. Hoode looked down at the hunk of bread and the cup of brackish water.

'What is this?' he asked.

'Food,' grunted the keeper.

'Is this all that I am to be served?'

'Unless you have some garnish about you.'

'I have to bribe you in order to eat?'

'This is prison, sir.'

Hoode bridled. 'Fetch the warden,' he said. 'I wish to complain. I also wish to know exactly why I was brought here and how long I am to be kept in this disgusting hole. It is not fit for the meanest animal. Fetch him at once.'

The man let out a cackle of amusement before throwing the bread on to the ground and tipping the water after it. Hoode was still protesting when the door was slammed in his face. He kept on yelling until the rising stench of his cell made him cough uncontrollably. The Marshalsea accorded him no respect whatsoever. He was just one more nameless victim of its grisly regime. As he collapsed to the floor in a dejected heap, he wondered what other tribulations lay in store for him.

Nicholas Bracewell left London early that morning on a bay mare he had borrowed from Lawrence Firethorn. He rode at a canter and paused only once to take refreshment at a wayside inn and to water his horse. When he reached Greenwich, he

spent time exploring the village and admiring its verdant setting. He also took the opportunity of asking after Orlando
Reeve. The local vintner told him that the fat musician lived in
a cottage just outside the village. Nicholas thanked him and
rode over to the house, giving it a cursory inspection before
continuing on past Greenwich Park to the palace itself. The
Queen's summer residence looked serene and stately in the
morning sunlight but it held dark secrets inside it. He knew that
he would have to plumb some of its mysteries before his work
was done.

Returning to the village, he went along the main street to the
Brinklow house. The servant who answered the front door
carried word of his unheralded arrival to Emilia. She was
highly surprised to learn that he was on her doorstep but agreed
at once to see him. Nicholas was shown into the parlour and
greeted by the mistress of the house. Emilia looked drawn and
jaded. Her red-rimmed eyes had obviously shed many a tear
during the night. Her voice was brittle.

'Please take a seat,' she said, indicating a chair.

'Thank you.'

'I hardly thought to see you here again.'

'It was needful,' said Nicholas, sitting opposite her. 'I am glad
to find you at home. Is Master Chaloner here?'

'Of course not,' she said. 'Why should he be? Simon and I
are betrothed but it would be most unseemly for us to live
beneath the same roof until the proper time. I hope that you
did not think otherwise.'

'I thought only of yesterday's sad events. In view of those, I
wondered if Master Chaloner felt obliged to remain here in
order to offer you his protection.'

'He has done that every night for months but I have always
refused. I need no protection. I am not afraid. This is my home.
I am quite safe here.'

'That is what your brother believed,' he said softly.

Emilia recoiled slightly as if from a blow. Nicholas chided

himself for such a tactless remark and reached out an appeasing hand. Making a swift recovery, she waved it away and stared levelly at him. He sensed once again the single-minded determination that had reminded him so much of Anne Hendrik. Most women would be frightened to be alone in such a large house filled with so many bitter memories but Emilia Brinklow was not. She loved the home and wrapped it around her like a garment.

'Why did you come, sir?' she asked.

'To speak with you and Master Chaloner.'

'Do you not have problems to deal with in London?'

'They can only be solved here.'

'In Greenwich?'

'In this house—and at the palace.'

'How?'

'That is what I have come to find out.'

A considered pause. 'You may certainly count on my help,' she said at length. 'I am racked by guilt at the way that West-field's Men have suffered at my hands. If there is any way in which I may alleviate that suffering, you have only to tell me what it is.'

'I need to put some more questions to you,' he said.

'You will find me ready in my answers.'

'Necessity compels me to be blunt.'

'That will not vex me.'

She held his gaze for a long time and he felt the pull of her attraction. It was patently mutual. Completely alone for the first time, each felt a surge of affection for the other which was at once incongruous yet perfectly natural. Nicholas wished that he could have met her in another place and in different circumstances. The smile in her eyes told him that she read and approved his thoughts.

'Very well, Nicholas,' she said, using his name for the first time. 'Do not spare me. Be blunt.'

'On the night of the murder, you were not in the house.'

'That is true.'

'Where were you?'

'Staying with friends at a cottage in Dartford.'

'When did you learn of the tragedy?'

'The same night,' she said. 'One of the servants rode out to fetch me. I came back with him at once to find the house in turmoil. You can imagine my grief. Thomas, my dear brother, so full of life and feeling—murdered.' She bit her lip as the memory stung her afresh. 'It was unbearable.'

'When had you last seen him?'

'Seen him?'

'Your brother. Before that terrible discovery.'

Emilia hesitated. 'Two days earlier,' she said finally, 'Thomas had been away on business.'

'In London?'

'Yes.'

'Do you know that nature of that business?'

'How should I?'

'You took such an interest in his work.'

'I was proud of it,' she said vehemently. 'Thomas was a brilliant man. He excelled at everything he touched. But he was also very secretive and only let me see what he wanted to show me. He never discussed his business with me.'

'What was he working on when he was killed?'

'I cannot say.'

'Have you no idea at all?'

'None. Why do you ask?'

'Because I think it has a bearing on his murder.'

'Sir John Tarker instigated that.'

'He was involved in the plot certainly.'

'It was all his doing,' she argued. 'You have seen the evidence that Simon collected. It cannot be denied. Sir John Tarker had my brother killed. *The Roaring Boy* proved that.'

'The play may have been wrong.'

It was a mild statement but it ignited a spark of anger in

Emilia, casting out any vestige of affection for him and replacing it with an icy disdain. She was shaking as she rose to her feet and stood over him.

'What do *you* know about it, sir?' she demanded. 'Have you learned more about this case in five minutes than I have in five months? Have you risked life and limb to gather all the facts as Simon has done? What gives you the right to tell us that we are mistaken? If Sir John Tarker is not the villain here, why did he have the play destroyed before it could pronounce his detested name?'

'Calm down,' he soothed. 'I spoke not to rouse you.'

'Well, that is what you have done.'

'It was a suggestion only.'

'Then you have seen my estimation of it.'

'We are on the same side,' he urged. 'If we are ever to see this matter resolved, we must work closely together.'

Her rage subsided and she nodded her agreement, sinking back down on to the chair. But her cheeks were still inflamed and her manner was far more watchful. Nicholas set about repairing some of the damage.

'I spoke out of turn and accept your just rebuke.'

'You touched unwittingly on raw flesh.'

'My clumsiness distresses me.'

'It did not deserve such fury,' she apologised.

'Perhaps it did. I know now where I stand.'

Emilia Brinklow looked at him with a curious amalgam of suspicion and wistfulness, still hurt by what he had said while remembering his many good qualities. She made a visible effort to subdue her irritation and even managed a smile of conciliation.

'This is a poor welcome after your long journey.'

'I brought it upon myself.'

'No, Nicholas,' she said wearily. 'I have been too bound up in this affair to view it coolly from without. The slightest breath of criticism is like a dagger in my breast. My wrath was ill-judged. Forgive me.'

'There is no need.'

'For me, it is *everything:* for you, it is just a play.'

'It is far more than that,' said Nicholas firmly. *'The Roaring Boy* has put my friend in prison, my fellows into the street and our whole future in jeopardy. No mere play could do that. This is a matter of utmost significance to us and that is why I have taken such trouble to come here. I was eager to talk with you and this house is the only place where I may reach Master Chaloner.'

'Simon lives but five miles' ride from here.'

'Can he be sent for?'

'I'll despatch a servant straight.'

'He cannot be spared from this debate.'

'Nor will he be.'

Emilia crossed to the door and and opened it to call for her maidservant. Agnes came running at once, took her orders, then rushed off to convey them to the ostler.

'He will be in the saddle within minutes.'

'Let us pray that he finds Master Chaloner at home.' Nicholas stood up and glanced through the window. 'I have another favour to ask of you.'

'It is granted.'

'Show me your brother's laboratory.'

'But you saw it on your last visit here.'

'Only from the outside,' he said. 'I would go within.'

'If you wish. Follow me.'

Emilia led him down a corridor, through the kitchens and into the buttery. The locked door that now confronted them was clad with steel. Nicholas was struck with its thickness.

'This door would keep an army out,' he observed.

'It saved the house from the fire.'

'What needed such careful protection?'

'His privacy,' she said. 'And his work.'

She produced a key from a pocket at her waist and used it to unlock the door. It opened on to ruination. Nicholas took a few steps into the laboratory, then paused to look around him, trying to reconstruct in his mind its fallen walls and its shattered windows. Emilia moved familiarly around the room, noting with pleasure that her orders for the removal of weeds had been followed to the letter. Valentine and his assistants had plucked up nature from around the ankles of science.

Nicholas walked forward in silent wonder. Even in its devastated state, the laboratory preserved a strange order and pattern. Burned-out tables were aligned, charred stools knew their place, wrecked equipment of all kinds stood in unforced symmetry. The punctilious mind of Thomas Brinklow survived the fire intact. Nicholas crouched down before a forge.

'Your brother smelted his own metals?'

'The forge was always busy.'

'He had some assistant to feed its hunger?'

'No,' she said fondly. 'Thomas looked after it himself like a favourite pet. He would let nobody near his forge.'

'Not even you?'

'Not even me. His workshop was sacrosanct.'

'He would need the finest metal if he built a compass.'

'That is what he produced.'

'A remarkable man,' said Nicholas with admiration. 'I begin to feel his presence. Where did he keep his papers?'

'In that desk,' she said, pointing to pile of cinders.

'All destroyed?'

'Lost forever. His inventions died with him.'

Nicholas thought long and hard before he spoke again.

'I have one last favour.'

'Ask anything if it helps our cause.'

'Who wrote *The Roaring Boy?*' he said, stepping closer to her as she pursed her lips and lowered her head. 'I must be told. Was it Master Chaloner? He said that the author had gone away but no man deserts a work like that at such a fatal hour. Did Master Chaloner pen *The Roaring Boy?*'

She looked up at him in evident distress. Before she could speak, however, Nicholas was distracted by a noise in the bushes. Fearing that someone was eavesdropping, he ran to the remains of a wall, jumped quickly over it and pushed his way into the undergrowth. Nobody was there. When he came out the other side, however, he saw a figure no more than twenty yards away, tying some rambling roses back on their trellis-work and apparently absorbed in his task. Valentine became aware of his scrutiny and turned to acknowledge him, touching his cap in deference with a gnarled finger and flashing the infamous grin once more.

Frustration finally provoked Simon Chaloner into action. Long months of hard and dangerous work had come to fruition in the yard of the Queen's Head, only to be squashed out of recognition by the man he was trying to convict of a murder. *The Roaring Boy* was a legal and highly public means of calling Sir John Tarker to account. Since that had signally failed, a more irregular and private means had to be used. There was no point in discussing it with Emilia because she would never condone such a course of action. Chaloner had to strike on his own.

He felt certain that his quarry would be at hand. With a Court tournament in the offing, Sir John Tarker would be practising in the tiltyard at Greenwich Palace once more. Having knocked *The Roaring Boy* from its saddle, he would be trying to unseat other challengers to his position. Chaloner might not get such an opportunity again. It had to be seized on ruthlessly. One shot from a pistol would achieve what five acts of a play would never do.

Having been in the palace many times, Chaloner knew how to find his way through its courtyards and apartments if only he could gain entry. That depended on good fortune. Armed and excited by the prospect of revenge, he rode out that morning in the direction of Greenwich, skirting the village itself so that he would not be seen by anyone from the Brinklow household and trotting on to find a copse where he could tether his horse and approach the palace on foot.

The main entrance was in the riverside frontage but there were postern gates at various points around the building. As he approached the rear of the palace, he saw a small crowd of people listening to a tall, distinguished man who was delivering some sort of lecture. Chaloner was in luck. A group of foreign visitors was being shown around the premises by the chamberlain. From their attire and general deportment, Chaloner guessed that they were Dutch, most probably the ambassador and his entourage. Intermingled with them were a few other nationalities. The ostentatious garb of one man combined with his extravagant gestures to mark him out as an Italian. His two companions also had a Mediterranean cast of feature.

Simon Chaloner did not hesitate. He walked slowly towards the group until he could merge quietly into it. The chamberlain was too caught up with listening to the sound of his own voice to see the intruder and the visitors assumed that he was a legitimate member of the party who arrived late. Chaloner had picked up snatches of Dutch and Italian in his army days. An occasional phrase and a benign smile were all that he needed to employ by way of response.

'Let us now step back inside the palace,' droned the chamberlain, leading them through the gate. 'I mentioned earlier that Duke Humphrey had called it Bella Court . . . '

The visitors followed, listened and gaped. Secure in the middle of them, Chaloner kept his head down and his hand on his sword. He was in. It was only a matter of minutes before he could detach himself from the knot of foreigners and slip into the building itself. He walked along a corridor with a confidence that suggested a legitimate right to be inside a royal palace. Doublet and hose of a colourful and expensive cut would not look out of place at Court and he had the true bearing of a gentleman. When two guards marched past, they did not even throw him a second glance. Now that he was inside Greenwich Palace, he was invisible.

The noise of mock battle rose up from the tiltyard to guide his footsteps. He came out on the leaded roof where Henry VIII loved to stand and he gazed down on the assembly below. Men in armour were fighting on foot or practising on horse-back with the lance. Retainers were everywhere. There was no sign of Sir John Tarker but the watching Chaloner sensed that he would be there. He hid behind the corner of a chimney-pot to keep the yard under surveillance while remaining out of sight himself. His intended victim was bound to emerge in time.

It was only a matter of waiting and watching.

Five hours of acute hunger made Edmund Hoode pick up the hunk of stale bread which had been flung to the ground. It was as hard as rock and his teeth could do little more than chip off a few crisp edges. He began to wish he had more politic in his dealings with the keeper. Hoode had money about him and would willingly part with it for wholesome food and restorative drink. Since he could be locked away in the Marshalsea for some time, it was important to keep body and soul together. He longed for the man's return and listened in the meantime to the accumulated misery of the prison as it reverberated along the gloomy corridors. The only time he had heard such wild cries before was when he had visited Bedlam to observe the behaviour of madmen.

It seemed an eternity before anyone recalled his existence. The footsteps were more ponderous this time and the key scraped in the lock before it engaged. Hoode was standing so close to the door that it caught him a glancing blow as it creaked open. The same keeper regarded him with mocking eyes. The man had no meal with him this time.

'Do you have any garnish?' he said.

'What will it buy me?'

'Depends how much you pay, sir.'

'A shilling?'

'That will keep you well fed for a day or two.'

'No more than that?'

'We have rates here in the Marshalsea,' said the man before spitting on to the floor. 'Any prisoner who is an esquire, a gentleman or a wealthy nobleman can eat heartily for a weekly charge of ten shillings.'

'I do not look to be here as long as a week.'

'It is good fare, sir. Bone of meat with broth. A piece of bone beef. A loin or breast of roasted veal. Or else a capon. As much bread as you will eat and a quarter of beer and claret wine.' He leered at Hoode. 'How like you that?'

'Indifferently.'

'Then you must stick to bread, water and some meat.'

'I cannot stay alive on that.'

'Buy yourself more, sir.'

'I'd rather buy some information,' said Hoode, putting a hand into his purse to pull out some coins. 'I am dragged here by the sheriff and thrown into this cell without due explanation. Why am I here?'

'Waiting, sir. Like all the others. Waiting.'

'For what?'

'Justice.'

'In a loathsome privy like this?'

The man eyed the coins. 'What do you wish to know, sir?'

'When I am to be released.'

'That is a secret.'

'Sell it to me.'

'I would not part cheaply with it.'

Hoode added another coin to the others and jingled them in his palm. 'Tell me, my friend, and the money is yours.'

'First give it to me,' said the man, extending a grubby palm.

'Not before I have your secret,' bargained Hoode. He jingled the money again. 'Come, sir. When will I leave the Marshalsea? When will I get out of this accursed cell?'

'Tomorrow.'

'Is that the truth?'

'As God is my witness!'

'Tomorrow!' Hoode was delirious with joy. 'I get out of this prison tomorrow. Here, friend. Take the money.' He put the coins gratefully into the man's hand. 'You have earned every penny. I am to be released from this hell tomorrow.'

'Not released, sir.'

'But you just said that I would. Did you lie!'

'When will you leave the Marshalsea, you asked.'

'Why, so I did and so you answered.'

'Tomorrow.'

'Aye, so there's an end to it.'

'You misunderstand me,' said the keeper, relishing the other's bewilderment. 'You leave here but are not released.'

'Where, then, will I go?'

'To visit a certain gentleman.'

'For what purpose?'

'He would have conversation with you in his house.'

'Who is this gentleman? Why does he seek my company?'

'Only he knows that, sir.'

'What is his name?'

'That I can tell you if you have courage enough to hear.'

'Courage?'

'Some shake at the very sound of his name.'

'Why? Who is he?'

'Master Topcliffe.'

Hoode began to sway. 'The torturer?'

'Interrogator,' corrected the other. 'You are honoured. Master Richard Topcliffe only invites very special guests to his house. It is your turn tomorrow.'

He went out laughing and pulled the door shut. Edmund Hoode did not even hear its loud bang as he went down in a dead faint.

Morning passed at the house in Greenwich and the afternoon soon dwindled away but there was no sign of Simon Chaloner. The ostler sent to fetch him returned with the news that the latter was not at home. Chaloner's servant had no idea where his master had gone or how long he would be away. Emilia Brinklow grew anxious at this intelligence. Her betrothed was in such close and regular contact with her that she always knew where to find him. It was most unusual for him to quit his house without leaving details of his whereabouts. She scented trouble.

'He may come here of his own accord,' said Nicholas.

'Then where is he? Simon could have been here hours ago. Something has happened to him, Nicholas.'

'Do not run to meet fear,' he cautioned.

'But I know Simon. This is not like him.'

'He may have had business elsewhere that detained him.'

'That is what worries me.'

They were back in the parlour and Emilia's calm and collected front had been fractured by her concern. Nicholas wanted to pay a visit to Orlando Reeve in the hope of catching the musician at his house but he felt unable to leave her alone in her distress. Evening was approaching and a man who called at the house every day had still not put in an appearance. It was puzzling.

'Simon is in danger,' she said. 'I know it.'

'Master Chaloner can take care of himself,' he assured her. 'Rest easy. He is young, strong and well-armed.'

'He is also impulsive. Far too impulsive. I fear me that he has finally run out of patience.'

'Patience?'

'Yes, Nicholas. He has waited so long.'

'For revenge?'

'For me,' she said. 'And I will only be his when the matter is finally and completely resolved. Even then . . . ' She bit back what she was going to say and paced the room instead. 'Simon has wearied of this interminable delay. He is distraught at the collapse of all our hopes. I demanded too much from him.'

'So what do you believe he has done?'

'Proceeded against Sir John Tarker on his own.'

'That would be lunacy.'

'Simon has more than a streak of that.'

'He would stand no chance of getting near him.'

'That will not check his ardour,' she said, coming back to him. 'He does not only wish to avenge Thomas's death. He has another score to settle. Concerning me. I will never forgive myself if anything happens to Simon. He is the dearest friend I have in all the world. And I am his.'

'He covets the day when he can make you his wife.'

'So do I.'

She manufactured a smile of enthusiasm but it was far too strained to convince Nicholas. In any case, he had seen her and Chaloner together. They were not like most couples on the verge of marriage. Emilia seemed to tolerate his love instead of requiting it. Nicholas wondered if her attitude to him would change in time but it was not his place to say so. What he did convey in a glance was his own admiration of her. Over half a day had now been spent in her company and it had seemed like minutes.

'You have been a good friend to me as well, Nicholas.'

'I will do all in my power to help you,' he said.

'I know and I am grateful. After what happened at the

Queen's Head yesterday, most people in your position would loathe the very sight of me.'

'I could never do that.'

'Even though I have caused you so much upheaval?'

'Sir John Tarker did that. Not you.'

He looked deep into her eyes and found an answering glint of affection. Nicholas mastered his curiosity. It was not the time to investigate his feelings for her. Emilia's bethrothed was missing and his safety was their immediate priority. He became businesslike.

'Where else could Master Chaloner be?'

'I do not know.'

'Might he not be with friends? With relations?'

'His friends are all in London, his family in Dorset. He would visit neither without telling me. Simon is a creature of habit. He is always here at this hour of the day.'

'I will gladly renew the search on your behalf.'

'You do not know the area.'

'Let your ostler be my guide.'

'No, Nicholas,' she said. 'Stay here in the hope that he will soon return. Your presence is comforting. I am most grateful that you came to Greenwich today.'

'So am I.'

She assessed him for a moment, then gave a sad smile.

'You asked me a question in the garden,' she said. 'I refused to give you a proper answer.'

'And now?'

'Simon Chaloner did not write *The Roaring Boy*. He has many sterling virtues but he is not a creative man. His talents run in other directions, as you have no doubt observed. He is far too restive to be a playwright.'

'It is work that requires a certain stillness.'

'Simon cannot keep still for one minute.'

'I thought it too solitary an occupation for him.'

'Too solitary and too safe,' she said wryly. 'I may not give you the author's name because I have vowed to shield him but it was certainly not Simon. He thought the play too slow a means to catch Sir John Tarker in a trap. That is why I am so anxious now. I fear he seeks a speedier solution.'

From his hiding-place on the roof, Simon Chaloner looked down on a panorama of controlled violence. Knights in splendid armour practised for hours to improve their skills, keeping strictly to the rules of jousting. Points were awarded for striking an opponent's helmet; for striking a coronel, the crownlike safety device at the end of his lance; for unseating him by legitimate means; or for breaking a lance by striking him in the permitted area from the waist upwards. Those who deliberately or carelessly struck an adversary's legs, saddle or horse had points deducted.

At any other time, Chaloner would have enjoyed the occasion and savoured its finer nuances. Now it was merely a tedious spectacle that dragged on and on into the evening. Sir John Tarker was there, resplendent in his new armour and invincible in the saddle, but Chaloner could not get near him without discovery. Tarker would have to be confronted in a more private part of the building. The knight could not ride up and down the tilt forever.

When the erect figure of Sir Godfrey Avenell came into the gallery above the yard, he caught the attention of his friend and beckoned him over. Chaloner was close enough to observe but not hear the exchange between the two friends. It was soon over. Two other spectators came into the gallery to join Avenell and they were soon deep in conversation with him. Chaloner watched them long enough to recognise the newcomers as two of the Dutch visitors earlier being shown around the castle, then he switched his gaze to the yard.

Sir John Tarker had finally come to the end of his practice. Dismounting from his destrier, he handed the reins to his esquire, then crossed to one of the armourers who was standing on the sidelines. There was an animated discussion as Tarker appeared to complain about some problem with his breast-plate, gesturing at it with his gauntlet. Contrite and apologetic, the brawny armourer pointed towards the workshops as if suggesting that he effect the necessary adjustments there and then. Chaloner was delighted when Tarker agreed to go with the man. The desired opportunity might have come at last.

He gave them plenty of time to reach the workshop because Tarker could only walk slowly in his suit of armour. Most of the other knights stayed in the tilting yard and the viewing stands were dotted with palace guards or servants, stealing a moment away from their duties to enjoy the impromptu tournament. Sir Godfrey Avenell was still talking with the Dutchmen in the gallery, all three of them now oblivious to the combat down below. Chaloner judged that the workshop would be largely deserted. He and Sir John Tarker might meet on equal terms at last.

'Why is your armour so expensive?'

'Because it is the best, Sir John.'

'It costs a king's ransom.'

'That is because it has to be tailored to each knight,' said the armourer in a guttural voice. 'And we have to import the metal. That only adds to the price. Only finest and strongest metal is used and that cannot be found in England.'

'The finest and strongest knights are English!'

Sir John Tarker let out an arrogant laugh, then ordered the armourer to look more closely at the part of the breastplate that was chafing the side of his chest slightly. They were in one of the workshops, a vast and cavernous place filled with glowing coals and curling smoke. Armour and weaponry of all kinds stood around the walls. Hammers and anvils abounded. The two men were beside a forge with their backs to the door. Chaloner let himself into the chamber, then eased the door shut again as quietly as he could before slipping home the bolt. They were completely safe from intrusion now.

Pulling out his rapier, he closed on Tarker.

'Turn, you vermin!' he shouted. 'Show your vile face!'

Tarker had removed his helmet so the expression of amazement showed when he spun round. His hand went for his own sword but Chaloner was too quick for him, wielding his rapier to first strike the gauntleted hand away from its weapon, then flick upwards into the knight's face. Tarker yelled as a gash opened up in his cheek to send a stream of blood running down his breastplate. He shook with rage. Grabbing a stave from a pile against the wall, he swung it viciously at his attacker. Chaloner ducked and used the rapier to prick the other side of Tarker's face. More blood flowed.

Howling even louder, the knight flung the stave at him and pulled his own sword from its scabbard, using its heavier blade to knock the rapier from Chaloner's hand. When he raised his weapon to smite his young adversary, however, he found himself staring into the barrel of a pistol. It was the weapon that Nicholas Bracewell had remarked upon and it was aimed directly at Sir John Tarker's forehead.

'Drop your sword!' ordered Chaloner.

'We should have killed you at the start!'

'Drop it or I shoot.'

Tarker glared at him. 'You do not have the courage.'

Simon Chaloner looked into the swarthy face with its coal-black eyes and its taunting smile. He thought of Thomas Brinklow lying butchered in his own home and he thought of Emilia being molested. The pistol remained steady in his hand as his finger tightened on the trigger. Retribution was indeed sweet. His finger tightened again but he did not fire. Before he could discharge the weapon, Chaloner was hit from behind by a swinging blow from armourer's tongs. In concentrating all his attention on one man, he had forgotten the other. He went down with a thud and rolled over on the floor. The armourer raised the tongs again to smash at the unconscious figure.

'No,' said the grinning Sir John Tarker. 'Leave him to me.'

[CHAPTER SEVEN]

Owen Elias set out that evening on the trail of an escaped murderer. He was in the unlikely company of George Dart. The assistant stagekeeper was alarmed to be pressed into service and taken off to the stews of Southwark with the exuberant Welshman. Dart was a short, thin, drooping youth in ragged garb with the timidity of a church mouse and the modesty of a vestal virgin. Bankside was not his natural milieu. Though he enjoyed those privileged occasions when Westfield's Men played at the custom-built Rose Theatre, he never tarried with his fellows to explore the taverns and ordinaries. Roistering made him fearful and whores made him blush. Since Bankside was notorious for its combination of the two, Dart flew into a panic before they reached London Bridge.

'Why me, Owen?' he said in his reedy voice.

'Why not, George?'

'You need someone strong and skilled with a sword.'

'I need you.'

'Bankside frightens me.'

'That's why I'm taking you.'

'But you say we are on the trail of a killer.'

'That is so,' confirmed Elias.

'If he has killed once, he may kill again.'

'You will be safe from harm, boy.'

'Will I?'

'Maggs would never lay a finger on you.'

'Why not?'

'He would not kill his own son.'

George Dart gulped. 'His *son?*'

They were on the bridge now, picking their way between the shops and houses, and dodging the occasional horse and cart that rattled along the narrow gap between the various buildings. Owen Elias explained that they were picking up a trail already abandoned by the officers of the law. Until he was caught up in the Brinklow murder, Maggs was a denizen of Southwark, well-known in its darker haunts and in its most disreputable company.

'They were as arrant a pair of knaves as any in London,' said Elias. 'Freshwell and Maggs. Freshwell was the roaring boy and Maggs was a sly little rat of a man. You should have chosen your father with more care, George.'

'My *father?*'

'I see only faint resemblance to him in you.'

'But I have never met this Maggs.'

'You have something of his fierceness,' teased Elias.

'My father worked for a fishmonger in Billingsgate!'

'Not tonight. You play a different part.'

'Why?'

'It keeps us both alive.' Owen Elias chuckled as Dart's face whitened. 'Be ruled by me, George, and you will see the wisdom of my device. We rub shoulders with true villains. They would steal the clothes off each other's backs but they have a code of loyalty. If we barge in there and demand to know where Maggs is, we will finish up in a ditch with our throats cut. My trick protects us.'

Dart was terrified. 'What must I say?'

'Nothing. Leave all the talking to me.'

'What, then, must I do?'

'You are already doing it.'

Elias let out another chuckle and pounded him between the shoulder-blades. They were soon leaving the bridge and heading for the sinful streets and lewder lanes of Bankside. The Welshman strode along with the sure-footed confidence of a man who knew the area well but his companion trotted nervously along beside him like a fawn in a forest of lions. The first few taverns they visited yielded nothing more than curses at the mention of the murderer's name. One innkeeper confidently claimed that Maggs was dead, another that he had fled the country. Nobody spoke of Maggs or Freshwell with affection.

As the brothels became fouler, the trail became warmer. They eventually began to meet with some success. Maggs was definitely still alive. Several people vouched for that. One man boasted that he had actually seen him though he would not disclose where. It was in the most revolting place of all that they finally got some real help. The Red Cock was an unashamed den of vice, a dark, filthy, smoke-filled hole of a place, where constant drinking, gambling and debauchery were interrupted only by the occasional brawl.

George Dart began to retch when he inhaled its fug and he jumped a foot in the air when a bold female hand caressed his trembling thigh in the gloom. Owen Elias was unperturbed by the sordid surroundings. He ordered beer, found a table in a corner and invited the oldest and fattest punk to join them. A trawl through the stews had taught him something of his quarry's taste in women. The diminutive Maggs liked to spend his nights on top of huge mounds of flesh.

Her name was Lucy and she had a rich cackle that made her whole body shake violently. When the massive powdered breasts leaped free from their moorings, George Dart covered his eyes with his hands. Elias spent some time working his way into her friendship before he dropped out the name he had brought with him to Bankside. Lucy became defensive.

'I may have known such a man,' she said. 'Why?'

'Because we have good news for him.'

She snorted. 'For Maggs? What is it—a royal pardon?'

'No,' said Elias, 'but it is a pardon of a kind. From beyond the grave, as you might say.'

'What mean you, sir?'

'We have a small legacy for him.

'Legacy?'

'Part of it sits beside you,' he said, pulling Dart's hands down from his eyes. 'This is his son.'

She was sceptical. 'Maggs? A son? He never married.'

'A bastard child. Born out of wedlock.'

'He had enough of those, I daresay,' she said with a cackle. 'Maggs was a lusty little rogue. I miss him.' She peered at George Dart. 'So this is his son, is it? He's as skinny as Maggs for sure, with the same mean face, but I doubt that he could stand to account in a woman's arms like his father. Maggs had a pizzle the size of a donkey's. Does this lad have anything between his legs at all?'

'Yes,' said Elias. 'He's no gelding.'

Cheeks like beetroot, Dart put his hands over his ears this time. Lucy was the most frightening woman he had ever met in his life. Her vivacity was overwhelming.

'What is this legacy you speak of?' she asked.

Elias dropped his voice. 'From the boy's mother. She died of the sweating sickness. Poor wretch! She had cause to hate Maggs yet she still loved him. And she doted on his issue here. Did she not, George? On her deathbed, she made her son promise to take a small sum of money to Maggs as a token of her love. Thus it stands.'

'If that is all,' she said obligingly, 'I'll save you the trouble. Give me the money and I'll see that Maggs gets every penny of it. You have my oath on that.'

Elias shook his head. 'We would happily do that, for I am sure that we could trust you, Lucy, but there is a solemn oath involved here. George is compelled to hand over the bounty himself. How else can he get to meet his father?' He put a familiar arm around her shoulders. 'Tell us where he is and we will be more than grateful. So will Maggs.'

She eyed them for a moment, then let out another cackle.

'I know where his father dwells but it would not help the lad to know. This dribbling booby would not get within a hundred yards of Maggs.'

'Why not?'

'He would be eaten alive as soon as he ventured there.'

'Where, Lucy?' coaxed Elias. 'Where is Maggs?'

'The Isle of Dogs.'

Darkness had fallen on the house in Greenwich but Valentine was still moving stealthily around the garden. It was his true home. Plants and flowers blossomed under his ugliness. Trees gave forth their fruit without recoiling from his touch. Nature accepted him in a way that human beings could not. Valentine lived alone in a hovel nearby but he often neglected it for days in summer months, curling up instead under a bush in the garden with one eye on the house itself. His vigil was sometimes rewarded with the sight of Agnes, the maidservant, coming to her window at the very top of the house to close the curtains or to tip a bowl of water out on to the grass far below. Moonlight once gave him a fleeting glimpse of her naked shoulders. It kept him below her window every night for a month.

As he looked up at the house now, light was showing in various rooms. Through the windows of the buttery, candles were throwing a ghostly glow out on to the ruins of the laboratory. Agnes would still be at her duties and it might be hours before she was allowed to retire to her own room. Valentine would wait. She might despise him but she gave him an enormous amount of pleasure, albeit unintended. It was enough. Night under the bushes brought rich compensation.

This particular night also brought a surprise. As he took up a vantage point in the undergrowth, he was alerted by a noise that seemed to come from the front of the house. Living so close to nature had given him the instincts of an animal and his back arched for a moment in fear. He quickly recovered and set off through the darkness towards the source of the disturbance. Valentine heard it more clearly now. There was the faint jingle of harness mingled with an unidentifiable dragging sound. Someone grunted under a strain, then he caught a few words that baffled him. Feet moved away from the house and a horse neighed as it was mounted. Two riders departed quickly into the void.

Valentine moved close enough to the front door of the house to pick out the shape of something on the hearth. It made him step back quickly into the bushes to consider what he should do. If he went to investigate more fully, he might be caught and unfairly blamed. If he knocked on the door to rouse the household, awkward questions would be asked about his presence there at that time of night.

He opted for another solution. Bending to gather some stones, he threw one at the lighted window beside the door. It bounced off harmlessly but produced no enquiry from within. He took a bigger stone and hurled it with more force at the door itself. Its thud was heard throughout the house and response was swift. The front door was opened by a manservant. Light spilled out from his lantern to illumine the figure on the ground. Valentine saw that it was a dead body which had been dragged up to the hearth.

The servant was so shocked that he let out a shriek.

Nicholas Bracewell was the first to react to the noise. He told Emilia Brinklow to remain in the parlour, then he ran along the corridor to the front door. The servant was now backing away in horror. Nicholas took the lantern from his quivering grasp and knelt down to hold it over the supine figure. Simon Chaloner lay on his back. Sightless eyes gazed up at heaven with a look of supplication but it was the grotesque wound in the forehead which transfixed Nicholas. A pistol had been fired at point-blank range into the skull to lodge deep in the brains. Dripping with blood, the gaping hole was like a third eye. Whatever else happened, Emilia had to be prevented from seeing such horror.

He stood up to give a stern order to the manservant.

'Go to your mistress,' he said. 'Bid her stay where she is until I return. Say nothing of what you saw or you will answer to me. Do you understand?'

'Yes, sir.'

'About it straight.'

The man scurried away and Nicholas used the lantern again to make a closer inspection of the corpse. Matted blood in the hair at the back of the neck showed that there was another wound. He wondered if Simon Chaloner had first been knocked senseless before being shot. When he searched for the German cavalry pistol, it was gone from its holster. Sword and dagger were also missing from their scabbards. His killer was obviously fond of souvenirs. Yet the dead man's purse had been left unmolested. He was not the victim of thieves.

Stifled gasps made Nicholas turn round. Other servants had now come to see what was happening and they were deeply shocked. Simon Chaloner was a regular and popular guest at the house but it was this last gruesome visit that would stick in their minds. Nicholas urged them to say nothing to Emilia, then sent most of them back into the house. The ostler stayed behind to guard the body while the book holder conducted a search of the front garden. The lantern failed to pick up the bloodstains on the grass but it clearly showed the route along which the body had been dragged.

Nicholas came to a verge in which eight hooves had gouged their autographs. Two horses had been spurred away from the spot only recently. They had galloped off in the direction of Greenwich Palace.

Two priorities existed. The murder had to be reported and—a far more difficult task—Emilia had to be informed of the death of the man she was betrothed to marry. Nicholas went back to the house. He told the ostler to let nobody near the corpse, then sent a manservant to fetch the local constable. Noises from inside the parlour told him that Emilia was protesting bitterly at being kept there without sufficient reason. When Nicholas went in, she was upbraiding the manservant for daring to give her orders in her own house. Anger faded to alarm when she saw the book holder's grim expression.

The manservant left them alone and closed the door behind him. Nicholas conveyed the message with a glance. Emilia swallowed hard and her eyes filmed over.

'Simon?' He nodded. 'Where is he? I must see him.'

'No,' said Nicholas, catching her as she tried to run past him. 'It is better if you do not. There is nothing that you can do. His body lies at your door. Who put it there, we do not yet know. The constable is on his way.'

Emilia almost swooned. 'Simon is dead?'

'Shot through the head.'

'Dear God!'

She collapsed in his arms and he helped her to a chair. Fate was cruel. Before she had even come to terms with one violent loss, another had been rudely visited upon her. A brother and a betrothed had been murdered. Emilia was in despair. Her life no longer had direction or meaning. There suddenly seemed to be no point in going on.

'Simon was such a good man!' she said. 'A brave man.'

'Perhaps too brave for his own good.'

'I *knew* that he would do something too wild in the end. I

stopped him a dozen times from riding off to confront Sir John Tarker on his own. I warned him this would happen.'

'We do not know the precise details yet,' reminded Nicholas, still with an arm around her. 'We must not make a hasty judgement. I admit that suspicion points only one way but we must be certain of our evidence before we proceed.'

'Why did Simon have to be killed?'

'Because he got so close to the truth.

'When they tried before, he always fought them off.'

'He was one man, they came in numbers.'

'But why bring his body to lay at my door?' she said.

'Two reasons,' he suggested. 'First, it is a warning to us of what we may expect if we pursue our case against a certain person. Second . . . ' His voice trailed away.

'Go on.'

'That concerns you.'

'In what way?'

'Sir John Tarker—if this is indeed his work—is sending you a personal message. When he insulted you at this house, your brother was here to take your part and throw him out. Master Chaloner then offered you his strong arm to protect you.' He glanced towards the door. 'It is no longer there. That is the message—you are highly vulnerable.'

'I am not afraid of him,' she said, recapturing a little of her spirit. 'He now has two murders to pay for and I will not rest until he has been brought down.' Her voice cracked and her eyelids fluttered. 'But what can one lone woman do against the power that he has at his command?'

'Call on her friends.'

She looked at him with the most profound gratitude. A man who might well be ruing the day she ever came into his life was actually offering his service to her. Nicholas Bracewell was a rock in shifting sands. She had lost Simon Chaloner but there was still one source of strength to cling to her in her hour of need. Emilia reached up to place the lightest of kisses on his cheek. Nicholas was touched but she pulled back in embarrassment, as if unsure about the rightness of what she had just done. Grief battled with affection for a second, then she fell to sobbing again.

There was a knock on the door. Nicholas looked up.

'Come in,' he said.

Agnes entered and curtseyed. 'The constable is here.'

'I will speak with him. Stay here with your mistress.'

'Yes, sir.'

'Let nobody else into this room.'

'I will not.'

Nicholas crossed to the door. Emilia got up and tried to go after him. He restrained her gently and shook his head.

'Not now. Take your leave of him at another time.'

George Dart could not believe his ears. Sitting in Lawrence Firethorn's house, he was actually being praised for once. The lowliest and most misused member of Westfield's Men was being congratulated on his performance by the greatest actor in London. The humiliation in Bankside was now being followed by acclaim in Shoreditch. It was all too much for him. Dart became light-headed and almost keeled over. Owen Elias was just in time to catch him.

'The lad is tired, Lawrence,' he said. 'Rightly so.'

'Yes,' added Firethorn. 'You have done a worthy deed this night, George, and it has exhausted you. Go home, boy. Sleep in the knowledge that you have rendered Westfield's Men a wondrous service.'

'Is that it, Master Firethorn?'

'Your bed awaits you.'

'Will I have to play the part of his son again?'

'That little drama is done.'

He escorted the assistant stagekeeper to the door and showed him out into the street before returning to his other guest. Firethorn was delighted with the progress that they had made even though Maggs still had to be confronted. At least, they now knew where to find him. Lucy had more than repaid the money that Elias had spent on her.

Left alone together, the two men could now talk more freely. The Welshman gave a much fuller account of the visit to the Red Cock than was tactful in front of George Dart and the actor-manager laughed royally. When it was time for him to take up a tale, however, his mirth evaporated.

'Lord Westfield has busied himself at Court,' he said.

'Without success, I fancy.'

'Our patron succeeded in getting the information that we needed, Owen, but it brings little joy. Nick Bracewell was right. A more powerful voice than Sir John Tarker's had to put Edmund in prison.'

'Say on.'

'He was arrested at the suit of Lord Hunsdon.'

'The Lord Chamberlain himself!'

'No less. Henry Carey, first Baron Hunsdon.'

'But he is not even mentioned in *The Roaring Boy*.'

'That makes no difference,' said Firethorn. 'When a member of the Privy Council takes out a suit, the law jumps to obey him. If Hunsdon wanted to arrest your grandmother on a charge of treason, he could do so.'

'Not without a spade and a peg on his nose. We buried the old woman thirty years ago.'

'You take my point, Owen.'

'Indeed, I do.'

'The injunction against us also serves Hunsdon well. He has his own troupe of players vying with us for fame and advancement. With our company becalmed, Lord Chamberlain's Men can steal a march on us.'

'It is iniquitous!'

'It is politics.'

'Is there no remedy?'

'None, sir. Lord Westfield's writ cannot contest that of a Privy Councillor. When Nick was wrongfully imprisoned in the Counter, our patron had influence enough to haul him out again. With some help from my dear wife, Margery, if I recall aright.'

'Can he not also free Edmund from gaol?'

'The Lord Chamberlain is too big a padlock.'

'How has he become involved, Lawrence?'

'Because it is to his advantage.'

'There must be deeper workings than that,' said Elias. 'Is Sir John Tarker so close with the Lord Chamberlain that he can demand such large favours from him?'

'Sir John served under him in the north.'

'And fawns upon his old commander.'

'They are both enamoured of jousting.'

'That gives them interest in common but not complicity in a murder.' Elias was mystified. 'Will a man as eminent as Lord Hunsdon stoop to protect such a guilty man from punishment?'

'It is not what he is doing, Owen. I doubt if the Lord Chamberlain knows any of the fine detail. A friend makes a demand on him, he obliges. And since there is gain for his own company in our disappearance, he is happy to do so.'

Owen Elias sat back on his chair to scratch his head.

'Something is missing,' he decided.

'Any whiff of hope for us.'

'A stronger link.'

'Link?'

'Between Sir John Tarker and Lord Hunsdon,' said Elias. 'I return to Nick's argument. Sir John is but on the outer fringe of the Court. He would not have the ear of the Lord Chamberlain. Someone else is involved here.'

'Who?'

'Someone whose name does have enough substance.'

'Who, Owen?'

'Someone who does his devilry behind the scenes.'

'I agree, man' said Firethorn. 'But who on earth is he!'

'We must find the rogue.'

Sir Godfrey Avenell held the ball-butted pistol up to the light of a candle so that he could study it in detail. He was in his apartment at Greenwich Palace. Delighted with the news he had received, he was equally pleased with the present which Sir John Tarker had just offered him.

'Thank you,' he said, fondling the butt. 'It is a most welcome addition to my collection.'

Tarker sniggered. 'I can vouch for its efficiency.'

'Good. I am only interested in weapons of death.'

'This pistol proved itself but hours ago.

'And it is of German design,' said Avenell. 'That is a happy coincidence. It lends a symmetry to this adventure.'

'It put an end to Master Chaloner's interference and that is all I am concerned with. He came to play the hero and went away as the victim. He will trouble us no more.'

'What about Mistress Emilia Brinklow?'

'I will pay my respects to her one of these fine days.'

'That was not my meaning.'

'She will lose all heart now.'

'Can you be certain of that?' said Avenell, putting the pistol on the table and turning to him. 'She has Brinklow blood in her, remember. You know how stubborn her brother could be. Thomas would not be moved.'

'Emilia will be. Chaloner was her right arm.'

'She still has a left one to hold you at bay.'

'Not for long,' said Tarker. 'I am too used to having my own way to be baulked. It is only a question of time.'

'You may have met your match in her.' Avenell flicked the

matter from his mind. 'We have both had a good day. You have removed the largest thorn in our flesh and I have done excellent business. What more could we ask?'

'The position of Queen's Champion.'

'That is beyond even my gift!'

'I wish to earn it, not be granted it as a boon.'

'Shine in combat and it may one day be yours.'

'I have no peer in the saddle.'

Avenell grinned. 'No man wears more expensive armour, I know that. Be worthy of it and I will forget the cost.' He picked up the pistol again. 'This weapon has a deadly voice but it lacks the beauty of a lance. You should have killed Chaloner in a joust. There would have been a poetry in that.'

'He is gone,' said Tarker. 'Why care by what means? Master Chaloner's brains are hanging out and all is well.'

'Not quite, sir. You are remiss.'

'How so?'

'I called for the name of an author.'

'That is in hand.'

'*The Roaring Boy* was too sharp a piece for comfort. Find the man who wrote it and silence his tongue as well.'

'Master Hoode is my assistant here.'

'He has revealed his co-author?'

'He will do in the morning,' said Tarker with another snigger. 'I used your name with the Lord Chamberlain to secure another favour. He was quick to oblige you.'

'So I should hope. We have always been close friends.'

'He has arranged for Master Hoode to have a meeting.'

'With whom?'

'Someone who is practised in the art of digging the truth out of even the deepest shafts. He is the ablest miner in London and uses only the sharpest pick.'

'Topcliffe!'

'You approve?'

Sir Godfrey Avenell smirked. 'The perfect choice.'

Even the most delicious food could not have tempted Edmund Hoode to eat. The name which the keeper had dropped into his ear was like a slow poison, working its way into his brain to paralyze his body and deprive it of all appetite. As the night wore on, he sat hunched up on the floor in the position he had occupied for several hours, wondering what he had done to bring such affliction down upon himself, vowing that he would never again write a play of any kind and wishing that he had been more regular in his devotions. Prayer was his last resort but he was so out of practice in communing with the Almighty that he could find neither the right words nor the appropriate tone. The Marshalsea was truly punishing his spiritual just as much as his theatrical misdemeanours. Her felt humbled.

Richard Topcliffe! The name was an act of torture in itself. What appalling crime had Hoode committed that required the intervention of such a vile man? Topcliffe was the most feared and odious government official in England. Taken into the service of Lord Burghley, he made his grisly reputation by the systematic and merciless torture of Roman Catholics, breaking the bones of his victims for gratuitous pleasure and squeezing confessions out of them along with large amounts of their blood. Innocence was no bulwark against Topcliffe. An hour at the mercy of his gruesome instruments could have even the most blameless of people pleading guilty to the blackest of crimes.

This was the man who had sent for Edmund Hoode. The fact that the playwright had been invited to Topcliffe's house made the prospect even worse. The interrogator so dedicated himself to the finer points of his work that he had a torture chamber built in his own home. Those rare few who resisted the rack and thumbscrews in the Tower were introduced to deeper realms of suffering in the privacy of his abode. Topcliffe was a one-man Inquisition.

Hoode was not a brave man. The wonderful speeches he had written for his martial heroes on the stage were mere empty words now. He could not hold out against any form of torment let alone that applied by a master of the art. The whirligig of time brought hideous changes. On Saturday, he had been the harmless co-author of *The Roaring Boy,* proud of its qualities as a play and committed to its nobler purpose. His infatuation with Emilia Brinklow had given the whole venture a sense of elation. That abruptly vanished. On Sunday, he was locked in a stinking cell at the Marshalsea before being handed over to a cruel monster who preyed on religious dissidents. What justice was there in this?

The one faint ray of hope came from Westfield's Men. They would be working assiduously on his behalf. Their efforts had not yet secured his release but they would continue the struggle. The prisoner was not forgotten. His friends loved him. One of them, in particular, would not rest until he had saved Hoode from his dire predicament. What worried him was that Nicholas Bracewell might not be in time.

'Help me, Nick!' he murmured. 'Help me! Soon!'

Nicholas Bracewell took charge of the situation at Greenwich in order to expedite matters. The local constable was a willing and good-hearted man but quite unequal to the task which had been thrust upon him. Minions of the law were not known for their efficiency even in London. Their provincial counterparts were even less equipped to deal with any crime of a serious nature. The plodding incompetence of the constable at least proved something to Nicholas. Even with the help of his two assistants, roused from their beds to join in the latest investigation, the man could never have solved the murder of Thomas Brinklow. Their success must have been engineered by someone else. This trio of law officers would need a week even to begin their pursuit of the killers, let alone to make an arrest.

The book holder lapsed into his customary role. He cued in the constable to take a statement from the manservant who found the body on the doorstep, then he prompted the former to ask the relevant questions. Nicholas himself gave a succinct and straightforward statement, omitting all mention of the deductions he had already made. The murder of Simon Chaloner involved complexities that were far beyond the capacity of the three men to understand. A surgeon was summoned to examine the dead man and to pronounce an interim verdict on the nature of his death, then Simon Chalenor was removed to the crypt of the nearby church. There, at least, he would be accorded the respect due to the deceased.

After a lengthy and wholly unproductive search of the immediate area, the law officers suspended their inquiry and went home with their lanterns. There would be much further questioning in the morning when sworn statements would need to be given to the local magistrate but there was nothing more to be done that night. Nicholas saw the men off the premises and wondered how they had ever been selected to represent law and order in Greenwich. Their inadequacy brought one blessing. It enabled him to shield Emilia Brinklow from any form of questioning. Instead of taking a statement from the person who knew Simon Chaloner best, and who might therefore give them the most accurate and useful information, they accepted Nicholas's explanation that she had taken to her bed in a state of shock and must on no account be disturbed.

The situation compelled him to stay in Greenwich. He would first acquaint Emilia with his decision, then collect his horse and ride to the nearest inn. As he walked back to the house in the moonlight, however, he became aware that he was being watched. It was the same feeling that he had when he and Emilia were in the ruined laboratory. Sudden movement had frightened the person away on that occasion and so he adopted a different approach. When he heard the rustle of bushes off to his right, he did not lunge off in their direction. He simply strolled past and went around the house, pretending to walk towards the stables but ducking into the first doorway that became available.

Stealthy footsteps came after him. Nicholas slipped his dagger into his hand and waited until a figure loomed up out of the darkness. He pounced quickly, pushing the man against a wall and holding the dagger to his throat.

'Do not harm me, sir!' cried a voice.

'Who are you?'

'Valentine the gardener.'

'What are you doing here?'

'I sleep here, sir.'

'In the open?'

'On warm nights like tonight.'

'Why were you creeping up on me?' demanded Nicholas.

'To speak with you, sir,' said Valentine. 'Search me, if you wish. I am not armed. I want to help.'

Nicholas ran a hand over the man's body to feel for weapons but found none. Taking his dagger from the other's throat, he pulled the gardener out into the moonlight to take a closer look at his face. The repulsive visage was split by its disgusting grin. Nicholas remembered the man and held the point of the dagger on him again.

'You have eavesdropped on me before,' he accused.

'It was not deliberate, sir.'

'Whose spy are you?'

'Nobody's, I swear it. I could not help hearing.'

'How much did they pay you to betray your mistress?'

'Heaven forfend!' said Valentine, bursting into tears and clutching at his sleeve. 'I would not hurt her for the world. She and her brother have been kind to me. A man with a face like mine does not find work easily. Master Brinklow was my friend. I worshipped him and his dear sister. Please believe me, sir.'

The plea was evidently sincere. Nicholas sheathed his dagger and took pity on the man. He gave the latter a moment to recover before he continued.

'You wished to speak with me?' he said.

'If I may, sir.'

'But you do not even know who I am.'

'You are a friend of this family and that is enough for me. I saw the way you took control this night. I watched you deal with those foolish constables. You are Master Bracewell and I want to help you all I can.'

'How?'

'I heard them come.'

'Them?'

'Dragging the dead body.'

Nicholas grabbed him by the arms. 'You saw them?'

'No, sir. I was too late.'

'What did you hear?'

'Voices only. Then the horses galloping off.'

'These voices. What did they say?'

'I do not know, sir. The language was unknown to me.'

'Foreigners?'

'Deep and gruff.'

'Can you you remember no words at all?'

'None, sir. Except "smell." They were in a hurry. One of them kept saying "smell" or something much like it.'

'Could it have been "schnell"?' asked Nicholas.

'Indeed, it could. Say it again.'

'Schnell. Schnell.'

'That was it, sir!' said Valentine. 'What language?'

'German.'

'Why should two Germans kill poor Master Chaloner?'

Nicholas said nothing. He was quite certain that the men were only delivering the corpse of someone who had been murdered elsewhere by another hand. Their nationality was an important clue, however, and he took due note of it.

'I wish I could tell you more,' said Valentine.

'You have been most helpful and I thank you for that.' His tone became much sterner. 'But that does not excuse your eavesdropping. Why did you listen to me when I talked with Mistress Brinklow earlier in the ruins of the laboratory?'

'I did not, sir.'

'You admitted it only two minutes ago.'

'I said I overheard you by accident. But not today. It was when you first came to Greenwich. You and your friend talked in the arbour with the mistress and Master Chaloner.'

'Where were you?'

'Caught nearby and forced to listen.'

'Why did you not discover yourself and leave?'

'It would have thrown suspicion on me, sir,' said the gardener. 'Once I had heard a little, I had to hear all. Besides, sir, I was interested. Master Brinklow was like a father to me. I mourn him every day.'

Nicholas warmed to the man. Disfigurement was only skin deep. Valentine was a loyal and compassionate man underneath his repellent exterior. He could yet be of more help.

'Why do you sometimes sleep in the garden?' he said.

'I like it, Master Bracewell. I am at peace here.'

'There must be another reason.'

Valentine grew restless. 'I'd blush to acknowledge it.'

'Why?'

'Come, sir, you are a man. You may guess at it.'

Nicholas was surprised. 'This concerns a woman, then?'

'Yes, sir,' said the other, strangely bashful. 'Not that the woman in question knows anything about it. Nor must she or all is lost. I'll say no more unless you keep my secret.'

'The matter will go no further.'

'Then hear her name.' The grin broadened. 'Agnes.'

'The maidservant?'

'As fine a piece of flesh as any in Greenwich.'

'You and she have some . . . understanding?'

'Oh, no, sir,' said Valentine with bitterness. 'She looks at my ugliness and blames me for it. I am never allowed near her. Agnes goes out of her way to abuse me. Why, only today she caught me near the window of the parlour and chided me for trying to listen to your conversation within.'

'Mistress Brinklow and I?'

'Agnes chased me off down the garden.'

'Then what did she do?'

'I have no idea.'

Nicholas did. It was conceivable that the maidservant had cleared Valentine away from the vantage point outside the window so that she could take it up herself. If she had overheard the conversation in the parlour, she would have known that they moved on to the laboratory. Someone had been listening to them in the bushes. Since it had not been the gardener, it may well have been Agnes. She had always been in the vicinity on his previous visit to the house. When he and Hoode had first arrived, the maidservant had actually been in the arbour with Emilia.

'It is Agnes who keeps you in the garden at night?'

'Yes, sir. I cannot but be fond of her.'

'Even though she rails at you.'

'That is the fault of my face and not her temper.'

'You are very forgiving.'

'All I want is to see her now again,' said Valentine in a conspiratorial whisper. 'To catch her unawares at some simple task. Opening her window, closing her curtains, even just blowing out her candle. In those moments—though Agnes will never know—she is mine.'

'Where is her chamber?'

'At the top of the house. I see her from the garden.'

'I cannot think she would enjoy your surveillance.'

'What harm does it do?' He plucked at Nicholas's sleeve and let out a chuckle. 'I watched her window for a whole month once. She did the same thing every night bar Fridays.'

'What was different about those?'

'She did not sleep in her room. Or if she did, she entered it in darkness and came not to the window. Why do the same thing six nights a week and not the seventh?'

'Haply, she was released from service on Fridays.'

'No question of that, sir. It is one of her busiest days with Saturday even more so. We work a full week here, sir. Sunday morning is our only time of rest and part of that must be spent in church.'

Nicholas was fascinated by the information. The insight into the weird emotional life of Valentine had started a line of thought which led in only one direction. If there was a spy in the household, the maidservant was best placed to perform the office.

'Thank you, Valentine,' he said. 'I am glad we met.'

A grim chuckle. 'Nobody has ever said that before.'

'Tell nobody else what you have told me.'

'I must ask the same of you, Master Bracewell. This is my domain out here. I stalk it like a cat. Do not take it away from me, sir. It is all I have.'

Nicholas nodded. He had no reason to rob the gardener of anything, especially as Valentine had helped him. They shook hands to seal their bargain and parted.

Emilia Brinklow was dogged by fatigue but kept awake by remorse. The murder of Simon Chaloner was devastating. Coming as it did in the wake of the attack on the play, it completely disoriented her. She did not know what to do or where to go next. Agnes sat with her in the parlour and tried to offer some words of comfort but they fell on deaf ears. All that Emilia could hear was the fearful thud on the front door which had announced the arrival of Chaloner's corpse.

Guilt coursed through her like molten lead. She blamed herself for his death. But for her, he would never have been drawn into the long and fretful search for justice with regard to her brother's murder. Chaloner had now joined Thomas Brinklow on a premature slab. Emilia believed that it was all her fault, that she should somehow have prevented him from taking such precipitate action against an enemy far stronger than him. She even wished that she had agreed to marry him sooner instead of offering him conditions. Her anguish was proof against all solace.

There was a tap on the door and it opened to admit the head of Nicholas Bracewell. She sat up with a start.

'Have they gone?' she asked.

'Their enquiries are over for tonight,' he said, coming into the room. 'I made sure that they did not trouble you.'

'Thank you. I appreciate that.'

'I will not disturb you any longer.'

'Where are you going?' she said anxiously.

'To the inn at the end of the main street. If I can rouse the landlord, I am sure he will give me a bed for tonight. I will then be on hand in the morning to lend further assistance.'

'You will stay here, Nicholas.'

'I have no right to intrude.'

'I insist,' she said, turning to the maidservant. 'See that a bed is made ready at once, Agnes. Hurry.'

As the woman went off about her task, Nicholas thought he detected a slight reluctance. He surmised that she was unhappy about his continued stay in the house and annoyed to be sent too far away to overhear what might be a valuable conversation. He took swift advantage of her absence.

'Speak to nobody,' he warned. 'Confide nothing.'

'Why?'

'It is a sensible precaution. Master Chaloner told me that this house has ears. I know that to be true.' He moved in closer and looked into her face. 'How do you feel?'

'Sick with grief.'

'Retire to bed.'

'How can I rest on such a night as this? What sleep do I deserve? I killed Simon,' she said simply. 'I killed him.'

Nicholas was firm but gentle. 'That is nonsense and you must not even think it. What you did was to give him an excellent reason for living. Remember the times you shared together and reflect on what they meant to him. Master Chaloner was deeply in love and that is the stoutest armour of all. He died ignobly but he also died happy. He had you.'

'I could have been kinder to him.'

He shrugged. 'Let us talk again in the morning.'

'Do not pack me off to bed, Nicholas. I am not ready. I am not disposed.' She took his hand impulsively. 'Stay with me for a little while yet. I need you.'

'My presence here occasions some disquiet.'

'You do not wish to stay?'

'Nothing would content me more,' he said, feeling the warmth of her hand, 'but I would not make you the object of comment. You thought it improper for your betrothed to stay beneath the same roof with you. How more unsuitable am I?'

'Nobody could be more suitable.'

He looked down into a face almost haggard with fatigue.

'Then I will stay.'

'I want your guidance.'

'Call on me for anything. I am here.'

He released her hand but she did not move away. Emilia continued to stare up at him. Her eyes were still awash with grief but he saw something else in them now. Nicholas was touched. What he caught was a signal that she was ready to trust him more completely, to let him closer than she had ever dared before. Simon Chaloner had been her confidant in the past. Now that he had died, his mantle was being handed to Nicholas. The book holder reached out boldly to take it.

'Tell me who wrote *The Roaring Boy*,' he said.

'I think you already know.'

It dawned on him at last. Emilia Brinklow loved the theatre.

She visited London regularly with her brother to watch plays. When Nicholas had asked why she did not feature as a character in *The Roaring Boy,* she was not coy or evasive. She gave him a sound technical reason for her absence from the *dramatis personae.* The play was far more than an obsession for her.

'*You* are the author.'

She smiled quietly. 'Women do not write plays.'

'One of them wrote *The Roaring Boy* and that makes the achievement all the more remarkable. I have read hundreds of plays in my time. Yours is not disgraced by any of them.'

'I wrote from the heart.'

Nicholas gazed at her with a new admiration. Emilia Brinklow was a talented woman. Her brother might have been a genius in the sciences but she had the talent for the arts. She also evinced rare courage in forcing her way into such a closed world. Theatre was an exclusively male preserve. Plays were written and performed entirely by men. For a woman even to attempt to emulate them was an act of bravery. To succeed in the way that Emilia Brinklow had done was quite astonishing.

'You see now why the author had to vanish,' she said.

'Clearly.'

'Who would even read a play penned by a woman?'

'I would,' he reminded. 'And I did.'

'Only because you thought it the work of a man. That is why I needed Edmund Hoode's assistance. He not only made the piece work on the stage. His name lent it credence.'

Nicholas Bracewell understood many things for the first time. His anger at having being misled was quickly smothered beneath his increased respect for her. Emilia Brinklow was not just a beautiful woman with a self-appointed mission. She was also a professional colleague. The implications of it all were not lost on him. She was in immense danger. Because he gathered the material for the play, Simon Chaloner was murdered. Because he reworked the drama, Edmund Hoode was imprisoned in the Marshalsea. Both had suffered from their association with *The Roaring Boy*. If its true authorship were revealed, Emilia would be hunted down without mercy.

Nicholas felt that it was his duty to protect her.

'I will stay until this affair is over,' he said.

'Here in Greenwich?'

'This is where it begins and ends.'

'My house is at your disposal.'

'There is nowhere that I would rather be.'

She gazed wistfully at him until a tap on the door told them that Agnes had returned. Emilia moved away and kept her back to them. The maidservant had prepared a room for the guest and waited to conduct Nicholas up to it.

He turned to Emilia to bid a polite farewell.

'Good night,' he said.

She acknowledged him with a faint wave of the hand. He went out with Agnes and the door was shut behind them. When Emilia swung round to look after it, tears of remorse were running freely down her face.

The bed was soft and the linen clean but Nicholas was quite unable to sleep. His mind was exercised by the events of the day. The murder of Simon Chaloner was paramount. There would be no adulterous lovers waiting to be caught this time. The law officers of Greenwich would have make their enquiries without any help and that made the likelihood of an arrest virtually non-existent. Additional men might be drafted in to assist them but there was no way that they would ever follow the tortuous path that led back to Greenwich Palace. Nicholas had to work alone, a daunting prospect until he remembered that he did, after all, have some associates.

Emilia Brinklow herself was more than a friend. Tragedy had yoked them together. A mutual affection which had been sown at their first meeting had pushed up its first shoots in unpromising soil. He felt it somewhat unseemly to have such warm feelings about a woman so soon after the death of her betrothed and he tried to put them aside but they remained beneath the surface. Only a woman of singular determination could have waged the battle that she had. The fact that she had actually made her own ammunition—*The Roaring Boy*—impressed him even more. Thomas Brinklow had created wonders in his workshop but his sister's invention came from the laboratory of her mind.

Valentine was a useful if unprepossessing ally. The gardener's nocturnal habits had paid dividends. Nicholas not only knew who had dragged the corpse up to the front door, he believed that he had unmasked the informer in the house. In the morning, he would confront another spy. Orlando Reeve had penetrated Westfield's Men to learn their plans. Nicholas Bracewell was looking forward to giving the musician a message from the whole company. In their own ways, Agnes and Reeve might turn out to be valuable associates as well.

His mind turned inevitably to Edmund Hoode. It was the playwright who was bearing the brunt of the punishment. Having been imprisoned in the Counter himself, Nicholas had some notion of the miseries of confinement. He had withstood them but Hoode was a weaker vessel. Nicholas wanted to rush back to London to bend all his energies to secure the release of his friend but it would be a pointless journey. The only way to liberate Hoode from the Marshalsea was to solve a second murder in Greenwich.

He was still contemplating the possibilities of the day ahead when he finally drifted off to sleep. An hour or more drifted by in blissful slumber. A clicking noise brought him awake. He opened his eyes but the darkness weighed down in them. When he sat up, he could still see nothing. What he did do was to catch her light fragrance. Emilia Brinklow had come of her own volition into his bedchamber.

She moved in silence across the room, then gently peeled back the sheets. Climbing in beside him, she lay quite still. He heard her breathing deepen as she fell asleep. Nicholas was moved. She had come to share his bed. Emilia wanted nothing more than his company and the protection that it conferred. The moment she was beside him, she was able to relax. She trusted him.

Nicholas was surprised how unsurprised he felt. Her arrival seemed like the most natural thing in the world. Had he tried to analyse it, the situation would have yielded up all sorts of warnings and contradictions but he was in no mood to spoil an affecting moment. She was there. At a time of real crisis, she chose the place where she most wanted to be. Nicholas accepted that fact with gratitude. He soon faded back into sleep himself.

Sunlight was fingering the curtains when he awoke next morning. He felt refreshed and invigorated. How long he had slept he did not know but one thing was certain.

Emilia Brinklow no longer lay in the bed beside him.

Lawrence Firethorn and Owen Elias set out on horseback at first light. Their rough and nondescript attire had been borrowed from the costume stock of Westfield's Men. With their plain caps and coarse jerkins, they looked like two watermen taking a day off from their oars. As they rode side by side along the street at a rising trot, Firethorn gave a snort of contempt.

'Look at me, Owen!' he exclaimed. 'To what depths have I fallen! I am accustomed to the robes of an emperor or the armour of a soldier king. At the very least, I play a duke or an earl. But this! I feel like a dung-collector!'

'That is exactly what we are, Lawrence.'

'I deserve better.'

'You will get it if this day's work bears fruit.'

'One rotten apple is all we seek. Maggotty Maggs.'

'Then we must dress the part.'

'I'll wear my Freshwell face.'

Firethorn insisted on being involved in the adventure in place of Nicholas Bracewell. Expected back the previous night, the book holder did not appear and they rightly assumed that he was detained in Greenwich by urgent business. In the interests of speed, they elected to take on the pursuit of Maggs by themselves. Owen Elias was glad of Firethorn's company even if the jogging of the horse did set off the latter's toothache again. The Welshman would not dare to take George Dart on this outing. He needed strength beside him and there were few more powerful men in the company than the barrel-chested actor-manager. The son of a blacksmith, Lawrence Firethorn had all the attributes of that occupation allied to a taste for danger. His skill with sword and dagger was no mere stage illusion.

'What do we say to him?' asked Elias.

'Leave that to me.'

'Tell him that Lucy sends her love.'

'At the sign of the Red Cock.'

'What other kind is worth having?'

They guffawed loudly and kicked their horses into a canter. Now that they were outside the city gates, their progress would be much quicker. They struck eastwards with the river on their right hand, its smell never far away. It was not a journey they would make by choice but necessity compelled them. Their whole careers were at stake. If one man could help to save them, they had to be prepared to track him down in his unsavoury hiding place.

It was the distinctive reek that first told them they were within reach of their destination. The stench came out to meet them like an invisible fist that punched them on the nose. They coughed and spluttered for a moment.

'How can anyone live in a place like this?' said Elias.

'They get used to it.'

'Not me, Lawrence. Diu—that stink!'

'When we hunt a rat, we must expect a sewer.'

It was a not unfair description of the Isle of Dogs. The low, marshy peninsula jutted out obstructively into the Thames at the bend between Limehouse and Blackwall reaches. It was directly opposite Greenwich on the south bank and the contrast between the two places could not have been harsher. Greenwich was affluent and graced by royalty: the Isle of Dogs was poverty-stricken and haunted by outlaws, punks and fugitive debtors. The latter was also swilled by all the sewage and detritus that came downriver from London. Sailors cursed the Isle of Dogs because it obliged them to make a long, time-consuming loop in their journeys. If they were forced to anchor nearby, it would always be in mid-stream or they would be pillaged from the northern shore.

Greenwich and the Isle of Dogs represented extremes of society. Only the rich and influential rose to attend the banquets at the palace: only the poor and the desperate sank to the ignominy of the Isle of Dogs. One was the home of privilege while the other was a lair for masterless men.

Lawrence Firethorn was revolted by the unredeemed squalor.

'Bankside can be bad enough,' he said. 'And there are parts of Clerkenwell that can turn your stomach but this is worse than both. What are we *doing* here, Owen?'

'Trying to find someone.'

'In this swamp! We'll be infected with every disease known to man and beast. The air is so thick and stale we may cut it with our daggers and feed it to those mangy hounds.'

Fierce dogs were scavenging in the putrid lanes. Small children were playing in the dirt. Stagnant water lent its strength to the general whiff of decay. Wild-eyed men and ragged women roamed the streets. Even at that early hour, the sound of violence rent the air. Firethorn saw the wisdom of their disguises. In the flamboyant doublet and hose that he usually wore, he would have been ridiculously out of place in the Isle of Dogs and that would have rendered him a certain target. As it was, they collected hostile glares from the beggars lying in the doorway of an ordinary. When the two strangers refused to toss them any money, the glares became loud imprecations.

They stabled their horses at a decrepit tavern and proceeded on foot to attract less attention. Owen Elias had suggested a morning visit in the hope that the area would be more quiescent but it was already bubbling with crude life. Lucy had provided the name of a street but no number. They were grateful to find only nine tenements in the street and two of those had collapsed against each other like drunken revellers. That left seven, each building with several occupants. They split up, knocked on doors and endured ear-shattering abuse. When only one door was left in the very last tenement, they converged on it without ceremony.

Elias's strong shoulder hit the door with such force that it broke the bolt. Firethorn was first in, his sword in one hand and his dagger in the other. Elias was on his heels. Both men froze in their tracks. They could not believe what they were seeing. Quite undisturbed by the commotion, two figures were rutting enthusiastically on a mattress. A big, bosomy woman of middle years was lying on her back with her taffeta dress pulled up to her waist and her chubby legs in the air while a small, thin, naked man with a bald head and a back covered in sweat and scabs, was pumping vigorously into her as if his life depended on it. He suddenly stiffened his back, let out a wheeze of pleasure, jiggled around for a moment and then broke wind.

Maggs rolled over on to the bare floorboards and gasped for air. Owen Elias was on to him in a flash, kneeling beside him and pricking his scrotum with the point of his dagger.

'Hello, Maggs,' he said. 'Visitors.'

'Who are you?' gabbled the disadvantaged lover.

'We ask the questions.'

Elias jabbed his dagger and produced a yell of pain.

'Don't kill him yet,' said the woman resentfully. 'He hasn't paid me.' She nudged her client. 'Come on, Maggs. Where is it?'

'Away with you!' said Firethorn, thrusting a few coins into her hands and shoving her out through the door. 'This is a private conversation.'

Maggs took stock of his oppressors. They had the upper hand. He began to squeal and plead for mercy. Firethorn stood over him with a swordpoint at his chest.

'How much mercy did you show to Thomas Brinklow?'

'I didn't kill him!' said Maggs. 'It was Freshwell.'

'The pair of you did it,' said Firethorn.

'I merely held the man. Freshwell struck him down.'

'Who paid you?'

'I do not know his name.'

'Who was he?' said Elias, grabbing the man by the throat to lift him upright and thrust him against the wall. 'We do not have time to argue, Maggs. His name!'

'Sir John Tarker,' mumbled the other.

'Louder!'

'Sir John Tarker!'

'Who else?' demanded Firethorn.

'Nobody,' said Maggs. 'He paid Freshwell and me to kill Brinklow and get his papers. But we were disturbed and had to run away. When we went back later, someone had burned part of the place down. All his papers were destroyed.'

'What papers?' said Firethorn.

'How should I know? We just followed orders.' Maggs became bitter. 'Sir John turned nasty. He betrayed us. Because we only did one half of what he asked, he handed us over to the law. I escaped but old Freshwell danced a jig on fresh air.'

'You may well join him,' said Elias.

'Hanging can be no worse than the Isle of Dogs.'

'These papers,' said Firethorn, feeling they had made a valuable discovery. 'Where were they kept? Were they to do with Master Brinklow's work, by any chance?'

'I've told you all I can,' whimpered Maggs. 'And I speak the truth. If you don't believe me, there's a letter in my breeches there from Sir John Tarker himself. I'll carry it to my grave. Pass the breeches to me and I will show it you.'

The two friends exchanged a glance and decided to comply with the request. A letter was crucial evidence. Elias kept his quarry pinned to the wall while Firethorn retrieved the tattered breeches from the floor. The latter handed them to Maggs. It was a fatal mistake. With a speed and suddenness which took them both by surprise, Maggs hurled the breeches into Firethorn's face and aimed a kick at Elias's groin which had him doubling up in pain. Before either of them could stop him, the little man ran stark naked through the door.

He did not get far. Alerted by the woman, someone was waiting outside for him. One thrust with the long spike was all that it took. Maggs was impaled to the door through which he tried to flee, bleeding like a stuck pig and squirming the last few seconds of his life away. One murderer had finally paid for his crime.

[CHAPTER EIGHT]

Anxious to make an early start to the day, Nicholas Brace-well foresook breakfast and headed for the stables. Emilia Brinklow had not yet risen so he left word with one of the manservants that he would soon return. He did not anticipate that his errand would take long. The ride to the cottage was a relatively short one and the sound of a coranto told him that Orlando Reeve was at home. The musician was already at his keyboard to put the finishing touches to his latest work. Nicholas was about to introduce a few discordant notes into the composition.

A deferential old man answered the door to him.

'I wish to see Master Reeve,' said Nicholas.

'Is he expecting you, sir?'

'He is not but my business will permit no delay.'

'It must, I fear. My master is at his work and I am forbidden to interrupt him for any reason.'

'You may be,' said Nicholas. 'I am not.'

He brushed past the man and went into the room from which the sound of the virginals came. Orlando Reeve was

[200]

seated before the instrument like an acolyte before an altar. He looked up in shock at the sudden intrusion. It bordered on sacrilege.

'Who are you, sir!' he demanded. 'Stand off!'

'Not until we have exchanged a few words, Master Reeve.'

'Show the fellow out, William!'

'I will try,' muttered the old servant, eyeing the visitor's powerful physique with misgiving. 'Follow me, if you please, sir.'

'Leave us,' ordered Nicholas. 'I am acquainted with an old friend of your master—one Peter Digby.'

Orlando Reeve tensed at the sound of the name. After a moment's consideration, he dismissed his servant with a peremptory wave and stood up to confront his visitor. The room occupied virtually the whole of the ground floor of the house. It was well-furnished and spotlessly clean but its main items of interest were the three keyboard instruments. They were superbly crafted and clearly of great value. The musician had built the room around himself to create the most propitious conditions in which to work and practice.

Reeve lifted his chin and adopted a patronising tone.

'State your business, sir. I have not much time.'

'You found enough to visit the Queen's Head recently.'

'I may spend my leisure as I wish.'

'Peter Digby says you would never wish to see a play. Yet you sat through two in as many weeks. Why was that?'

'I do not have to answer to you,' retorted Reeve with a lordly sneer. 'Who are you that you should force your way into my home to interrogate me?'

'My name is Nicholas Bracewell and I am here on behalf of Westfield's Men. Peter Digby is a close friend of mine.'

'And of mine, sir.'

'Throwing him out into the street is a strange way to repay his friendship,' said Nicholas. 'For that is what you have helped to do. Because of you, one of our number lies at this moment in prison and the rest of us are denied a stage on which to play. We are fellow-artistes, sir. Why do you rob us of our occupation?'

'I did nothing of the kind,' blustered Reeve.

'Who sent you to the Queen's Head?'

'I went of my own accord.'

'Even though you hate the theatre and avoid it like the plague? You came to urge an old acquaintance in order to draw intelligence from Peter Digby.' He took a menacing step closer. 'I will not leave until I hear the truth.'

'You do not frighten me,' said Reeve, wobbling with fear and purpling around the cheeks. 'If you do not quit my house presently, I'll summon the constable and bring on action for assault.'

'He'll come too late to save you from certain damage.'

'Spare me!' cried the other, backing away as Nicholas moved towards him again. 'I have done you no harm. Do none to me!' He held out his hands. 'These are my fortune. If my hands are hurt, my livelihood dies. Do not touch my hands.'

'I will not touch you, Master Reeve,' said Nicholas as he raised a bunched fist high above the virginals. 'Your instruments will bear the suffering instead.'

'Stop!'

'It is only a box of wood and strings.'

'You destroy the most precious thing in my life!'

'Then we pay you back in kind. You helped to take our theatre away from us. I'll separate you from your music.'

He raised his fist even higher but Orlando Reeve flung himself in front of the instrument, his face now puce all over and his eyes bulging dangerously. He gabbled his plea for mercy but Nicholas brushed it aside. The book holder had come for information even if he had to smash everything in the cottage to get at it. Reeve finally capitulated.

'I'll tell you all,' he said, panting and perspiring. 'But you wrong me. I did not seek in any way the loss of your right to act at the Queen's Head. Until this moment, I knew nothing of it. I simply obeyed a summons.'

'From whom?'

Reeve took a deep breath. 'Sir John Tarker. He saw the playbills for *The Roaring Boy* and sent me to enquire further into its substance. That's all I did and all I would do, sir. I have no quarrel with Westfield's Men.'

'We have one with you.'

'Sir John *forced* me to go.'

'On both occasions?'

'The second only. The play was *Mirth and Madness.*'

'What of your first visit?'

'That was prompted by . . . another source.'

'I want his name.'

'He will never forgive me if I part with it. The man has been my patron for many years. I would not betray him.'

'Choose between them,' said Nicholas, holding his fist over the instrument again. 'His name or your virginals.'

Perspiration began to drip off the musician's face as he writhed in his quandary. Nicholas was an immediate threat but an even greater one might await him if he complied with his visitor's request. He was skewered on the horns of a dilemma and movement in either direction would cause him pain. Music eventually won the argument. The rescue of his beloved instruments was his paramount concern. They were quite irreplaceable. He lowered his head in defeat.

'Go your way, sir.'

'Only when I learn his name.'

'Sir Godfrey Avenell.'

'He sent you to the Queen's Head?'

'A rumour displeased his ears. I was sent to sound its depth. Peter Digby told me what I sought, that Westfield's Men *were* going to play the murder of Thomas Brinklow.'

'So you were Sir Godfrey Avenell's creature?'

'He loves my music, sir. I did him but a favour.'

Nicholas was scathing. 'It did not advantage us, Master Reeve. When the piece was staged, Sir John Tarker hired bullies to cause an affray and disrupt it. How would you feel if we did likewise when you were playing before your audience?' He stepped in close. 'Do you hate Peter Digby so much that you would see him thrown out like a beggar? Will you set no price at all on friendship?'

Orlando Reeve was shaken to the core. There had been a certain pleasure in worming the required information out of the gullible Peter Digby and he had been handsomely rewarded for his pains. For him, the matter ended there. He did not realise that such dire consequences might follow and he was astute enough to realise that Sir John Tarker would not have wrecked the performance of a play unless he had cause to fear its content. Reeve quailed. What had he got himself drawn into and how could he possibly get out of it?

Nicholas Bracewell glowered down at him in disgust.

'Where might I find Sir John Tarker now?'

'Nearby, sir. He stays at the palace.'

'And Sir Godfrey Avenell?'

'He is there, too. Practice for a tournament is afoot.'

'They'll stay for a day or two?'

'All week.'

Nicholas was content. He had found out what he needed to know and given Orlando Reeve a scare into the bargain. He left the cottage and mounted his horse. He was soon trotting back towards the Brinklow house. Nicholas felt that he was now able to enjoy his breakfast.

Noon found Sir Godfrey Avenell in one of the workshops at Greenwich Palace. Hammers pounded and fire raged all around him but he was not perturbed. Nor did the swirling smoke offend his eyes or nostrils. He enjoyed the clang of metal and the forging of new weapons. The workshop was his natural habitat.

The Master of the Armoury held an important post. His chief responsibility was to have a sufficient store of armour and weapons to fit out an army in the event of war. When the Spanish Armada sailed for England a few years earlier, Sir Godfrey Avenell had worked at full stretch to equip the force which had been hastily thrown together to guard strategic points on the mainland against the threat of invasion. When that crisis passed, he was able to concentrate on his other main duty, which was the organising and staging of Court tournaments.

Some Masters of the Armoury would have stood on the dignity of their position and delegated most of the mundane tasks to subordinates but Avenell liked to be involved at each stage. Instead of consorting only with the knights who used his weapons, he befriended those who made them as well.

'Is all ready here?' he said.

'I have the inventory in my hand, Sir Godfrey.'

'Read the items as they load them up.'

Under the supervision of a clerk, men were carrying piles of weapons across to a series of wooden boxes. A consignment was about to be stored in preparation for the forthcoming tournament. Avenell stood at the man's shoulder as the clerk read the inventory.

'One hundred pikes . . . two hundred tilt staves . . . eighty-five swords for barriers . . . sixty vamplates . . . one hundred coronels . . . one hundred and twenty puncheon staves . . . '

'Where are the mornes?' asked Avenell.

'Already in store, Sir Godfrey. Two hundred of them.'

'Good. We need them to blunt our lances. We must not fright the ladies with the sight of blood.'

'Our armour prevents that.'

Avenell waited until the full consignment had been checked

and stored. He then took the clerk aside and whispered something to him. The man produced a second inventory from inside his doublet. Taking it from him, the Master of the Armoury read it to himself.

'Five hundred pikes, four hundred spear staves, one hundred two-handed swords, one hundred rapiers . . . '

The list was long and comprehensive. Avenell handed it back to the clerk with a nod of approval. The man secreted it inside the doublet once again.

'Delivery is in hand?'

'Yes, Sir Godfrey. They'll be at Deptford by evening.'

'When will they leave?'

'Tomorrow on the morning tide.'

Sir Godfrey Avenell was pleased. Efficient and industrious himself, he set high standards for his many underlings. He demanded complete loyalty and commitment from them. Discretion was also imperative. Those who fell short in any way were soon discharged. The clerk had been with him long enough to be trusted. It was good to have such men around him as part of a smooth-running system which had evolved over the years. The workshops at Greenwich Palace were a source of continual joy to the Master of the Armoury.

A small shadow suddenly fell across that joy. As he left the workshop and came out into the fresh air, Avenell was met by a servant bearing a message. It was delivered at the main gate of the palace with a request for urgent attention. Avenell dismissed the servant and tore off the crude seal on the letter. Two lines of spidery script made him hiss with rage.

Marching back into the workshop, he tossed the missive into the burning coals of a brazier and continued on down the room. A door at the far end gave access to an antechamber used for the fitting of armour. Sir John Tarker was preening himself in a mirror while his squire was polishing the new suit of armour. Avenell stormed in with murder in his eyes. The squire did not need to be told to leave at once. He bolted from the chamber to leave the two men alone together. Tarker was bewildered by the dramatic intrusion and the blistering anger.

'What ails you?' he said.

'Maggs.'

'He cannot harm us. Who will listen to the word of a hunted outlaw? His spite can never touch us.'

'Maggs is dead,' said Avenell.

Tarker grinned. 'Then we have reason to celebrate, not to quarrel. If the rogue lies in his grave, all fear is gone. What benefactor took the life of that little rat for us?'

'I did.'

'You?'

'By indirect means,' said Avenell. 'I could not rely on you. When you hired those men, they failed us badly.'

'That is why I threw them to the law.

'You could not even do that properly. Freshwell was put in chains but Maggs broke free and ran.'

'To the Isle of Dogs. What harm could he do us there?'

'None until today. As long as Maggs stayed there and kept his mouth shut, I was content to let him live. But I took the precaution that you should have taken.'

'Precaution?'

'I had him watched.'

Tarker grew uneasy. 'What happened?'

'Someone tracked him down. They came to question him this morning about the murder. They may have wrung something out of him before my man could shut the villain's mouth forever.' He drew his rapier. 'In other words, they are still sniffing after our scent.'

'Maggs knew only part of the truth.'

'He knew enough to keep them coming after us.'

'Who *are* they?'

'People you swore would never bother us again,' snarled

Avenell. 'People who stand between me and my peace of mind.' He advanced on Tarker with his sword raised. 'People I would have put down once and for all.'

He slashed away with his weapon and Tarker jumped back involuntarily but he was not the target of the attack. Sir Godfrey Avenell was taking out his anger on the glistening armour, hacking away at the decorated breastplate until he knocked the whole suit over with a clatter, kicking the helmet free, then jabbing madly at the leg armour. Only when he had scored the metal in a hundred places did he pause to glare across at his alarmed companion.

'Next time,' he warned, 'it will be you. Kill them!'

Emilia Brinklow was waiting for him when he returned to the house and they shared breakfast together. Nicholas Bracewell told of the visit to Orlando Reeve but divulged nothing of what passed between them and she did not press him on the matter. They simply ate and talked together quietly as if they had been doing it every day of their lives. Emilia was transformed. The pale and dispirited creature of the night before was now poised and alert. Her cheeks had colour, her eyes hope and her whole being had acquired a new definition. Sadness still rested on her but its weight was no longer quite so suffocating.

She made no reference, either by word or glance, to their brief time together in bed and Nicholas started to wonder if it had really occurred. Was it no more than a pleasant dream sent to ease his troubled mind? Or was it some waking fantasy conjured up by the intense pressures of recent days? Had she indeed come to him and now regretted her action so much that she had blotted it out of her mind? Did their moment beside each other perhaps contribute to her apparent recovery? At all events, it was not a barrier between them and he was grateful for that.

They remained happily at the table until midday when the

constable and his two assistants arrived to resume their way-
ward investigation. After hours of questioning those who lived
in the neighbouring houses, they had divined nothing of any
significance. Nicholas again steered them through their halting
routine. He also ensured that their interrogation of Emilia was
neither too distressing nor robust.

The manservant who discovered the body then adjourned
with Nicholas to make sworn statements at the nearby home of
a magistrate. Valentine was sheltered from the need to give any
testimony even though he had been first aware of the arrival of
tragedy on the doorstep. Nicholas saw no point in dragging the
gardener into the investigation and thereby exposing his eccen-
tric sleeping arrangements to public gaze while only further
complicating the situation for the law officers. The book holder
had already taken long strides forward and he did not want
three well-intentioned buffoons around his feet to trip him up.

When he got back to the house once more, he was amazed
to see two familiar figures dismounting from their horses.

'Nick, dear heart!'

'We knew that we would find you at the house.'

Nicholas was thrilled. 'By all, it's good to see you!'

They exchanged embraces of welcome, then compared
news. Lawrence Firethorn and Owen Elias had not tarried in
the Isle of Dogs. The killing of Maggs made their own presence
at once unnecessary and dangerous. Survival was the only law
that existed in that human jungle. They left while they still
could and were ferried across the Thames on a barge with their
horses. Who dispatched the naked Maggs with such brutal
finality they could not tell but they felt that Freshwell's partner
in crime had somehow met his just deserts.

Nicholas took them into the house and introduced them to
Emilia Brinklow. She had expected to meet the whole company
after the performance of *The Roaring Boy* but she had been
hustled away from the fiasco by Simon Chaloner and had
forgone that pleasure. She was clearly honoured to meet Law-

rence Firethorn, an actor whose work she revered, and she delighted Owen Elias as well by complimenting him on a number of performances. Emilia had obviously been a keen follower of the fortunes of Westfield's Men for some time. For their part, they were charmed by her grace and composure. Firethorn was so taken with her that he even started to make flirtatious remarks. Nicholas cut short this standard reaction to female admiration by telling him about the second murder. The newcomers were duly outraged.

'Here on the doorstep?' exclaimed Firethorn.

'Slaughtered by the same hand,' decided Elias.

'Yes,' said Nicholas. 'Solve one murder, solve both.'

He saw that Emilia was sinking back into her grief once more and he quickly moved on to another topic. She rallied within minutes and remembered the duties of a hostess. Sensing that the men wished to be alone, she went off to the kitchen to order refreshment for the guests and to give them the chance to talk more freely.

'Where did you spend the night, Nick?' said Firethorn.

'Here at the house.'

Elias chuckled. 'We can see why you did not rush to get back to London. A warm bed here is better than a cold lodging in Shoreditch.'

'Mistress Brinklow invited me to stay.'

'Say no more, Nick,' advised Firethorn. 'We are green with envy already. On to our discoveries in the Isle of Dogs.'

'You found Maggs?' said Nicholas.

'Found him and lost him.'

Firethorn recounted the tale and the book holder was spellbound. Everything he heard tallied with what he himself had found out or suspected. Between the three of them, they had made substantial progress and they at last knew the name of the man who was the true author of all the evils that had beset the Brinklow household.

'Sir Godfrey Avenell!' said Elias. 'He's worse than Freshwell and Maggs together. At least, they were honest rogues. He hides behind his rank.'

'I'd like to meet up with the knave!' said Firethorn.

'You will get your chance,' promised Nicholas. 'Both he and Sir John Tarker are close by in Greenwich Palace. We three must find some way to smoke the two of them out. And we may not do that until we have first uncovered the deepest mystery of them all.'

'The deepest?' asked Elias.

'Why?'

'Why what?'

'Why was Thomas Brinklow killed?'

'The play explains that,' said Firethorn. 'He was the victim of a malignant enemy. Sir John Tarker hated him.'

'It is not enough,' argued Nicholas. 'Sir John would do nothing without the approval of Sir Godfrey Avenell. He is the key to all this. Why did *he* want Thomas Brinklow dead?'

'Were Sir Godfrey and Master Brinklow also at each other's throats?' suggested Elias.

'Far from it. They were good friends. They even dined in each other's company at the palace. Indeed, it was there that Master Brinklow was introduced to the lady who was to become his wife. And who brought the two of them together?'

Even as he asked the question, Nicholas caught a glimpse of an answer he had never even considered before. It made him revalue the whole situation. Before he could share his thoughts with his friends, Emilia returned with the promise of food and drink. They rose courteously from their seats and insisted that she rejoin them. When all four were once again seated, Nicholas explored an area which had been brought to light by the visit to the Isle of Dogs.

'When you showed me your brother's laboratory,' he said, 'you spoke of his papers having been destroyed.'

'Why, yes. In the fire.'

'What sort of papers were they?'

'Drawings, calculations, inventions.'

'None survived?'

'None at all, Nicholas,' she said. 'Thomas was a careful man, as I told you. His papers were like gold to him. He kept them locked away at all times out of fear.'

'Of what?'

'Theft by his rivals, jealous of his success.'

'Only rivals?' She looked perplexed. 'Was your brother ever commissioned to work for Sir Godfrey Avenell, the Master of the Armoury?'

'He was. On more than one occasion.'

'What was the nature of those commissions?'

'I cannot say. Thomas did not discuss his work with me. I explained that to you. All I know is that he paid regular visits to the workshops at the palace to consult with Sir Godfrey. And then those visits stopped.'

'Why?' asked Firethorn.

'Thomas would not tell me.'

'Did you have no inkling of your own?'

'None, Master Firethorn. It was not my place.'

Nicholas was curious. 'How soon after these regular visits broke off did your brother meet his death?'

'Less than a month.'

The three men were exercised by the same thought. Thomas Brinklow was not killed at the behest of a spiteful enemy who lusted after the former's sister. He was removed out of the way so that his papers could fall into the hands of Sir Godfrey Avenell. Something in among those drawings and calculations was a sufficient motive for murder.

Nicholas Bracewell spoke for all three of them.

'Have you *nothing* of your brother's work to show us?'

'Go to Deptford and you may see many examples of it,' she said. 'The royal dockyards worship the name of Thomas Brinklow. They will show you his navigational instruments.'

'I hoped for something here in the house.'

'It was all consumed in the fire.'

'Some tiny item must surely survive,' he continued. 'He lent his skills to the design of this beautiful house. Did he not also create something to use or display in it?'

'Nothing,' she said. 'Except one trifling gift for me.'

'Gift?'

'It is hardly worth mention, Nicholas. I would certainly not offer it as an example of Thomas's genius. He was a man who could invent telescopes to read the heavens and devices to plumb the depth of the sea. A simple knife is but a poor epitaph for him.'

'Knife?'

'He gave it me to unseal letters.'

'May we see it, please?'

'If you wish, but what interest can it hold for you?'

Nicholas was adamant. 'Send for it, I pray.'

'I'll fetch it myself directly,' she volunteered.

In the short time it took her to get the knife, the three friends had agreed on the likely motive for the first murder. It was grounded in the scientific and engineering experiments of Thomas Brinklow. He had been killed for his papers. Failure to steal them had led Freshwell to the gallows with his tongue cut out and Maggs to the Isle of Dogs. What was so important about the mathematician's work that justified such a wholesale waste of human life?

Nicholas Bracewell was made aware of another anomaly.

'Maggs told you that they found the place on fire?'

'Yes, Nick,' said Elias. 'It was not their work.'

'Whose then was it? Someone started that blaze.'

Emilia came back into the room bearing a long, thin knife with a pearl handle. At first glance, it looked no more than an attractive implement for domestic use but Nicholas had second thoughts when he handled it. The knife was unusually light in his grasp and gave off a peculiar sheen. He passed it to Firethorn who was quite intrigued.

'Your brother made this for you?' he asked.

'In his workshop.'

'From what metal?'

'He did not say.'

'It is lighter by far than any knife I have seen,' said Nicholas, taking it back into his own hands. 'Yet its balance is perfect and its edge well-honed. May I test it against my dagger? I am loathe to damage it if it is the only keepsake you have of your brother.'

'This house is keepsake enough,' she said, realising that the knife might after all hold significance. 'Do as you think fit with it, Nicholas.'

He slipped his dagger from its sheath and used it to clip the blade of the knife sharply. The latter withstood the blow without a blemish. Nicholas hit the blade much harder next time but it was still equal to the test. He passed the dagger to Owen Elias, then held the knife in front of him by its handle and its tip so that it lay horizontal. The Welshman lifted the dagger and smashed its blade down against the target.

'Aouw!' he yelled, shaking his hand. 'I have jarred my wrist. It was like striking against solid stone.'

Nicholas examined the two weapons. There was a deep nick in the blade of his dagger but the knife was unscathed.

'Germans,' he murmured.

'Speak up, Nick,' ordered Firethorn.

'Germans. The two men who brought Master Chaloner here last night spoke to each other in German.'

'This is Greenwich,' said Elias, 'and full of musicians from the palace. They come from all nationalities and you may hear a dozen languages in the streets. French, Italian, Dutch, Portuguese. Even German, I daresay.'

'They were no musicians, Owen. But armourers.'

'How do you know?'

'Because the best craftsmen in Europe were brought to the palace to make armour in its workshops. Most of them were

German. They are experts at their work. They know how to bend the finest metals to their will. The finest—and the strongest.'

He held the knife out on the palm of his hand.

When Topcliffe lifted the poniard from the table, Edmund Hoode went weak at the knees. Wrists manacled, he had been hauled out of the Marshalsea and taken by prison cart to the house of the interrogator. Richard Topcliffe was seated behind a long table when the prisoner was brought in by the two gaolers. He made Hoode stand directly in front of him so that he could appraise him in minute detail, searching—or so the playwright feared—for the points of greatest weakness and vulnerability about his anatomy. As Topcliffe picked up the little dagger, Hoode feared that it would be used to cut a first morsel of flesh but his host reached instead for one of the large red apples in a bowl. Slicing it in two, he looked up quizzically at his guest.

'Remove the manacles,' he said.

'We have orders to keep him restrained,' said one of the gaolers. 'He may be desperate.'

Topclife was curt. 'I will not have the fellow trussed up in irons before me. Remove them without delay and then remove yourselves.' The two men hesitated. 'Master Hoode will not try to run away. I can vouch for him.'

The playwright had neither the strength nor the will-power to take to his heels. He was grateful to have the manacles unlocked and pulled off the wrists that they were chafing so badly but he would have preferred his two companions to remain. As the gaolers left the room, he hoped that they would linger nearby. Richard Topcliffe was the last man in the world with whom he cared to be left alone.

His host bit into the apple and chewed it slowly. He was much older than Hoode had anticipated, perhaps sixty, and his grey hair had an almost saintly glow. The doublet and hose of black satin came in stark contrast to the whiteness of his face. His body was lean, his shoulders rounded, his hands covered in knotted veins. Hoode found it difficult to believe that a man who looked like a retired bishop could possess such an insatiable appetite for cruelty.

Then he looked into Topcliffe's eyes. They were dark whirlpools of malice that seemed to contain the frothing blood of his countless victims. Hoode felt as if he were staring at an evil force of nature. No further torture was needed to make him submit. Those eyes caused pain enough.

Topcliffe's voice was like a poniard between his ribs.

'Welcome to my home, Master Hoode.'

'Thank you,' gulped the other.

'I have been asked to speak with you in private.' He swallowed a piece of apple and sat back. 'How do you like the Marshalsea, sir?'

'I do not.'

'Are the food and company not to your liking?'

'Indeed, they are not.'

'Then let us see if we can improve your accommodation. If you help me, I will see what I may do to assist you. I do not like to see you suffer so.' He wrinkled his nose in disgust. 'And carry such an abominable stink.' He glanced down at a sheaf of papers in front of him and read something that made him click his tongue in admonition. 'You have been reckless, Master Hoode. Seditious libel is no light matter.'

'But I am innocent of the crime!' cried Hoode.

'That is for me to determine.'

'No libel was intended or employed, Master Topcliffe.'

'Then why are you here?'

Topcliffe raised a mocking eyebrow to silence Hoode. The playwright saw the sheer hopelessness of his position. If someone in authority had brought a charge against him, it was lunacy to imagine that the interrogator would take the play-wright's part. Richard Topcliffe did not make impartial judgements. Those who were sent to him were already presumed guilty and thus fit for extreme punishment.

The old man bit off another piece of apple.

'What is your opinion of pain, Master Hoode?'

'Pain?'

'Have you ever considered its nature or purpose?'

'No, sir.'

'A poet like you? A man whose profession must make him contemplate all the mysteries of existence? Yet you have never studied the philosophy of pain?' He swallowed his food and gave a faint smile. 'It has been my one true passion in life. Suffering is a most rewarding subject of study. If you can control and inflict pain, you have unlimited power. That is the great difference between us, Master Hoode. You have devoted your life to giving pleasure while I have dedicated mine to administering pain.'

Hoode was given a few minutes to weigh the import of the words he had just heard. The playwright was already in agony. He and the interrogator had indeed operated in two opposing worlds. What terrified him was the thought that they might now be united in one with Hoode providing pleasure to a fiend who revelled in pain. He shuddered as he felt the old man's gaze raking his body again. There was no escape.

'I always find it in the end,' said Topcliffe.

'Find what, sir?'

'The truth. No matter where a man may hide it, I will root it out. Sometimes I have to look in their heart and sometimes I have to prise open their brains. I will even lay bare a man's soul in order to get at it.' He stood up and came around the table. 'Where do *you* keep the truth?'

'About what, Master Topcliffe?'

'This play of yours, *The Roaring Boy.*'

'It is not my play,' insisted Hoode. 'I was merely the carpenter who made the necessary repairs. Another hand wrote the piece. Look for him.'

'I do, sir. That is why you are here.'

'But I do not know his name!'

'You will remember it in time.'

'The author preferred to remain anonymous. I have no idea who he was or why he wrote what he did. I will swear that on the Bible, sir.'

'They all say that.' Topcliffe grinned. 'Follow me.'

He walked to the end of the room and opened a door. Hoode went after him with reluctant footsteps and found himself in a passageway that led to a flight of steps. Topcliffe went down them with his victim in tow. They came into a long, low, stone-floored chamber that was lit by altar candles. One glance at the contents of the room was enough to make Hoode's stomach heave.

In the middle of the room stood a large, solid, wooden contraption with all manner of straps, spikes and ropes attached to it. Stout handles on all four sides of the rack allowed it to be tightened inexorably in all directions. Other devices were ranged around the walls. These further refinements of torture included iron bridles to fit over the head and deep into the mouth, an array of thumbscrews and a wooden coffin lined with razor-sharp teeth that could bite ever deeper into the flesh of its occupant when its sides were beaten with hammers. Red-hot tongs and pokers nestled in the brazier that stood in a corner.

It was not just the sight of these objects that made Hoode retch. The atmosphere in the room was unbearable. The smell of suffering was almost tangible. Richard Topcliffe thrived on it but his guest was inhaling the reek of a charnel-house.

The interrogator indicated the rack with immense pride.

'Have you ever seen such a wonderful machine?' he said. 'It is my own invention. Compared to this, the one at the Tower is child's play. Do you see what I have done here? Every part of a man's body can feel a separate agony. Look at this device for the hands, Master Hoode. You will be able to appreciate its cunning.'

'Will I?' Hoode murmured.

'You spoke of your carpentry on a play. Well, here is carpentry of a much higher order. Each finger slots into its own individual hole, as you may see. I simply turn this one handle and the subtlety of my design becomes apparent.' He was almost drooling now. 'All ten fingers are simultaneously crushed and a tongue is invariably loosened.'

Edmund Hoode was in such distress that he clutched at a wall for support. The fact that he did not know the name of the play's author was irrelevant. Richard Topcliffe would search for it with a cruelty and relentlessness that were their own justification.

'Go back to the Marshalsea now,' said Topcliffe.

'Back?' gasped Hoode in relief. 'I am released?'

'For the time being. Reflect on what I have said and you will soon remember the name that evades you. This visit has simply acquainted you with my methods, Master Hoode.' He gave his faint smile. 'You have seen my instruments.'

T he three men continued to question Emilia Brinklow about the nature of her brother's work but the help she could give them was limited. She was sometimes allowed to view the results of his toil but he never discussed the means by which he made them. Privacy had been the major preoccupation of Thomas Brinklow.

'What about his wife?' asked Nicholas Bracewell.

'Cecily?'

'Was she taken into his confidence?

'Even less so than me,' said Emilia, 'and that upset her deeply. She was always curious about the time he spent in his workshop but he never let her past that iron door. Cecily was locked out just as much as the rest of us. She protested bitterly but in vain.'

Nicholas thanked her for her help and asked if he could show his friends around the ruined laboratory. Emilia gave them the freedom of the house. She herself felt the need to pay an important call elsewhere.

'I will to the church,' she said. 'Simon lies there. I want to offer up a prayer for the salvation of his soul.'

'That is only proper,' said Nicholas.

'I feel ready to look upon him now.'

'Prepare yourself first. It is not a happy sight.'

'Duty bids me endure it.'

She gave him the key from her pocket and took her leave. They could easily have entered the ruin from the garden by stepping over one of its walls but it seemed sensible to approach it as its designer must have done. Lawrence Firethorn and Owen Elias both commented on the thickness of the door. When it was thrust open, they stepped into the wilderness beyond and marvelled. Nicholas indicated some of the apparatus at the far end of the workshop.

'Here is his forge where he fashioned that knife-blade,' said Nicholas. 'Close by are two more furnaces.'

'Was not one enough?' asked Elias.

'Not for a craftsman,' explained Firethorn. 'I grew up in a world of sparks and steel. My father was a blacksmith and taught me that iron is not simply a dull metal. If it is handled aright, it can come alive. My father knew how to make it hiss in the coals and sing on his anvil.'

'How many furnaces did he have?'

'Two, Owen. One firing will drive out some impurities from the metal. A second may refine it more and render it easier to handle. All depends on how much heat you apply.' Firethorn enjoyed a rare lapse into nostalgia. 'I watched my father for hours on end in his forge. Most of his time was spent in shoeing

horses and fitting iron rims on cartwheels but he was a skilled
metalworker as well. His wrought-iron screen still stands in the
village church.'

'Thomas Brinklow was no blacksmith,' reminded Nicholas.
'He had *three* furnaces to conduct his experiments, each one
different in size and shape to the others. What does that suggest
to you, Lawrence?'

'It goes well beyond my father's art. I'd say he found a way
to alter the properties of the metal by the separate firings.
Something may have been added in its molten state.' He knelt
beside one furnace and picked up a handful of small cinders.
'Here is one clue, sirs. I would expect to find a forge like this
burning charcoal. These cinders are the last remains of coal, a
fuel that causes untold problems.'

'Unless he found a way to cure them,' said Nicholas.

Firethorn felt the cinders. 'Or a new type of coal.'

'From Wales, perhaps,' said Elias. 'We have mines.'

'Or from even further afield,' added Nicholas. 'Ships carry
timber and other fuels into London every day.'

They continued the speculate for some time before Nicholas
drew his friends down the garden to the middle of the largest
lawn. He lowered his voice.

'Here we may certainly talk in complete safety.'

'Are we then overheard?' said Elias.

'There is a spy in the house. I believe I know who it is. She
will not be able to listen to us out here.'

'She?' repeated Firethorn.

'If I am correct.'

Valentine suddenly came out of the bushes some twenty
yards away with his wheelbarrow. He gave Nicholas the most
obsequious grin and ambled off in the direction of the house.
The book holder's companions were taken aback.

'Who, in God's name, is that?' said Elias.

'Valentine the gardener.'

'A hideous face like that does not belong in a lovely garden,' opined Firethorn. 'It should be set on the side of a cathedral with the other gargoyles.'

'Do not be misled by appearances,' said Nicholas. 'He is our friend. To business. I cannot tell you how it cheers me to have you both here. Three of us may contrive things that no one person could ever attempt alone.'

Elias grinned. 'Tell us what to do and it is done.'

'Then first, we must split up. I am known to be here in Greenwich, you are not. That gives us an advantage. One of you must go to the palace to see what may be learned there.'

'That will I,' volunteered Firethorn.

'They may not even admit you,' said Nicholas, 'but much may be gleaned if you hang about the quay. Ask what comes in and out by boat. Find out about the workings of the palace. Pick up even the tiniest scrap of news about Sir Godfrey Avenell. His face must be well-known to all. Ask why the Master of the Armoury spends so much time down here in Greenwich when his office is in the Tower.'

'I'll find out all that and more, Nick,' said Firethorn.

'What of me?' said Elias.

'Haunt the taverns here, Owen. You met with good fortune in the stews of Bankside. Try your luck in Greenwich.'

'What must I seek?'

'Any rumour, tale or idle gossip about Thomas Brinklow. Secretive about his work he may have been, but someone must have supplied him with materials. Who delivered the coal, for instance? Who built his equipment and machines? Who kept them in a state of repair? Someone must have got in here.'

'Drink and listen,' said Elias. 'Fitting work for me.'

'About it now.'

They arranged a time and place to meet up later. As they strolled back down the garden together, Firethorn remembered what Nicholas had said a little earlier.

'You are known, but we are not?' said the actor.

'Yes, Lawrence. Word of my presence here will already have

been sent to the palace. I am hoping that it will flush out some of the game.'

'We have been in the house awhile now. Has not the same person reported as much to her spymaster?'

'No,' said Nicholas. 'I set my own informer to watch her. Valentine may seem to be about his work out here but he is also keeping his eyes peeled. If a certain maidservant tries to leave the premises, I will be told.'

'You are a stage manager to your fingertips!'

'He is too comfortable here in Greenwich,' said Elias with a wink. 'How will we ever drag him back to London when he has a beautiful woman to care for him and an ugly gardener to act as his eyes and his ears?'

He and Firethorn went off laughing happily together but Nicholas did not share their mirth. The teasing remark had contained a grain of truth that almost embarrassed him. The book holder was becoming slowly drawn to Greenwich and the kind of life that it might offer him. More particularly, he was drawn to Emilia Brinklow. She was much more than a grieving young woman who needed his help at a difficult time. She had qualities that he found quite entrancing and his admiration for her had soared since her authorship of *The Roaring Boy* had been revealed. What impressed him was not just the extraordinary skill she had shown for a novice playwright but the way in which her writing had so carefully disguised her gender.

The moment alone together in the middle of the night had a profound effect on him. It was some time since he had shared a bed with a woman and, although they did not sleep in each other's arms as lovers, there had yet been a bond forged between them. Trust, affection and need had brought Emilia to his bedchamber. It was an open question whether or not they could mature into something more permanent.

As soon as he caught himself even considering such a possibility, he expelled it from his mind. Emilia Brinklow could never be his. She was a rich young woman with a large house and a recognised place in Greenwich society, while he was a humble book holder with a theatre company which did not even have a venue in which to perform. Emilia could offer him so much but he could never bring an equal portion of money or property to the match. On the other hand, there were deficiencies in her life that he could repair. Nicholas could provide the strength which her brother had obviously supplied and the love which hitherto had come from Simon Chaloner. Would he, however, simply be taking the place of others? To be at all worthwhile, he knew, a friendship had to be a merging of true minds.

With a conscious effort, he shook himself free of her for the second time. Emilia Brinklow did not intrude upon his concentration again because someone distracted him. It was Valentine, giving a pre-arranged signal to him that Agnes was about to leave the house for some reason. Nicholas could guess what her errand might be. With her mistress out of the house at church, she had the opportunity to slip out and send some sort of message to the palace. There was no chance of her going there and back on foot so he surmised that she must have an intercessory in the village.

Nicholas moved swiftly. Screened by a line of trees, he worked his way towards the house and was in time to see the maidservant letting herself out by the rear door. She looked furtively around before darting behind the bushes. Nicholas cut around the other side of the house so that he would be at the front when she got there. Agnes knew how to conceal her movements. Only the faintest disturbance in the bushes showed her progress. She emerged near the front gate and tried to scurry through it.

The solid frame of Nicholas Bracewell blocked her way.

'Where do you go on Fridays?' he asked.

She let out a gasp of fear, then burst into tears.

· · ·

Sir John Tarker was an arrogant man who had been utterly humiliated. Somebody now had to pay for that humiliation. Sir Godfrey Avenell had administered it but the real cause of it was Nicholas Bracewell. The book holder's name had cropped up time and again to irritate and confound him. After being soundly beaten at the Eagle and Serpent, he somehow had the resilience to bounce back. Tarker had gone to great lengths to effect the destruction of *The Roaring Boy* and the damage that had occasioned Westfield's Men was an incidental bonus to him. An affray, an arrest and an injunction had virtually killed the theatre company.

Yet its members still kept up their pursuit of him. He was certain that two of them had run Maggs to earth in the Isle of Dogs but the organising force behind them was Nicholas Bracewell. And the latter was back in Greenwich.

'I want him!' he barked.

'Leave him to me,' said a heavy-set man with a guttural accent. 'I'll break his back for him.'

'No, Karl. This man is my quarry.'

'Will you run him through with a lance?'

'It would be too kind a death for Nicholas Bracewell.'

'How, then, will you kill him, Sir John?'

'Slowly.'

The armourer grunted in approval. They were alone in one of the workshops at the palace and Tarker was venting his spleen. Nicholas Bracewell had helped to lose him his position, his pride, the finest suit of armour he had ever possessed and the invaluable friendship of the man who had bought it for him. Unless he could somehow cut himself a path back into the favour of Sir Godfrey Avenell, Tarker faced bankruptcy, forced retirement from tournaments and certain elimination from Court circles.

'How soon will you do it?' asked Karl.

'Tonight.'

'Is that not too dangerous?'

'Why?'

'We left Master Chaloner's body there but yesterday. The crime has been reported and law officers are looking for us. Will they not be lurking near the house still?'

'What matter if they were?' said Tarker. 'If some imbecile of a constable were guarding the house, he would point us the way to Nicholas Bracewell's bedchamber without a qualm. You would have to murder a man in front of their noses before the Greenwich constables would take notice.'

'Tonight, then.'

'It may be the last time my prey is still here.'

'The message said that he would stay until the whole matter was over,' said the German with a smirk. 'And my messages are usually correct.'

'The whole matter *will* be over tonight,' affirmed Tarker. 'When this Bracewell is removed from the scene, the rest soon collapse. They are cut adrift without him.' His eyes narrowed to pinpricks. 'And *she* is cut adrift as well. No brother to protect her. No Master Chaloner. No Bracewell.'

Karl chuckled. 'You will call there as often as I do.'

'Tonight we will both pay a visit.'

'What must I do?'

'Ensure that he is indeed in the house.'

'And?'

'Find us the means to get to his bedchamber.'

'Will a key to the front door be enough?'

'Can you get such a thing, Karl?'

'Of course,' boasted the other. 'I can get whatever I wish from her. She will deny me nothing.'

Nicholas Bracewell did not mince his words with Agnes. After taking her back into the kitchen, he sat her down and told her the consequences of what she had done. The maidservant blubbered all the way through and needed several minutes before she could even speak. She had been caught, trying to sneak away from the house with a message concealed up her sleeve. Nicholas had broken the seal, read the missive and seen its warning of the arrival in Greenwich of Lawrence Firethorn and Owen Elias. Agnes was an efficient spy.

'What have you got to say for yourself?' he demanded.

'Nothing, sir.'

'I, at least, will hear you out,' he said. 'If I hand you over to the law, they will lock you up for months until a trial can be arranged. They may even put you in a cell and forget that you are there, which would be no more than your wickedness deserves. Is that what you want?'

'No, sir!' she implored. 'I could not bear it!'

'Then tell me the truth.'

'I was not involved in the murders, I swear it!'

'Yet you supplied information to the murderers.'

'They said they were only after his papers.'

She went off into another paroxysm of weeping. Nicholas could see that her remorse was genuine. The woman had enough guile to act as an informer but no capacity for defending herself now that she had at last been exposed.

Nicholas took her by the shoulders to calm her down.

'Begin at the beginning,' he said. 'What is this about papers? Did they belong to Master Thomas Brinklow?'

'Yes, sir. He always kept them locked up. His wife could not get near them and she was nosey enough. I was told to borrow some of them but I could never even get inside his laboratory. Clever thieves were needed for that task.'

'Freshwell and Maggs?'

'That's what I thought they were. Thieves, not killers.'

'They were paid to be both.'

'Nobody told me,' she protested it. 'I was to leave the key for them to get into the house and steal the papers. That was all my part in the business. I went off to bed that night and slept soundly. The next thing I know, I am wakened by the master, yelling that he is being attacked by villains. I raised the alarm at once.'

'Too late to save Master Brinklow.'

'Would I have come running down the stairs if I had been a party to murder? I helped to put Freshwell and Maggs to flight. Because of me, they did not steal those papers. When they came back, the workshop was in flames.'

'Who set it alight?'

'Nobody knows.'

'One of the other servants?'

'They would have no cause.'

'What did you feel when you saw your master dead?'

'As if I had hacked him down myself,' she said as she relived the horror of it. 'Master Brinklow was kind to me. His sister has a sharper tongue at times but he was always very courteous with us. I was overcome when I saw what they had done to him. My conscience would not let me sleep for many weeks afterwards.'

'Yet you went on helping those who killed him.'

'No, sir!'

'You let two innocent people go to their deaths.'

'I could not stop them,' she argued. 'Who would have listened to me? When they caught the two of them together like that, their guilt seemed crystal clear. My testimony could not save them. What weight can you place on the word of a common maidservant?' A coldness came into her tone. 'That is what Mistress Brinklow always called me.'

'Emilia Brinklow?'

'Cecily, her sister-in-law. She had no time for me.'

'So you got your revenge by letting them drag her off to the gallows with Walter Dunne. Is that how it was?'

'No, sir, it was not. I was sorry to see them hanged but they had done wrong in the eyes of God.'

Nicholas exploded. 'You dare to make a moral judgement on

them when your own actions have been far more sinful? You betrayed your master. You betrayed his wife. And you have gone on betraying Mistress Emilia Brinklow ever since.'

'It was not like that!' she insisted.

'Then tell me what it *was* like.'

'It is too painful even to think of now.'

'Do not expect sympathy from me,' he said harshly. 'Pull yourself together or I will call the constables forthwith and throw you to their mercy. Now, speak!'

His stern command frightened her into obedience. Agnes took a deep breath, wiped away her tears and launched into her tale. There was no attempt to excuse herself. She was presenting the facts as she knew them so that he could judge for himself if she was as guilty as he assumed.

'I loved him,' she said with a fond smile. 'I loved him then and I love him now. His name is Karl. He is German, one of the armourers in the workshops at Greenwich Palace. He came to visit the master to discuss some business. I was collecting herbs in the garden when Karl arrived. We talked, he asked my name. I liked him from the start.'

'What business did he have with Master Brinklow?'

'He did not say. But later—when we had become close friends—he asked me to find out certain things for him. Karl said it would be proof of my love.' She shrugged helplessly. 'That is how it all began.'

'And it was Karl who asked you to procure the key?'

'Yes.'

'So that Freshwell and Maggs could commit murder?'

'No!' she denied. 'Karl told me that it was all a mistake. They had come here to steal the papers from the workshop when the master came home unexpectedly. He set on them in his anger and a fight developed. Freshwell and Maggs killed him trying to defend themselves.'

'That is what Karl expected you to believe?'

'He made it sound true.'

'And gave you some reward no doubt.'

'He did not offer me a penny,' she said indignantly. 'Nor would I take it. What I did was out of love for him. That is the height of my offence.'

Nicholas understood the significance of Fridays. It was the night when she stole away for a regular tryst with her lover. The woman was no practised informer who worked for gain. She put up with the disagreeable things she was forced to do in order to spend one night a week in the arms of her man. The plain, homely face and the plump body suggested that she might have had very few men in her life, perhaps none who took her as seriously as Karl appeared to do. She had given herself completely to him. It never occurred to her that he might be manipulating her cynically for his own ends.

Her admitted dislike of Cecily Brinklow raised an issue that had rather faded into the background. In the light of what Agnes had said, however, it took on a new importance.

'Walter Dunne was arrested with your master's wife.'

'They were taken in the very act, sir.'

'Who told the constables where to find them?'

She coloured and grew evasive. 'I have no idea.'

'Someone must have known the place and sent them to it. Do you not think it strange that they called at precisely the right time to catch two people in a moment of such intimacy?' He leaned in close. 'Why did you do it, Agnes?'

'It was sheer chance that they were found like that.'

'It was deliberate. Karl ordered it.'

'He . . . may have suggested it.'

'No, Agnes. He made you implicate two people who had nothing whatsoever to do with the murder of your master. And you went willingly along with such a pack of lies. I can see that you hated your mistress.'

'She was harsh with me. And unfaithful to her husband.'

'Did you never think of warning him about it?'

'He already knew.'

'Master Brinklow was *aware* of his wife's adultery?'

'He all but encouraged it.'

Nicholas was startled. Here was an entirely new slant on a murder which he thought he was finally sorting out in his mind. Thomas Brinklow had been portrayed to him as a brilliant inventor and an honest, generous, well-loved man, yet here was a maidservant claiming that he was also a complaisant husband. It compelled him to adjust his whole view of the domestic situation at the house. Agnes reached forward to clutch anxiously at him.

'What will happen to me, sir?' she whimpered.

'I do not know.'

'Will they chain me up? Will they beat me?'

'We shall see.'

'Is there no way that I can make amends?' she asked. 'I know I have done wrong but Karl made it seem so right. He has a way of explaining things to me.'

'How did he explain the death of Master Chaloner?'

'Karl had nothing to do with that!'

'He may well have dragged the body here himself.'

'No!' she cried. 'He would never do such a thing. Karl is kind and loving. You do not know him as well as I do. He would not dream of committing murder. It was not Karl.'

'Then who *did* kill Master Chaloner?'

Agnes was stunned. It was a question which she had blocked out of her mind. A look of total incomprehension spread over her features. Nicholas almost felt sorry for her. She had been pulled unwittingly into a complex plot over which she had no control and which she could not even begin to understand. Like Orlando Reeve, she was as much a victim as an accomplice but that did not exonerate her from blame or lessen the horror of the events in which she had been caught up.

She was now shocked, contrite and fearful.

'I cannot bring Master Brinklow back from his grave, nor Master Chaloner. But surely there is some way I can atone? Some means by which I can *help* you?'

Nicholas looked down at the scribbled message that he had found when he intercepted her. He held it up.

'Where were you taking this?'

'To the Black Bull Inn,' she said. 'There is a man, who is paid to carry my letters to the palace with all haste.'

'Give him another message,' said Nicholas.

'Another?'

'I will dictate it to you.'

Lawrence Firethorn was in his element. As he mingled with the small crowd at the end of the pier, he was playing a part that had been assigned to him. He might not win the applause of a packed audience at the Queen's Head but his performance was no less important for that. The tide was receding so the boat was moored well down the jetty in order to sit in deep water. Horse-drawn carts had brought its cargo from the palace and the heavy boxes were being winched aboard and lowered into a hold in the middle of the vessel.

The clerk from the armoury was checking his inventory as the cases were roped up in readiness for the huge hook on the winch. Firethorn sidled up to him in the most casual manner.

'Good day, sir,' he said.

'Good day to you,' said the clerk, sparing him no more than a glance. 'Stand aside, if you will. I am busy.'

'I see it well. What are your men loading here?'

'That is our business.'

Firethorn shrugged. 'I ask but out of interest, sir.'

'Then satisfy it and go your way. Those boxes are full of implements for the garden. Spades, hoes, rakes and the like.'

'Made here in the palace workshops?' said Firethorn with irony. 'What are your armourers doing with garden tools? If the

Spanish invade us, are we supposed to beat them off with rakes? Here's strange weaponry indeed.'

'Away, sir, or I'll call the guard!' snapped the clerk.

Firethorn mollified him with a gesture of conciliation. He drifted across to the boat itself and spoke to one of the sailors helping to bring the cargo aboard.

'Where do you sail?' he asked.

'Deptford,' said the man, spitting into the Thames.

'These boxes are for the royal dockyards?'

'Our journey ends there but they will travel on.'

'To what port?'

'Who knows?' said the man, guiding another load of boxes into the hold as it swung towards him. 'We put them into a larger vessel and our work is done.'

'Larger vessel?'

Firethorn had heard enough to arouse his suspicions. If a larger vessel were involved, the cargo must be destined for a port across the Channel. It was inconceivable that garden implements were being exported from Greenwich Palace to the Continent. An actor who dominated every stage on which he walked now made himself as inconspicuous as he could by walking to the very tip of the pier and sitting on its edge to stare out into the river. Across its murky water was the Isle of Dogs and Firethorn was grateful that he would not have to visit that reeking swamp again. On the other hand, it did not have a monopoly of evil. The opulent and respectable Greenwich housed villains as loathsome as any across the Thames.

When the cargo was loaded and the clerk departed with his men, Firethorn sauntered back towards the boat. The crew were making ready to set sail. He hailed the captain and requested to come aboard. The latter was a big, bearded man with a weather-tanned face and a distrustful eye. He allowed Firethorn to step over the bulwark but no further.

'What do you want?' he said.

'Safe passage to Deptford.'

'This is a cargo boat. We carry no passengers.'

'Make an exception and you will be well paid.' He opened his hand to show the silver coins on his palm. 'Well, sir? It is a good return on a short voyage.'

'Short, indeed,' said the man, clearly tempted by the money. 'But you could get to Deptford much quicker by horse. Why choose the slowest means?'

'Because I am in no hurry.'

Firethorn beamed at him and disguised the nudging pain he still felt from his bad tooth. The man looked him up and down for a moment before snatching at the coins.

'Stay aboard,' he said, 'but keep out of our way.'

'I will be invisible.'

The boat set sail and Firethorn leaned against the bulwark in its stern. Sea-gulls followed them away from the pier and wheeled around the vessel as the wind filled its canvas. The short journey to Deptford was not wasted by the lone passenger. He drifted across to the hold, which was so shallow that part of its cargo protruded up on to the deck. Firethorn rested against one of the boxes and pretended to survey the teeming life around them on the river. When he was certain he was not being watched, he searched the box for splits or knotholes but its wood was sound.

He needed a surreptitious dagger to gain entry. Inserting it below the lid of the box, he worked it up and down until he felt the timber loosen. A tiny gap had been opened up but it was sufficient. He peered quickly into the box and saw the rapiers lying side by side.

'Garden implements!' muttered Firethorn. 'What will they do with them? Challenge the weeds to a duel?'

[CHAPTER NINE]

Edmund Hoode was so reduced by hunger and anxiety that he barely had the strength to move. As the finger of light slowly withdrew from his cell in the Marshalsea, he lay on the floor in a disconsolate heap and mused on his sorry plight. "Disasters come triple-tongued" he wrote in one of his plays and that line now returned to haunt him. *The Corrupt Bargain* was his first disaster, a mediocre play made far worse by the death of its central character. Ben Skeat, however, was fortunate. The old actor had died while exercising his art. It was more than Hoode would be allowed to do.

Infatuation with Emilia Brinklow presaged his second disaster. Meeting her had swept aside all reservations about *The Roaring Boy*. It seemed like an exciting challenge and revived his creative urge. Pleased with the result of his reworking of the play, he had seen it felled on the stage at the Queen's Head before his own eyes. One play stricken by the demise of its main character and another stopped in its tracks by a brawl. These were not unrelated phenomena. Some malign curse had clearly been put upon his work. Whatever his pen touched soon crumbled to dust.

He could have borne the two disasters if a third had not arisen to join them. His name was Richard Topcliffe and he had left the playwright in a state of cold hysteria. The memory of those instruments in the cellar had burned itself into Hoode's brain. Simply to look at them had been torture enough. To be subjected to their venom would be unendurable. He knew that his heart would burst asunder long before his body was rent apart on the rack.

When he tried to compose his own epitaph, it served only to deepen his melancholy. No words could sum up the agony of his last hours alive, no conceit could describe his self-contempt, no clever rhyme could adequately express the folly of his existence. All was lost. A man whose plays and playing had delighted audiences for a decade or more would give a final, inglorious performance before a lone spectator. Only an excruciating death would draw applause from the watching Topcliffe.

Hope was a cruel illusion. Westfield's Men were still toiling on his behalf but their efforts were futile. If the influence of their patron could secure no comfort for their doomed playwright, then his situation was beyond recovery. Edmund Hoode was to be a scapegoat, a blood-covered warning to every other author to work more guardedly and to eschew libelous comment on figures in authority. It was a savage injustice. He was being sacrificed for a play he did not write about a man he had never met.

He looked up at the barred window. The last few rays were quitting his cell along with the last strands of belief in his friends. They had let him down signally and the greatest disappointment came from the man in whom he had reposed his highest expectations. A fury rustled deep inside him and slowly built until it burst through his sorrow and made him clamber to his feet to yell with all his might.

'Nicholas! Where *are* you!'

Everyone had something to say about Thomas Brinklow but all comment led in the same direction.'

'Which was?'

'He was a recluse. In love with his work.'

'Why, then, did he marry?'

'It was a blunder. All agree on that.'

'Could he have been happy with another woman?'

'No,' said Owen Elias. 'Nobody spoke it outright but their nudges and winks were eloquent enough. Our Master Brinklow was not for marriage with any woman. It is certain that his match fell short of consummation.'

'Small wonder that his wife looked elsewhere.'

'She did not need to, Nick.'

'Why?'

'Walter Dunne came with her. Or so the rumours would have it. He was the steward of her former household and warmed her bed as part of his duties. When she took a husband, she did not lose a lover.' Elias chuckled. 'The common report is that Master Brinklow was cuckolded on his wedding night. What sort of husband would tolerate that?'

'A man content to be husband in name only.'

Nicholas Bracewell was reminded of the maidservant's remark that Thomas Brinklow had condoned his wife's affair. If that was so, it cleared the lovers from even the faintest vestige of suspicion. Why did they need to kill a man who actively promoted their relationship? Instead of being an obstacle that needed to be removed, the husband had been a most effective cover. Aspects of Brinklow's character were emerging which had not found themselves into the play.

'What else did you learn, Owen?'

The two men were back at the house in Greenwich at the agreed hour. Lawrence Firethorn's absence was puzzling but they hoped that he would arrive in due course to pool his findings with theirs. In the meantime, Elias held the floor. The Welshman had been assiduous, visiting all the taverns in the vicinity and soaking up dozens of assorted recollections of Thomas Brinklow.

'He did employ builders,' said Elias, 'he did engage suppliers, he did pay someone to maintain his equipment. But it was only ever under his personal supervision. Nobody ever got into that workshop on his own.'

'What was he hiding?'

'It was his way, Nick. That's what everyone says.'

'His way.'

Elias retailed a number of anecdotes about Brinklow's obsessive privacy. He also discovered that the murdered man was an unusually devout Christian, visiting the church every day and often staying an hour alone in prayer. His wife had been far more erratic in her attendance.

'Even though she had more to confess,' said Elias.

'Confess?'

'Lustful embraces with Walter Dunne.'

'It seems that she had already confessed those to her husband,' said Nicholas. 'To confess them before God would have brought an end to them.'

They were still discussing the idiosyncrasies of the Brinklow household when a dishevelled Lawrence Firethorn was shown into the room. Dust-covered and perspiring, he yet had an air of triumph about him.

'Where have you been?' asked Nicholas.

'Why have you kept us waiting?' said Elias.

Firethorn sat down beside them. 'I have been to the very *fons et origo* of evil. We do not just deal with rogues and murderers here, gentlemen. We fight against treason.'

He checked to ensure that nobody else was listening.

'Rest easy,' said Nicholas. 'That little spy has been disarmed. You may speak freely now. What is this treason?'

'The most damnable crime I have ever encountered, Nick.'

Firethorn told them about his vigil at the quayside. His brief voyage to Deptford had not only revealed the true nature of the cargo aboard the boat. When he reached the dockyards and saw it unloaded into a larger vessel, he discovered its ultimate port of call.

'Flushing.'

'The weapons are going to the Netherlands?' said Elias.

'Where, then, is the treason?' asked Nicholas. 'If swords and pikes are sold to the Dutch, they are bought by those who are friendly to our nation. Nobody can question that.'

'Unless that cargo is unloaded on Dutch soil,' argued Firethorn, 'to be carried to another country over land. If those weapons are part of some legal trade, why do they have to be costumed as garden implements? And why should weapons be sent to the Continent when we have a greater need for them in Ireland? There's treason brewing here, have no doubt. Another fact supports it.'

'What is that, Lawrence?' said Elias.

'Sir Godfrey Avenell. Nick bade me enquire after our Master of the Armoury and so I did. Every guard and servant around the palace has a tale about the man.'

'Do they call him traitor?' said Nicholas.

'Far from it,' said Firethorn. 'They respect the noble knight. He is diligent in his office and fair-minded with those who work beneath him. Sir Godfrey has a flair for staging tournaments and a knowledge of jousting that is based on years of experience.' He turned to Elias. 'One of his old opponents in the saddle was Lord Hunsdon. I had forgot our Lord Chamberlain was also a notable jouster in his younger day. Their friendship started in the tiltyard.'

'How does Lord Hunsdon's name come in?' said Nicholas.

'He signed the order sending Edmund to prison.'

'Yes,' added Elias. 'Our patron found that out. The Lord Chamberlain is also responsible for the injunction that keeps us out of the Queen's Head. He is giving Sir Godfrey full return on their friendship.'

'Lord Hunsdon will have the reddest face in Christendom when the truth about that friend is published,' observed Firethorn. 'Do you know what they all ask about the Master of the Armoury? Where does he get his wealth? Why does a man who has but a modest income for his duties keep a house in the Strand and another in the country? How can he afford to dress as well as he does, to ride on such fine coursers and to afford suits of armour for his favourites?'

'I begin to see your reasoning,' said Elias.

'His money comes from selling arms to our enemies.'

'Can this be proved?' said Nicholas.

'It already has been to my satisfaction.'

'We'll need more evidence yet,' continued the book holder, 'but it certainly explains why Master Chaloner met his death. He strayed too close to the truth. Sir Godfrey Avenell is not just concealing his part in the killing of Thomas Brinklow. He may be hiding this appalling treason.'

Elias was vengeful. 'A man who betrays his country is no better than a dog. Sir Godfrey should be hanged, drawn and quartered. Think of the wickedness of it! Those weapons he has sold abroad may be used to kill his own countrymen!'

Firethorn nodded. 'We must stop the devil forthwith.'

'He must wait his turn,' said Nicholas. 'First, we must catch Sir John Tarker in our snare. He is a party to the murders if not to the treason. He is also the chief shield used by Sir Godfrey. Remove him and we may see what evil and corruption lie behind it.'

'Sir John stays at the palace,' said Firethorn. 'How do we entice him out? We have no means to gain entry there. We can hardly expect him to come calling at our invitation.'

Nicholas grinned. 'Yes, we can. And he will.'

. . .

Sir John Tarker mounted his horse by the light of the torch in the wall-bracket. Karl made final adjustments to the girth of his own mount. Midnight was approaching and all the gates of the palace were sealed but they were about to leave by a postern at the rear. Clouds drifted lazily across the moon. Tarker grunted with pleasure. Darkness was a good omen.

'Heaven blesses our enterprise,' he said. 'We thought to ask for a key to the house and one is offered.'

'Agnes is a good woman,' said Karl, putting a foot in the stirrup and hauling himself up. 'She has never let me down before.' He gave a cruel laugh. 'But, then, I have never disappointed her. Agnes will be well-rewarded for this night's work.'

'I've a mind to reward her in bed myself,' said Tarker, 'if I had not already set my eye on someone else in the house. Once Nicholas Bracewell is out of the way, all else falls into my hands. Come, Karl.'

The guard unbolted the postern gate and the two of them went through it. The horses were soon cantering across the grass in the direction of the village. Sir John Tarker was in good humour. The message that had been sent by Agnes had come at exactly the right moment. The maidservant claimed that she had overheard Emilia Brinklow confess to Nicholas Bracewell that her brother's papers had not all gone up in flames. Records of his most recent work had been hidden elsewhere in the house because of their importance. According to the letter, Nicholas Bracewell insisted on taking the papers to his bedchamber for safekeeping. Agnes promised to leave a key near a side-door so that Karl could slip into the house to steal the documents.

Sir John Tarker was delighted. Nicholas Bracewell and the missing papers, which had caused so much trouble. If he could kill the former and retrieve the latter, he would be back once more in Sir Godfrey Avenell's charmed circle. One night's work would restore all that had been taken away.

They came into the village and slowed to a trot. When the

silhouette of the house rose up before them, they dismounted and tethered their horses to some bushes. As they approached silently on foot, both felt their blood race at the prospect of action. A soldier and a jouster, Tarker always revelled in combat but Karl was just as keen to be involved. When he had knocked out Simon Chaloner with a blow from his tongs, the armourer had wanted to finish him off. Deprived of that pleasure, he was eager to be involved in the slaying of Nicholas Bracewell.

Both wore dark attire which allowed easy movement and blended with the night. They circled the house warily to check that nobody was still awake. The whole place was in darkness. Karl led the way back into the garden to await the signal promised in his lover's message. Only when a lighted candle appeared at her window was it safe for them to enter. They crouched in the bushes and looked up at the top of the house, cursing the delay and wondering if something was amiss. Absorbed in their vigil, they did not realise that they were themselves under surveillance and that Valentine was curled up like a dog in the undergrowth only yards away.

'Hurry, Agnes!' Karl muttered under his breath.

'Where *is* the woman?' hissed Tarker.

'She will come.'

'When?'

He got an immediate answer. A flickering candle was held in the topmost window for a few seconds before the curtains were drawn to hide it. Tarker jabbed his companion and they trotted towards the side-door of the house. It was the work of a moment to locate the key that the maidservant had left for them. Karl put it into the lock and turned it slowly. When the door opened, they went noiselessly in.

Their entry was not unobserved. Eyes accustomed to the darkness, Valentine saw them go into the building and knew his role. He threw a ball of moss up to a window on the first floor so that its gentle tap on the glass could act as a warning. The gardener had been thrilled to be given such responsibility by Nicholas Bracewell. Having discharged it, he withdrew once more into his hiding-place.

Tarker and the armourer moved furtively along a dark passageway. Since Karl has visited the building more than once, he was familiar with its design. Fortune favoured them. They knew that Nicholas Bracewell was in the bedchamber at the top of the first flight of stairs. They could be in and out without disturbing anyone else. Emilia Brinklow slept in a room farther along the landing and all the servants were up in the attics. Tarker led the way up the stairs, feeling for each step with his foot and taking care to make no sound. Karl's breathing quickened with excitement.

When they reached the landing, they paused to take stock of their surroundings. Karl checked the door to the attic rooms and found it securely shut. They would have no interference from any men in the house and Emilia was the only other person on the first floor. It was time to execute their plan. Nicholas Bracewell must be despatched before a search of his chamber was made by candlelight. They would soon be riding back to Greenwich Palace with their double mission accomplished.

'Stand ready!' whispered Tarker.

'I have the cloth in my hand '

'Then use it!'

Tarker eased the door open and they saw the outline of the sleeper in the bed against the wall. A few swift steps got them to the place of execution. Karl held the piece of cloth over the mouth of their prey to silence him while Tarker stabbed repeatedly with his dagger. No human being could survive an attack of such savagery. Had he been in the bed, Nicholas Bracewell would have been dead within seconds.

As it was, the joint ferocity of the attackers was wasted on a pillow and a sack of hay. Before the two men realised that they had been duped, light poured in from half a dozen candles and the room was boiling with bodies. Owen Elias and Lawrence Firethorn grappled with the armourer and quickly managed to disarm him. Nicholas Bracewell launched himself at Tarker, grabbing the wrist that held the knife and smashing it down across his knee so that the weapon was knocked free. The two of them rolled on to the bed and fought with their bare fists.

The ostler and the three manservants each held a candle in one hand and a sword or club in the other. The local constable held another, while his assistant carried two. They illumined a scene of vigorous activity. Sir John Tarker was fighting hard but Nicholas was the stronger and the more athletic. Without his weapon, the former could never master his assailant. He made a supreme effort to push Nicholas off him and struggled to his feet, dodging the club that was swung at him by a servant and grabbing a small table to swing at all and sundry.

Nicholas dived beneath it and tackled him around the legs, bringing him crashing to the floor before raining blows to his body. Tarker punched, gouged and bit his opponent but his energy was starting to wane. He was riding no fine horse in the tiltyard now. He had no magnificent armour for defence and no lance for attack. In unarmed combat with Nicholas Bracewell, he was being comprehensively beaten.

The book holder rolled over until he was on top of his man. Sitting astride Tarker's chest, he grabbed the black hair and began to pound the head against the floor. Dazed and weary, his adversary was unable to unseat him.

'Why did you come here?' demanded Nicholas

'To kill you!' gasped Tarker.

'The same way that you murdered Master Chaloner?'

'With even more pleasure!'

Sir John Tarker tapped a last reserve of strength and heaved upwards with all his might but Nicholas was equal to the manoeuvre. As he was forced back, he jumped quickly to his feet, hauled Tarker after him, then delivered a punch to the jaw that took all resistance away. As the man slumped to the floor, the two constables gave a ragged cheer.

Fighting was not yet over, however. Firethorn and Elias had overpowered the armourer and pushed him against a wall. Karl saw the situation all too clearly. He and Sir John Tarker had been lured into a trap with law officers present to act as witnesses. What galled him was that Agnes had been part of the deception. Rage at her betrayal gave him fresh energy and he suddenly burst from the grasp of the two men who held him and raced to the window. Throwing it up, he flung himself out and landed on soft ground below.

Firethorn roared his annoyance and sought to go after the man but pursuit was unnecessary. As the armourer tried to make his escape, the flat of a spade swung at him out of the darkness and hit him full in the face. Valentine stepped into the pool of light thrown down by the candles and looked up at the faces in the window.

There was a wealth of indignation in his apology.

'He jumped in my flower-beds!'

Edmund Hoode shrank back against the wall as he heard the tread of the keeper's feet. They sounded more urgent than usual. The playwright was being sent for again by Richard Topcliffe. He was going to be torn slowly apart on the rack while the torturer searched in vain for a name that Hoode had never even heard. It was better to die swiftly in the prison than in such agony on the murderous contraption at Topcliffe's house. When the door opened, therefore, Hoode tried to hurl himself at the keeper in the hope that the latter would draw his dagger and relieve him of his agonies with one sharp thrust. The plan soon foundered. He was now so weak that his violent assault was no more than a drunken fall against the keeper, who steadied him with his arm.

'Be careful, sir,' he said. 'I warned you to eat more.'

'I refuse to go,' mumbled Hoode.

'You have no choice. Orders have come.'

'I will never go back to that accursed house again.'

'Lean on me and you will find it easier.'

'Let me stay here,' pleaded Hoode. 'Lock the door and throw away the key. Or lend me your dagger that I may do the deed myself. Do not make me go!'

The keeper was used to such protests. He got the prisoner in a firm grasp and more or les carried him along the dark passageway before ascending a flight of stone steps. An iron door was opened by another keeper and Hoode was taken through it. The Marshalsea was a barrage of noise but the playwright could only hear the voice of Topcliffe in his ear. When he thought about the device he had been shown at the house, his fingers began to throb in protest.

'One more flight of steps, sir,' said the keeper.

'Spare me, friend. Take pity on me.'

'Out we go!'

The man kicked a door at the top of the steps and it was opened by a colleague. Hoode came into a room where the prison sergeant sat behind a desk. The man looked up before consulting a paper in front of him.

'Edmund Hoode?' he asked.

'No, no!' denied the latter. 'I am someone else.'

'This is the man,' confirmed the keeper.

'You are released,' said the sergeant.

'To go to that abominable house again?'

'I do not know where they will take you, sir.'

Hoode threw himself to the floor in front of the desk and put his hands together in prayer. Humiliated when he was thrown into the Marshalsea, he was now begging to stay there.

'Do not let them take me! Please! Let me stay!'

'Get him out!' said the sergeant impassively.

The keeper picked him up bodily and hustled him through

another door into an antechamber. Two figures converged on Hoode at once. He thought they were the gaolers who had taken him to Topcliffe on the previous occasion. This time they would not bring him back alive. With the last ounce of his strength, he tried to beat the two of them away.

'Edmund, dear heart!' said Lawrence Firethorn 'You are free. We are here to take you home.'

'Look at the state of him!' said his wife in horror. 'You poor creature! Come to me!'

She enfolded him in an embrace that knocked all the breath out of him but her warmth and maternal affection soon began to have an effect. Hoode blinked at them in disbelief.

'They will not take me to Master Topcliffe again?'

'No, Edmund,' said Firethorn. 'You are safe now.'

'Your suffering is at an end,' added Margery. 'We will take you home to wash and feed you. Then you will have the softest bed in the house on which to lie your head.'

'Welcome back, Edmund. Welcome back to Westfield's Men!'

Nicholas Bracewell arrived at Avenell Court before any of them. Officers would soon be sent with a warrant for the arrest of its owner but he was determined to have a private interview with him first. Lawrence Firethorn had been left to implement the release of Edmund Hoode. Nicholas reserved a more dangerous assignment for himself. Leaving his horse in the stable-yard, he made his way to the front door and rang the bell. A massive door swung open. Nicholas gave his name and was invited to step inside. He was taking an immense risk in arriving alone at the house of Sir Godfrey Avenell but he knew enough about the man's character to believe that he would at least be admitted to his presence.

His instinct was sound. Instead of having his unwelcome visitor overpowered by his men, Sir Godfrey asked the servant to conduct him to the main hall. Nicholas walked along the corridor with its display of armour and weaponry. When he was taken in to his host, he was given a mild shock. Sir Godfrey was sitting in his high-backed chair near the fireplace as he listened to some dances being played on the virginals by Orlando Reeve. The Master of the Armoury was serene and relaxed but the musician was soon discomfited. When he glanced up and saw Nicholas enter, Reeve immediately began to hit the wrong notes on the keyboard.

'Enough!' said Avenell. 'Stop that cacophony!'

Orlando Reeve obeyed and sat nervously on his stool.

Avenell looked at the newcomer. 'So you are Nicholas Bracewell,' he said. 'I had the feeling that we might meet sooner or later.' He turned to the servant. 'Take his weapons. I will not be accosted by an armed man in my own home.'

Nicholas Bracewell held his arms out wide so that the servant could take the sword and dagger that hung in their scabbards from his belt. The man departed with the weapons and closed the door behind him. What he had not taken, however, was the knife which Thomas Brinklow had made for his sister and which Nicholas had concealed up his sleeve. The book holder anticipated that he might need a second mode of defence and was taking no chances.

Avenell stood up in front of the fireplace, framed by its marble bulk. More weapons stood on the mantelpiece and a pike rested against it like a giant poker.

'Why have you come?' he said calmly.

'I needed to speak with you, Sir Godfrey,' said Nicholas. 'They told me you had left Greenwich Palace to return home. You have missed much activity in the night.'

'Activity?'

'Sir John Tarker is under lock and key for the murder of Master Chaloner and for the attempted murder of myself. With him is an armourer by the name of Karl. Their part in the killing of Thomas Brinklow will also be looked into.'

Avenell was unruffled. 'Why should any of this concern me in the least?'

'Sir John was a close associate of yours.'

'That is no longer the case.'

'He was acting on your orders.'

'Is that what he has claimed?'

'He will admit it under questioning.'

'I doubt that, Nicholas Bracewell. You will find it very difficult to link anything that Sir John has done with orders that I am supposed to have given. No court in the land will arraign me. I have important friends.'

'Not any more, Sir Godfrey.'

'Why do you say that?'

'Because Lord Hunsdon has already repudiated some of the actions you made him take. The injunction has been lifted from Westfield's Men and Edmund Hoode will have been released from the Marshalsea within the last hour.' He saw Avenell's jaw tighten slightly. 'Do not look to the Lord Chamberlain this time. He does not befriend traitors.'

'Guard your tongue, sir!'

'That is what they are calling you in Deptford.'

'What are you talking about, man?'

'*The Peppercorn.*'

'I have never heard that name.'

'It is the vessel that was bearing your latest shipment of arms to the Netherlands,' said Nicholas. 'When it set sail from Deptford early this morning, it was intercepted. A quantity of weapons made in the Greenwich Palace workshops was found aboard. Those weapons did not tally with the items listed in the manifest.'

'Blame that on some idle clerk and not on me.'

Nicholas admired his self-control. 'Two people were arrested aboard *The Peppercorn,*' he continued. 'Dutchmen, who had been staying in Greenwich with you to do business. They were sailing to Flushing with those arms but they were not going to make delivery in the Netherlands. Their business was with other nations, as you well know.'

'This is wild speculation,' said Avenell. 'I have yet to hear or see one scrap of proof being offered for my involvement. If any weaponry has left Greenwich illegally, I will be the first to track down the culprit and have him thrown into prison.' He gave a defiant smile. 'Where is your proof, Nicholas Bracewell?'

'At the home of Master Thomas Brinklow.'

'Brinklow was a fool!'

'He was also a genius,' said Nicholas. 'He invented a new process for smelting iron ore. It produced a metal that must have dazzled your eyes. A metal that was lighter and stronger than anything your armourers can produce. Easier to work, I suspect, for I have seen the results.' He gazed levelly at the other man. 'You coveted that process. Because he would not hand it over, you had Master Brinklow killed.'

'The man was an idiot. I offered him a fortune.'

'He found out what you meant to do with his invention.'

'That process was our key to a treasure-house.'

'Yes,' said Nicholas. 'If you produced such superior weapons, you could have sold them at a much higher price to hostile nations. When Master Brinklow realised that, he broke with you and refused to let you near his invention. He knew too much about you to be allowed to live.'

'He is not the only one, sir.'

'Information has been laid with the authorities. They will soon be here to arrest you on a charge of high treason and bear you away to the Tower.'

Avenell smiled. 'They will not keep me there for long, I do assure you. Everything you have alleged may be placed at the door of other people. There is no proven link with me.'

'Sir John Tarker thinks otherwise,' said Nicholas. 'He said that he murdered Master Chaloner at your behest.'

'Then it is a case of his word against mine.' Avenell put a hand against the fireplace and leaned back. 'You will have to do better than that, sir. Groundless accusations will get you nowhere. Search wherever you like. You will never be able to connect my name with the death of Master Chaloner.'

Nicholas Bracewell looked steadily at him, then let his gaze drift upwards. On the mantelpiece, directly above the head of Sir Godfrey Avenell, was an object which did more than connect a name with a corpse. The ball-butted German cavalry pistol, a souvenir of Chaloner's army career, was now part of the private collection of the Master of the Armoury. Nicholas was staring up at the murder weapon itself.

Sir Godfrey Avenell's composure vanished. When he realised what his visitor could see, he grabbed the pike from beside the fireplace and advanced on him. Thunderous knocking could be heard in the distance and voices were raised. Officers had patently arrived to effect the arrest of a presumed traitor. It all served to make Avenell more frenzied.

'Whatever happens,' he sneered, 'you will not live to see it. Goodbye, sir!'

He thrust at Nicholas with the pike but the latter eluded it and backed away. Avenell followed, circling him with the weapon at full stretch. When Nicholas veered towards the dais at the end of the hall, Orlando Reeve let out a squeal of fear and jumped off his stool. He cowered in a corner as he watched them. Noises in the passageway became louder and more urgent. Help was fast approaching.

Avenell jabbed with the pike again, then swung it in a vertical plane to try to knock his quarry over. Nicholas ducked under the whirling weapon just in time but the older man quickly adjusted his attack. A second swing of the pike took Nicholas's legs from under him and sent him sprawling on the marble. Doors were now flung open and a detachment of armed officers marched in. Avenell stopped them with a command.

'Stay there!' he ordered. 'Keep out of this!'

Their arrival gave Nicholas the opportunity to get to his feet.

He was glad of the presence of more witnesses. Orlando Reeve's gibbering testimony would not have been enough. The officers could clearly see that Nicholas was at a disadvantage and that any action he took would be strictly in self-defence.

Avenell closed on him with the pike, using it to describe small circles in the air. He had moved his grasp down the shaft now so that he could use it more like a staff. When he lashed out and missed with the blade, he quickly brought the other end of the shaft into play and caught Nicholas a glancing blow on the shoulder. It send him falling back into a suit of armour which collapsed on to the floor with a loud clatter. Avenell was on him at once, sensing his chance to finish off the man who had pursued him so remorselessly.

He raised the pike, leaped in and brought the blade down with devastating force. Nicholas reacted like lightning. As the weapon descended, he rolled over, flicked the concealed knife into his hand and thrust it upwards. The pike clanged harm-lessly on the floor but the knife that Thomas Brinklow had made struck home. Sir Godfrey Avenell had taken possession of the discovery at last. He gave a strangled cry and dropped his weapon. The Master of the Armoury lay twitching on the ground in an island of his own blood, clutching vainly at the knife which had gone clean through his neck and which bore the proud name of his victim.

The spectators filled the yard of the Queen's Head an hour before the play was even due to start. Such was the scandal that surrounded it—and the reverberations that its first attempted performance caused—*The Roaring Boy* was the biggest attraction in London. Lord Westfield was up in his accustomed position with his entourage. Emilia Brinklow was in the front row of the lower gallery, waiting to see how much of the second version of the play resembled her own original draft. Restored to liberty and resuscitated by the gratitude she heaped upon him, Edmund Hoode had been more than ready to resume work on the piece to rewrite it in the light of new evidence. His health improved markedly under Margery Firethorn's care and his apprehension was greatly stilled by the news that the egregious Richard Topcliffe had actually been arrested because of his excessive cruelty to those he interrogated. Emilia was looking forward to seeing Edmund Hoode in a new role in their joint creation.

Alexander Marwood had vowed he would never let any theatre company through his portals again but the prospect of naked commercial gain soon modified his verdict. Westfield's Men were not just a viable troupe once more. They were brave heroes, who had helped to solve two murders and uncover a shameful act of treason by no less a personage than the Master of the Armoury. The repercussions were enormous and they ensured huge audiences for anything that Westfield's Men cared to present. In the case of *The Roaring Boy*, it was impossible to get even half of the would-be spectators inside the yard. They would have to wait for later performances, for the piece would surely enjoy a long and successful run.

The Roaring Boy still held to its original shape but its scope was vastly wider. Beginning as a domestic tragedy about a man with a wanton wife, it broadened out into a complex political drama. The Stranger—played by Hoode once more—was now openly called Sir Godfrey Avenell and Tarker's role was more subordinate to his master. Emilia Brinklow herself still did not appear in the story but one other new character had been created. Glowing with pride and grinning ridiculously, Valentine the gardener was standing in the yard to see himself brought vividly to life on stage.

The play was a sensation, the performances uniformly excellent and the whole occasion memorable. The only thing which threatened to disrupt the event was a sudden recurrence of Lawrence Firethorn's toothache. Weeks of intermittent pain had made him prod and pull at the aching molar until it was barely hanging in his mouth but it would not be dislodged completely. When he stepped on stage as Freshwell, one side of his mouth was the size of an inflated bladder. The distorted visage was very much in character and the swollen gum made him speak out of the side of his mouth. But the pain got steadily worse as the play progressed. Like the true professional that he was, he managed to turn it all to good account in the end.

Act Five brought the piece to a horrifying conclusion. As the roaring boy was dragged up to the gallows, he fought off his guards to make a moving speech of denial, freely admitting his own guilt while nobly trying to save Cecily Brinklow and Walter Dunne from their undeserved fate. Freshwell's mouth was now a furnace of pain. The tooth burned with such intensity that it seemed to be on the point of exploding inside his mouth. Lines written in prose by Edmund Hoode turned the actor into his own surgeon.

> *Hang this guilty man on high but spare the innocent. I'll not go to my grave with their deaths on my conscience. Sooner than speak against them, I will pluck out my tongue so that it can speak no lies!*

His hand went into his mouth, his fingers grabbed the pounding tooth and he pulled for all his worth. There was a cry of utter amazement from all who watched. He really did seem to have done what he had vowed. Blood gushed out of his mouth in a torrent and splashed forward on to the spectators in the front rows. It was accompanied by a roar so loud and so chilling that it brought hairs up on the back of every neck in the yard. At a moment of supreme pain, Lawrence Firethorn had achieved an effect that no actor in the world could match. The dripping tooth which he held up in his hand looked like the tongue he had sacrificed for his art. It was a fitting climax to the crescendo of violence and duplicity which had preceded it.

Applause of that wildness and length had never been heard

at the Queen's Head before. As Firethorn led out his company to drink it in, the blood was still streaming down his chin. He did not mind in the least. The pain had finally gone and he could float on a sea of exquisite pleasure. His companions shared the ovation. Edmund Hoode beamed up at Emilia Brinklow. Barnaby Gill bowed low to Lord Westfield. Owen Elias waved to Valentine. George Dart cried with joy. *The Roaring Boy* had vindicated the reputation of Westfield's Men and carried their art to a new pinnacle. It was such an unequivocal triumph that it even brought a smile to the face of Alexander Marwood. The ultimate accolade had been achieved.

Nicholas Bracewell found her in the private room which she had hired at the Queen's Head. While everyone else was moving into the tavern itself to celebrate an extraordinary event, Emilia Brinklow had withdrawn to be alone. The book holder knew where to find her. There were tears in her eyes as she admitted him to the room.

'I hoped you would come, Nicholas,' she said.

'We have been waiting for you down below.'

'There is no place for me there.'

'Indeed, there is,' he argued. 'But for you, *The Roaring Boy* would never have come into being. Put off your modesty. This triumph is largely yours and you may bask in it. You are the only true begetter of this play.'

'No,' she said firmly. 'I am content to let it stand as Edmund Hoode's work. He has earned the right by the misery that he endured because of me. Only you and I must know the secret of *The Roaring Boy*. It is our bond.'

She reached up to kiss him tenderly on the lips and let him embrace her in his arms. Nicholas was moved. The event at the Queen's Head that afternoon had been the culmination of months of hard work and setback for her. Emilia Brinklow had seen all her hopes flower in the sunshine. She was entitled to be the guest of honour at the celebrations, yet she preferred to be alone with him. He put a hand under her chin to kiss her again but she allowed the merest brushing of the lips this time before pulling gently away.

'Have I offended you?' he said with disquiet.

'You have pleased me more than I can say, Nicholas.'

'All your distress is now over. Your brother and Master Chaloner have truly been avenged. They may rest at peace in their graves.' He took her hand. 'It is time for you to start living your own life again.'

'It can never be separated from them.'

'It must,' he said. 'You are at last free.'

'You do not know the chains that bind me.'

'Can they not be broken?'

'Alas, no!' She came to him again to look deep into his eyes. 'If any man could do it, his name would be Nicholas Bracewell. But I could not ask you to share my burden or to be stained with my shame.'

'Shame?'

She nodded. 'Do you remember when you stayed the night at my house in Greenwich? Someone came into the bed-chamber.'

'I will never forget it.'

'I need forgiveness also.'

'Why?' he said. 'It answered a need in both of us and I will cherish the memory because of that. You wished to lie beside me, Emilia, and you did.'

'I did,' she whispered, 'and I did not.'

'What do you mean?'

She lowered her lids. 'Do you know in whose bed you lay that night?'

'You said it was your brother's.'

'Thomas always slept in there. But not with his wife. Cecily had another bedchamber. Though he agreed to marry her, they privately contracted to sleep apart.'

'She with Walter Dunne, if she chose?'

'My brother closed his eyes to their love.'

'Why?' he asked.

'Because his heart had already been given to another.'

As she looked up at him again, realisation hit him with the force of a blow. Emilia Brinklow had not come into his bed to be with Nicholas himself. She was lying beside her brother again. Theirs was a passion forbidden by law and frowned upon by nature but it had withstood both. Thomas Brinklow's extreme privacy was now explained. Marriage was just one more shield against the prying eyes of the world. He chose a woman who did not want a proper husband in her bed because he was already wholly committed to his sister.

Nicholas was deeply shocked but not disgusted. Here was a love he could not understand but neither could he condemn it. *The Roaring Boy* was its issue. Emilia Brinklow had not written it simply to avenge the death of a brother. She was fuelled by her enduring passion for a lover.

'Now you may see why I was betrothed to Simon,' she said. 'I needed him to help me but I could never requite his love. It was a cruel irony. I loved him only as a brother while it was brother only that I loved.' She searched his eyes. 'Do I repel you now?'

'No!' he assured her.

'Do you think me evil and corrupt?'

'You are brave and honest.'

'And so are you, dear Nicholas. I knew it when I first saw your kind face. Do you recall what I said?'

'That I reminded you of your brother.'

'It is not the only reason that I shared your bed.'

Nicholas was touched that she should confide in him but he was hurt as well. He had lost her. Emilia Brinklow could never give herself to any man now. The house in Greenwich was a monument to her brother and she would tend it lovingly for the rest of her days.

'One thing more,' she confessed. 'I set fire to the workshop that night. Thomas had commanded it. He knew he was in danger and made me swear to destroy the place if anything should happen to him. He did not wish his discoveries to fall into the hands of Sir Godfrey Avenell.'

'But you were not in Greenwich that night,' said Nicholas. 'You claimed that you stayed with friends.'

'One friend, Nicholas. His name was Thomas Brinklow. We came back to the house that night by separate means. Thomas had told the servants that he would return from business in London. That intelligence was passed to the killers.'

'By Agnes?'

'By Cecily,' she said. 'She was a spy without even knowing it. That is why Sir Godfrey Avenell contrived to get her inside the house. When he wanted to know anything about Thomas, he simply had to ask his wife. That was why Cecily pestered my brother so about his work. She had no interest on her own account. It was Sir Godfrey's curiosity that she was trying to satisfy.'

Nicholas was intrigued. 'Agnes, then, was innocent of complicity in the murder. When she provided the key for Freshwell and Maggs, she thought she was simply letting in two thieves to borrow papers from the workshop.'

Emilia nodded. 'She will stand trial and must take her due punishment but Agnes was only used by others. Freshwell and Maggs knew my brother would return that night. What they did not know was that *I* would follow soon after.' She grimaced at the memory. 'When I got back, the house was in disarray. I knew the cause at a glance. I honoured my promise to my brother. Everything went up in flames.'

Nicholas felt as if his own plans and aspirations had just been set alight. Emilia was an even more remarkable woman than he had imagined. Her play had just thrilled a packed audience but it had drawn a complete veil over a fundamental part of the story. He now understood why she was so anxious not to appear in it as a character herself.

'Do not think too harshly of me, Nicholas.'

'I will never do that,' he said gallantly.

'You will visit me in Greenwich one day?'

'If I may. But you will surely come here again to see Westfield's Men perform your play.'

'I think not.'

There was no more to be said. Nicholas placed a kiss on her hand and took his leave of her. His place was downstairs in the taproom with his fellows: hers was back in Greenwich with her brother. The book holder was wistful but not abashed. Emilia had trusted him enough to let him look into her heart and he would always be grateful to her for that.

Celebrations were reaching the rowdy stage when he got into the taproom. Lawrence Firethorn had bought drinks for the entire company and Barnaby Gill was entertaining them with one of his jigs. Peter Digby played the accompaniment, delighted to be working once more for a company he feared he had inadvertently betrayed. George Dart was so euphoric that he did not mind having his ear clipped by Thomas Skillen, the ancient stagekeeper. Edmund Hoode was resting on his laurels in the corner and finding them a softer couch than he had enjoyed at the Marshalsea. Owen Elias was making some of the hired men laugh at his merry tales. The spirit of Ben Skeat seemed to float above the joyous gathering.

Margery Firethorn handed a cup of wine to Nicholas. He waved away enquiries about Emilia and submerged himself in the jollity. The company had been through a long, dark tunnel of pain before it emerged into this blaze of light. It was entitled to sing and shout until its lungs burst. Nicholas was so happy for them that his own sadness was forgotten.

He made his way across to Hoode and sat beside him.

'This is your finest hour, Edmund,' he said.

'I want to share it with Emilia. Where is she?'

'Too exhausted to come. *The Roaring Boy* thrilled her but it also drained her emotions. It was a brother's murder she was watching on that stage.'

'My work distressed her?' said Hoode in alarm.

'It pleased her beyond measure,' said Nicholas, 'and she asked me to tell you that. It pleased and harrowed everyone who saw it, Edmund. Today you have become the most famous playwright in London.'

'Yet the piece is not mine.' He clutched at the book holder's sleeve. 'Come, Nick. It is time to let me know the secret. You will have divined it by now, I am sure. Speak a name into my ear and it will go no further. Who is the true author of *The Roaring Boy?*'

'You swear to lock the truth away?'

'On my oath!'

'And you will never ask me again?'

'Tell me who he is and I am satisfied.'

'Then hear it,' said Nicholas, cupping his hands over his friend's ear to whisper into it. 'Edmund Hoode.'

'You mock me!' complained the other.

'I give you right and title.'

'Another hand fashioned *The Roaring Boy* at first.'

'You have made it your own,' said Nicholas. 'That other hand wrote another play. What you have done is to breathe fresh life into it. Take all the honour that is due, Edmund. No man here has deserved it more. Look how your fellows acclaim you.' He took in the whole room with a sweep of his arm. 'Besides, you did something on that stage this afternoon that no author could ever have done and Westfield's Men are eternally in your debt.'

'For what, Nick?' said Hoode. 'For what?'

'Writing a play that cured us all of the toothache!'